Roger Ormerod is the author of over thirty novels.

He was born in 1920 and left school at seventeen to join the Civil Service in which he had spent most of his working life. He retired in 1970 and later worked as a postman and in the production control department of a heavy industry factory. He lives in Wolverhampton.

SHAME THE DEVIL

To Richard Patton, the inheritance of
George Tate's camera equipment at first
seems inexplicable. They had only known
each other for three weeks, and that had
been sixteen years before. But the Chief
Super must have had a valid reason, and
when Richard discovers what it was,
that is when the trouble starts. He has
inherited much more — the tag-end
of an investigation into an unsolved
kidnapping . . .

Books by Roger Ormerod
Published by The House of Ulverscroft:

ROGER ORMEROD

SHAME
THE
DEVIL

Complete and Unabridged

ULVERSCROFT
Leicester

First published in Great Britain in 1993

First Large Print Edition
published 2001

The moral right of the author has been asserted

British Library CIP Data

Ormerod, Roger, 1920 –
    Shame the devil.—Large print ed.—
    Ulverscroft large print series: mystery
    1. Detective and mystery stories
    2. Large type books
    I. Title
    823.9'14 [F]

    ISBN 0–7089–4436–1

Published by
F. A. Thorpe (Publishing)
Anstey, Leicestershire

Set by Words & Graphics Ltd.
Anstey, Leicestershire
Printed and bound in Great Britain by
T. J. International Ltd., Padstow, Cornwall

This book is printed on acid-free paper

1

'It all sounds very strange to me,' said Amelia, as we walked out into King Edward Street.

It did to me too, but I was reserving my reactions. 'What's strange is that he remembered me at all. Where did we leave your car? Along here, was it?'

'Let's look for a café first.' My wife always looks for cafés. She can then sit opposite to me and analyse my expressions. 'No hurry, is there?'

'It's just . . . ' I smiled at her as she took my arm. 'I was wondering whether we ought to go and see his widow, while we're here in this district.'

'Umm!'

'Not keen?'

'It would seem . . . well, a bit too eager, don't you think, Richard? Can't wait to get your hands on your legacy, that sort of thing. We can always come again. Phone first — that would be better.'

But here, at the town of Potterton, we were sixty miles from home. I said nothing. What I was eager to get was some sort of an

1

explanation. It was nearly sixteen years since my brief encounter — if twenty-three days can be called brief — with George Charles Tate. I hadn't even known his Christian names, then. To me he had been 'Sir'. Or 'Chief', short for Chief Superintendent. I'd been 'Sergeant' to him, not even *his* sergeant, come to think of it, as I'd been seconded to him as part of the blanket coverage he'd requested. He had wanted a liaison officer, in charge of communications. So I had spent three weeks with him, in control of phones and radios and reports, and half a dozen constables, in our operations unit, which had been a mobile office. And most of that time he had spent outside on the job, sometimes with me, more frustrated every day, more exhausted, gaunt and distressed. Yes, we'd worked very close together during that short period. We'd suffered together. Towards the end, in so far as there'd been an end, he had been calling me Richard.

But that didn't explain why, after all those years, he should have left me his photographic equipment in his will.

'This looks a pleasant place,' said Amelia, and, as I held open the door for her, she added, 'In any event, you really need a hobby. You know how niggly you get when you've got nothing to occupy your mind. Well

. . . now you can take up photography.'

But the bequest had been added in a codicil, tacked on at the end of his will during those last days in hospital. 'To Richard Patton, who will remember our brief period of duty together, and who will know what to do with my photographic apparatus.'

Damn it all, he'd linked the two together, the bequest and the memory. And I didn't know a thing about photography.

Over coffee and buttered scones I said, 'It wouldn't really be too soon to visit her, you know. It's taken that solicitor three months to trace me. And widows can get lonely.'

She pouted at me. 'I know you, Richard, through and through. I can almost see your nose twitching. What's on your mind?'

'He had a reason, my love. A reason. How did he put it? 'Who will know what to do with my photographic equipment.' '

'Apparatus, was the word he used.'

'Well then.'

'Don't be obscure, please. Explain yourself,' she instructed.

I reached for my pipe, remembered where we were, and dropped it back into my pocket. 'It's got a different sound. Apparatus. Equipment. Different. Apparatus suggests to me something's that put together for a purpose. Equipment . . . oh, something you

3

buy for a particular purpose.'

'You're playing with words.'

'I don't think George Tate was. We'll see. Perhaps there'll be something obvious. Something he rigged.'

'All right, all right.' She put up a hand. 'I give in. We'll go and see the widow. But . . . if we seem to be causing any distress, any at all, then we must apologize and retreat. Don't you think?'

'I'd have done so in any event.'

'Of course you would.' But she didn't sound certain of that. I suppose I have a tendency to be persistent.

This town was strange to Amelia, and had changed considerably since I'd last seen it, so though we had the address we had no idea how to find it. We strolled on as far as the main square, which seemed to be in the throes of transition to a pedestrian precinct. Being only half-way towards their objective, they had excluded motor vehicles, but the buses still came through, and the taxis, I saw, and the pedestrians had to maintain a high standard of agility. We circled the outskirts, so that I was beginning to forget in which direction we had left Amelia's Granada. But help was at hand. They had a patrolling policeman. Yes, he knew Primrose Drive, and yes, when I mentioned the name of our

4

car-park, he knew that too. So his directions began from the car-park, very precise, very detailed, and given to me as though he thought I looked a bit dim. I thanked him. We continued on our way, the car-park being just round the corner. I said, 'I hope you can remember all that,' and Amelia assured me she could.

Her memory took us three miles into rolling countryside, where the roads opened out and swept around the flanks of the hills, or plunged us down into the valleys amongst the trees, losing their leaves now, nestled tight-packed and almost concealing the houses crouched there. Executive and higher executive dwellings, these. In an hour's time — it was a little past three o'clock — these roads would hum to the expensive treads of Mercedes and BMW and Jaguar. Now it was quiet. We could ease down to walking pace in order to scan the side roads for the sign: Primrose Drive.

And there it was, one of those in the valley. It was built along one side only of the road, the other side being the river, which flowed dull and quiet in the failing light, at the bottom of a gorge. The house was called Penhallow. It was not one of the larger homes, but was detached, as were all of them, and in its own group of ancient oak and beech, with a short drive curving between high yew hedges in need of a trim.

There was a porch light on, welcoming, waiting for somebody. For us? Had the solicitor phoned ahead? We parked on gravel and got out to have a look. The front door opened before we reached the porch, and she stood there waiting for us. It was a little disconcerting, she having anticipated my eagerness.

'Good afternoon,' I said.

'You'll be Mr and Mrs Patton.' It was a statement. 'Do come in.' She stood aside.

A ginger cat came to look at us, then retreated back to its warm spot. Mrs Tate smiled an empty smile and told us, 'Dennis Finch phoned.' This was the solicitor. 'Did he tell you I wanted to see you as soon as possible?'

No he hadn't, but it was a relief to hear we were not intruding. I caught Amelia's eye. This didn't sound encouraging to her. We hadn't come for any other business but the collection of a camera and maybe a couple of unused films, had we? But already there was a suggestion of something more. I raised my eyebrows at her, and she shrugged.

'I'm Jennie,' said Mrs Tate. 'Please call me Jennie. Will you come in here? It's cosier in this room.'

I introduced us by Christian names as we walked the length of the hall, and she took us into their living-room. It was indeed a room that was lived in. The general impression was of casual ease and relaxation. Nothing was new, but the age was one of venerable dignity. The furnishings and ornaments indicated more background wealth than I would have expected from a retired policeman, even a Chief Superintendent, and he had retired early. I'd heard that somewhere. Less than a year after the fiasco we had shared, he had resigned. The rumour that trickled along the grapevine was: washed-up. His failure had broken George Charles Tate.

Before we were properly settled Jennie said she would put the kettle on.

'No, please,' said Amelia quickly. 'We're fine. We've just come from a café in town.'

It clearly suited Jennie Tate, who had something she wanted to say. She was a tall woman, stately, and moved with a confident tread that hinted she might have been in the police force. Her eyes seemed to confirm this; they examined us, assessed us, and docketed us. Then she sat, and we did, side by side on a settee facing her.

'So you're Richard Patton.' She gave me a pallid smile.

I felt a little self-conscious, feeling I had

been much discussed, and I couldn't help wondering whether in flattery or denigration. She couldn't have heard about me except from her husband.

'He spoke of you,' she confirmed softly. 'Oh . . . often. Particularly at the beginning. I mean, the beginning of his retirement. You know he retired early?' She waited as I nodded. 'He used to say, 'Richard Patton would understand.' As though no one else might.' She pursed her lips. It was a tiny smile, rueful. 'But of course, I did. It was a bad time, Richard. I had to keep reassuring him. It wasn't his fault . . . '

'Of course not,' I murmured, but she went on without a break.

' . . . that the little boy died.'

Amelia touched my arm. I heard her draw in her breath sharply. Then her hand caught mine and squeezed it. Hard. I had deliberately said nothing to her about the child.

But this woman was strong. She had boosted her husband at a time when he'd been close to a breakdown. She could certainly support herself now, and her eyes challenged me to suggest otherwise.

'Nobody can say positively that the little boy died,' I said quietly. 'We have to remember that the young woman disappeared at the same time. It's just possible that she

8

took Adrian with her. Adrian? Was that his name? It's been a long time.'

She nodded. Her eyes held mine, and she hesitated as though collecting her thoughts. She didn't want my encouragement; she would know every detail, would have analysed every contingency, would have swept her mind for the smallest traces of reason and logic . . . and sanity, I suppose. Because there'd been nothing sane or reasonable about the actions of the kidnappers, nothing predictable. It had been that difficulty which had very nearly driven Chief Superintendent Tate crazy. We had never, during those terrible three weeks, caught a glimpse of a logical pattern we could work to and explore. Jennie held my eyes, and almost implored me — yes, implored, I decided, not challenged — to discover or produce one tiny detail she had not torn to shreds of exasperation in an attempt to save her husband's sanity.

And I had nothing to offer.

'Yes,' she agreed quietly, 'that was the boy's name. Adrian Roland Spooner. Five years and seven months old. The girl was getting on for seventeen. It's not an age at which young women take other people's children away. Certainly not of his age. And usually it's when they've lost a child of their own. No . . . no, I don't think she took Adrian with her. Not at the end.'

I might have disputed one or two points in her statement. At seventeen a girl could well be yearning for a child of her own, and here was one ready-made, you could say. She had been taken along by the three kidnappers as someone to look after the boy. It had been twenty-three days before the hand-over was completed. There'd been plenty of time during which the two, the young girl and the boy, could have become closely attached to each other. I knew nothing about Adrian's home life, but what was happening to him at that time, as a captive but free from family restraints, could well have seemed more exciting than his normal existence. Oh yes, I kept my options open on that point. The girl might, at the end, have taken him away with her — as her own.

And yet, would he not, at some later time, have remembered he had real parents, and contacted them?

But Jennie was determined to get it all said.

'The ransom was paid,' she stated crisply, 'the money was collected, and there was no possible reason why the child should not have been handed back to the parents. But there was nothing, no sign, no hint of a sign, never any trace since then of the young woman or the boy.'

Amelia's fingernails were digging into my wrist. I could hear that she was breathing more deeply. I hadn't told her the background, leaving it until later, assuming that the widow would be anxious to get rid of us and would simply have thrust a camera and a tripod into my hands and said, 'Here, sign this receipt.' But no. She'd been waiting for us.

Why me? That was becoming obvious. I'd been the one closest to George Tate during the whole of those terrible days. It was the reason he had left me his photographic equipment. But that latter aspect of it wasn't yet clear to me.

'They did arrest the three kidnappers,' I murmured. 'Later. They were sent for trial and they were sentenced, and went to prison. But that was over fifteen years ago. They'll no doubt be free now — maybe on parole. But they got them.'

'Oh yes,' said Jennie. 'Through the back door, George called it. They all three lived in this town, and it was only a matter of finding out who worked together as a trio, and who were the ones missing from their usual haunts during those three weeks. But they didn't get out of them the really important information . . . the boy . . . the girl. Why didn't they force it out of them? Why?'

Her voice had been rising, anger taking over.

'George was a good policeman, Jennie. He wouldn't be able to put too much pressure on, without the risk of losing his convictions. He'd have been careful not to leave one tiniest loophole in his case.'

'Oh, I'm sure he was.' She tossed her head. 'If I'd been there, they'd have told *me*. Oh yes, I can be sure of that. They'd have told me where the child was, and the girl, and that wretched money. *And* where they had held him. I'd have got *that* out of them. Those four things. That, I would. But he had to treat them gently, afraid for his ridiculous case. Gently! So that George was left, all these years, with those questions unanswered and niggling at him . . . ' She dashed a hand across her eyes, raising her chin in proud defiance. 'All these years,' she went on, more contained now. 'And they — those three men — they're free again. Spending their money *now*, I bet. Laughing in the face of the law . . . '

Now she couldn't go on. She lowered her head, staring down at her hands, locked together — all she had to hold on to now.

'Usually,' I said, 'when they've managed to get away with large sums of money, they disappear to Brazil, or somewhere like that. If they're still hanging around, you can bet *they* haven't got the money.' I didn't know whether this would be any comfort to her.

'Then who has?' she demanded.

'The young woman you mentioned,' said Amelia brightly. 'She disappeared with the boy, so why not with the money, too? Richard — you've told me nothing about a kidnapping.'

I sighed. I'd hoped to keep it until later, alone. But it seemed I would have to enlarge on a few points. The money. That had been one of the farcical aspects of the case. Those three men, even the girl, had been in phone contact time after time with our mobile operations unit. With me on the receiving end, so that I am the one who knows the exact details. I'm the one who tried to reason with them. But no, they were stubbornly stupid. Any suggestions from our end they took as traps. So . . . it had had to be exactly as they demanded.

'Why not with the money?' I said to Amelia. 'That's one of the big snags we encountered.'

'I've never been clear about the details,' Jennie complained.

So the Chief Super hadn't confided fully in his wife. I wondered why not. But there was no reason now why I shouldn't supply the missing facts.

'It's like this,' I said. 'The father of the boy, Marcus Spooner, was . . . and still is, I suppose . . . a financier, a tycoon. It seemed to me he lived on debt, but I was told that what he lived on was an overpowering personality and an unshakeable self-confidence. Famous for his wealth and power, he was. The kidnappers demanded half a million pounds, though they might just as well have made it a whole million, or two or three. Spooner traded in billions. He'd only got to snap his fingers and his bankers fell over themselves to provide the money. That wasn't the problem. It was how the kidnappers demanded it that gave everybody a headache. D'you know . . . they asked for it, at first, in used pound notes. That was when we had pound notes, before the coins.'

'I wonder why George never told me this,' murmured Jennie. 'Smoke if you wish,' she added, and I realized I was turning my pipe in my fingers.

I smiled. 'It's just to play with. No, I don't suppose he would tell you, Jennie. It was his one big mistake — or so I've always thought — that he agreed to their demands on that. He had the idea it'd hamper them. And he was dead right there. Have you ever thought what half a million one-pound notes would be like? A hundred of them weighed three ounces. Five hundred thousand weighed getting on for a thousand pounds. That's eight hundredweight. And they took up around twenty-four cubic feet of space. Say a cubic yard. *That* was what we had to deal with. We split it up into four cardboard boxes, each one three feet by two feet by one foot. They weighed two hundredweight each. I remember the Chief Super saying, 'There — let 'em try handling that lot.' We'd had to use a fork-lift truck to get it all in position. Position! Where they wanted it left, which was in the pedestrian precinct in Alberville at midnight. Why those three idiots chose such a place we couldn't decide. We had them cut off as soon as they entered it. But there you are . . . '

I stopped. The memory was bitter. Alberville was one of half a dozen small towns scattered across that huge expanse of moorland in which the kidnappers were operating. On the face of it, you would've said it had to be simple to keep contact with them, either coming to the arranged hand-over locations (there were eventually three of these involved) or leaving them. But the moorland was not like that. It was crossed by half a dozen minor link roads, and riddled with thousands of disused tracks. The three men seemed to be able to melt away and dissolve into the ground. There one minute, gone the next. At first we'd been trying to track their movements with a helicopter, but that seemed to enrage them. They threatened to leave the boy's body lying on an exposed spot, so that we could find *that*. Then there'd been the difficulty that the press, to whom it was all very exciting, also wanted to use helicopters. We had to put a stop to that.

But the night of the first attempt to complete the hand-over had been a wash-out. Alberville pedestrian precinct. I was up on the roof of Woolworth's with George Tate, each of us with binoculars, so that we might get a sight of their faces. But of course they were masked. Ski-masks, if I remember correctly . . .

I must have been too long remembering. Amelia said, 'There we are, you said. Go on. Where are we?'

'Sorry. What was I saying? Oh yes — the pick-up details.'

And I could tell from Jennie's expression that this was something else she hadn't heard. So I explained the details of the first hand-over attempt.

'So what went wrong?' Amelia demanded.

'Have you ever tried lifting heavy cardboard boxes? They're slippy, and that trio were wearing gloves. Did I tell you it was winter? No? It was the end of November, midnight, and frosty. Of course, that'd been the Chief Super's — '

'Call him George, please,' put in Jennie.

'Yes. Right. George reckoned we might nab 'em while they struggled with the boxes. If all three came. We knew, by then, that there were three, and a girl. It'd all been going on for over a week, and there'd been a lot of negotiating over the phone. So we had three different men's voices, and a woman's. Our expert said a teenager. So there we were, waiting, at midnight. Hidden cars everywhere. It couldn't fail. George was certain that once he'd got his hands on 'em they'd tell us where they'd got the boy hidden. I didn't like the look on his face when he said that.'

'So what went wrong, dear?' asked Amelia. She rarely calls me 'dear', only when she intends to imply disapproval. Unfair, that was. It wasn't my organization we were discussing.

'They came prepared,' I explained. 'We never found out where they got it, but they turned up with an armoured ex-army personnel carrier. They stopped, they all three jumped out, and of course they couldn't lift the boxes. There wasn't room on each box for three pairs of hands. So they stood there for a

17

minute, shouting filth at the sky, and stabbing the air with their fists, then they simply jumped back into their armoured carrier, and away they went. And out popped the intercepting cars, and that damned armoured thing went ploughing through them, and disappeared into the night leaving a lot of wreckage behind. They dumped it two miles out of town, where they'd obviously left an ordinary car. And that was the end of round one. Crooks ahead on points.'

'It isn't amusing, Richard.'

I looked at my pipe and spoke quietly. 'It wasn't amusing at the time, no. There was that little boy shut up somewhere, and a young woman . . . '

During all this time, Jennie had said nothing, but she was staring at me with an expression of awed disbelief. So George Tate had never revealed any part of the truth to her. He would have been underlining his failure. But I could see she resented his silence.

'So what happened next?' she now said softly. 'What happened the other two times?' She made an impatient gesture. 'The other times they escaped.'

Escaped capture by her husband, she meant.

'Oh . . . ' I tried now to make light of it.

'The next time the drop, as we called it, was right out in the wilds, and in daylight. They reduced the handling difficulties, by demanding it in used fivers. But that was still quite a bulk and still too heavy. There was a phone box, way out on the moors, and nowhere for us to hide within striking distance, and that was where they wanted it left. George and I lay on the top slope of one of the surrounding hills, hidden behind a gorse bush, and the idea was that he would radio for his cars to close in when they stopped and picked up the money. It all seemed too easy. They turned up with a stolen Landrover. One look at that cardboard box — there was only one this time — and the three men went wild with fury. They laid into it with their boots, smashed in the sides of the box, and there was a great cloud of fivers floating in the wind. Then they jumped in their Landrover, and instead of driving off the way they'd come, along the road, they set off directly across country, and we'd got no vehicle that could stick with them.' I stopped. Amelia had made a sound of distress.

There was a short silence. Jennie's eyes were huge. She whispered, 'Poor George.'

'Exactly,' I agreed. 'His luck was right out. And of course, there was the other trouble.'

'What trouble?' Amelia demanded. She was

taking a very poor view of this.

'That was Marcus Spooner's money blowing about — and there was a strong wind. George had to call in all his men to chase it. Half a mile away, and they were still picking 'em up.'

The silences were now becoming cool and discouraging. I had to plunge in quickly. 'It was the money to buy the boy's freedom.' A feeble excuse, that was. I felt ashamed to use it.

'It was', said Amelia heavily, 'the father's money, and you said it yourself . . . he could call up millions. Your job was to rescue the boy . . . '

'Yes. But we couldn't chase them across country like that. We just didn't have the proper vehicles.'

'Hmph!' she said, whipping the hair angrily from her eyes, and Jennie whispered, 'George should have thought of that.'

I didn't mention that I had considered George's whole approach to be wrong. He had wanted to get his hands on them, all three, and hope he could force one of them to reveal the location of the place they were holding the boy. But what if they'd stubbornly refused? What if the two youngsters had been left stranded? No — I'd have made sure they got the money, then we'd have had a good chance they would release the boy unharmed. But I'd been only a sergeant, and he a Chief Super.

'And the third time?' asked Jennie, no tone in her voice at all. It was as dead and distant as an answering machine.

'The third time they picked a village. Somerford, or something like that.'

'Somerville Parva,' said Jennie distantly. 'It's a little more than a village.'

'Whatever it was, they decided the pick-up was to be there, all to be in position by half-past two, by the post-box outside the Junior School. It seemed stupid to us. There just were no bolt-holes for them, this time. One road in and the same road out. But we did exactly as instructed. By then, the three geniuses had worked it out, weight and bulk. They wanted it in used tenners, this time, which still weighed over a hundredweight. But now it was in something they could pick up. A suitcase. They'd even managed to work out the dimensions. So — the tenners in the suitcase, and we left it exactly where they asked. But . . . we got no luck on this thing at all.'

'It went wrong again?'

'It did, my love. There we were, hidden in a house opposite the school, George and I, me with the radio. We'd left the suitcase on the pavement, beside the post-box, as instructed, at two thirty. It came round to that time, and no sign of them. Then a quarter to three, and the kids were soon due out of the school — and we didn't want any more children involved. Then the school bus drew up, to pick up the ones from the neighbouring villages, and it blocked our view of the suitcase. George cussed the driver, and perhaps the cusses reached across the road, because he started his engine again and moved a few yards. Then it drove away altogether, and *then* the kiddie-winkies came rushing out and a crossing-keeper appeared with a stop sign on her pole . . . but they'd missed the bus. It'd left. We didn't understand it for a minute or two, because the suitcase was still there. The trouble was — looking at it more carefully — it'd changed colour. Crafty devils, they'd switched cases while the bus was hiding what was going on.'

'You should've had a policeman hidden in that post-box,' said Amelia, nodding.

'A tiny policeman?'

'I was trying to lighten the tone, Richard. You were beginning to sound quite angry.'

'Yes. Yes, I suppose I was.'

'And of course, you lost them,' she said primly. She was obviously envisioning how she would have laid it all on.

22

'We lost them,' I agreed. 'The bus was abandoned ten miles away, with the driver tied to his seat.'

Frankly, I'd been relieved at the time. Now, I was certain, all we had to do was wait for the phone call . . . where they'd left the little lad. But it never came.

'George told me nothing of this,' Jennie complained, on the edge of tears, 'just that they'd got away with the money.' It seemed to be the only criticism she could produce.

'He ought to have told you everything,' Amelia agreed, reaching over and putting a hand on one of Jennie's.

'Anyway,' I summed up, 'we lost the money, the three men, the boy and the girl. It was months later — I was back on my own patch then — when I heard the three had been arrested. They said they knew nothing about what had happened to the money, or the boy, or the girl. They revealed the name of the girl. What was it? Sylvia Craythorpe, that was it. She was the girl-friend of one of the gang, the sister of another. But all three insisted they didn't know what'd happened to her or to the boy. They wouldn't reveal where they had held him. Or rather, they said they'd never be able to find it again. It was my opinion that they'd hidden the money, and in their fury about what a fiasco it'd all been, and in the way of low-intelligence types, they'd killed the boy. The girl? I can't even guess. They surely wouldn't have killed *her*. Perhaps she was frightened — if they did kill the boy — and she just ran away. But if that was the case, she certainly couldn't have done her running away with a suitcase of money weighing a hundredweight. And the money's never turned up. It hadn't come to light during the time I was in the force, and you can bet we'd have heard of it. The information would've been circulated. And if — as I gather — they're now out of prison, you can be certain they're being watched.'

There was a long silence. In the end, Jennie sighed. 'He made a real botch of it, didn't he?' Now she was appealing. If he'd been ashamed to tell her, it was because he'd thought so, too.

'Not really,' I lied placidly. 'He did everything it was possible to do.'

But he hadn't, I thought, done the correct thing.

'He's never let it drop,' said Jennie softly.

'It would be difficult for him to forget — ' I began.

'No, no. I mean, he was still working on it when he died.'

'Working on it!' Abruptly I felt very depressed. There had been an implication in her statement. Amelia's hand felt cold in mine, and she shifted uneasily. 'In what way do you mean, Jennie?' I asked, trying to sound casual.

'Oh . . . out most evenings. Prowling around. He grew a beard and a moustache and went out in his old gardening clothes. Never an explanation to me. I resented that. But I knew he was snooping. Towards the end, the last few months, he'd been working a window-cleaning round, or something like that.'

'Window-cleaning?' I repeated it like a parrot. The neat and dapper Chief Super doing a window-cleaning round!

'Oh yes.' Jennie tried to laugh it off, to make light of it. But her grey eyes seemed darker, the pupils dilating. 'He bought his own van, second-hand. It's in the garage if you'd like to see it. I'm sure you would.' It was close to an instruction. 'He was driving it the night he died. He would go out with it, ladders on top, in old jeans and a black T-shirt and an anorak, and be out all day. Half the night, sometimes. Oh no, he hadn't let it drop. And . . . ' She hesitated, her eyes darting to Amelia's face, then to mine. 'I'm sure he must have discovered something, in the end.'

'Why do you say that?' I ventured.

'They told me he'd taken a corner too fast, and the van turned over and rolled down to the river and into the trees. An accident. I don't believe that. It wasn't an accident, Richard, I'm sure it wasn't.' And for some obscure reason she seemed unduly concerned that it wasn't even disturbed.

So this was it, what it was all about. And I was caught again. Was I going to jump to my feet and say, 'I'll just collect that camera, or whatever, and we'll get off home.'? I simply sat and stared, out of focus.

It was Amelia who spoke for me. 'And you think he meant Richard to carry it on for him?' You have to say this for my wife: her voice was quite steady, her tone that of a reasonable enquiry.

'I think he hoped that Richard might.' It was a whisper.

'So the bequest was just a lure?' Amelia persisted, getting it right out into the open.

'Oh no.' Jennie looked embarrassed. She even tried a dismissive laugh, but it didn't quite come off. 'A lure! To get your husband to take over his window-cleaning round? Quite absurd! For him . . . oh yes . . . he took it on seriously. I mean — who's better placed for spying through windows? Or taking photos through windows? He used to take cameras out with him. Two cameras. I know

26

that, because there was one in his van when he had his accident, and one in his anorak pocket. A compact, they call it. Here, let me show you. It's all yours now.'

She got to her feet. All of it? Did this include his investigations?

2

She opened the door and waited for us at the foot of the stairs. I detected Amelia's reluctance. She was still uncertain about the length of line attached to George Tate's lure. I smiled at her when she turned her head. She pouted. But we followed Jennie up the stairs.

George had a small back room rigged out as a dark-room. Jennie put on the light — white — though I had the idea he would use an orange one, or complete darkness, when working. It was all very neat, a bench and a table, an enlarger, drawers full of printing papers and photographs, which we didn't have time to look at, and cupboards beneath containing measuring flasks and dishes and trays and the like. Quite an expert, George must have become.

'And there are these,' said Jennie, opening a deeper drawer.

His cameras, two tripods, and an assortment of lenses and accessories, they were all there, together. He had — I can list the cameras now — a Pentax, which I discovered was a single lens reflex camera with a zoom lens and an automatic wind, a Contax T2 pocket camera, which was also motor-wound, and a Leica M6, which Jennie told me he took out at night because it had a very quiet shutter and a fast lens. By this, she meant an F/1, as they put it. Very fast, I later learned. The lens alone would have bought me about half a dozen suits and several pairs of shoes.

'Yours now, Richard,' said Jennie, smiling genuinely for the first time. 'And everything that's in this room.'

I was at the stammering stage, somewhat overwhelmed. 'But . . . I . . . I can't. Really. It's too much. These cameras . . . valuable. You could sell them, Jennie. And the enlarger . . . '

'They're yours. He left them to you for a purpose,' she reminded me. 'That one you're holding is the one they found in the van.'

She was referring to the Pentax. I was busy picking strips of black adhesive tape from it. I stopped picking. The tape could mean something.

'Not in the water?' I asked.

'No. The van didn't actually reach the river.' She was speaking calmly, in a detached manner that she'd acquired in self-defence. 'I think there's a film in it,' she warned me.

'Ah!'

'Would you like to see the van?' she asked.

'And you can come back for all this at another time.'

She meant she would like to see us again, but she didn't like to ask outright.

'Of course,' said Amelia. 'There's no hurry.' But she didn't seem anxious to see the van.

'I'll just take this one along for now,' I said, meaning the Pentax. It was the one he'd been using.

'Certainly. Take what you like.'

Then she took us down to look at the van. It seemed important to her. We went through the kitchen, out to a covered walk along the side of the house, and directly opposite was a door into the garage. She put on the lights.

We had entered at the rear corner. The garage was wide, with double doors, and we had to walk round a cherry red Sierra. The van was beyond. It was a light grey van, small, and its two ladders, rather distorted, were lying against the far wall. The remains of a rack still clung to the battered roof. Only one door of the two rear ones remained, and the driver's door had clearly been cut out, probably by the rescue team. But there had been no fire. George Tate had been crushed behind the wheel.

'Why do you have it here?' I asked. It should surely have gone straight to a scrapyard.

'I wanted it here. To show you, Richard. And it happened only two hundred yards away.'

I glanced quickly at her. She was nodding. Already, so long ago, she had had me in mind. Perhaps George had said something to her, something like, 'If anything should happen to me, let Richard Patton know.' Ah yes. Possibly. If he had realized he was in danger, that is.

'I wanted it as evidence,' Jennie added.

'Of what?' I was puzzled. Was she quite sane?

She pointed. 'That.'

It was a small round hole, a little under half an inch across, a foot behind the driving seat and a little higher up towards the roof. It was a depressed hole, the grey paint peeled evenly around it and darker grey priming revealed beneath. If that wasn't a bullet hole, I would have been very surprised. Amelia didn't need telling. I heard her draw in a shuddering breath.

'What did the police have to say about it?' I asked, not making an issue out of it.

'They said a twig must have gone through it. It *could* have been a twig?' she asked, almost imploring, I thought.

'A twig,' I murmured. 'A twig?' I straightened my shoulders. 'I'll just have a look inside.'

I climbed into the back, where the door was missing. Really, I was searching for an exit hole, it being reasonable to assume that twigs aren't strong enough to make two holes, one in and one out, though bullets are. But I was unlucky. The roof, which had taken most of the impact, was half torn off, and had taken part of the side with it. Disappointing. I turned away, tripping over something caught beneath the tangle that had been the driving seat. I looked down, and dragged it free.

I was holding a leather belt or strap, one that widened in the centre to four or five inches across. I tried to equate it with something in my memory, but couldn't quite retrieve it. It didn't seem to be anything involved with window-cleaning. I put it back where it had been.

'Well?' said Jennie.

I very nearly said, 'Well what?' And there would have been a snap in my voice. As a compromise, I shrugged. 'There's nothing, one way or the other.' She could decide, herself, how to take that.

The fact was that I was simmering with an internal anger. I knew that it was a bullet hole. All right, so it had missed its target, but I knew now that George Tate had been killed. Removed. Quiet, inoffensive and still-suffering George Tate had been murdered.

Haunting him to the day he died had been the basic truth: that there was still the unexplained disappearance of the child and the young girl. Missing, also, was half a million pounds — a relatively minor issue. It might, in any event, no longer be missing, as the three kidnappers were now free. George had probed too deeply. He had touched an exposed nerve.

But . . . was this for me, to pick up and carry on?

As I moved away from it, I noticed that something had been painted over on the van's flank. Inadequately. It was the blue and red logo of British Telecom. George had bought himself an ex-telephone engineer's van, probably already damaged. This linked with the leather strap, though we were half-way home before it clicked.

Nowadays the telephone cables are mostly underground, but there are still telephone poles around. The leather strap was what the men use to lean back against, when they are up a pole, leaving them with both hands free. And they use those little light grey vans with ladders on their roofs. As, apparently, did George Tate.

A man of all work, he had been. Policeman, window-cleaner and telephone linesman. And photographer élite.

But Amelia had already made her decision. This was not for me. As we drove away from Primrose Drive, she squeezed my arm, and I glanced aside to catch her uncertain smile.

'You'd be no good at cleaning windows, Richard, anyway,' she said. At home, she always complains that I don't get into the corners.

Yet it was not so easy as that to dismiss it. The whole set-up had an unsavoury background. *That* was not to my liking. It also involved firearms — one, in any event. That, too, was not to my liking. But George seemed to have trusted me. Why me? I kept asking myself that. What had I done to impress him with any background of reliability? I found it all very disheartening.

I was no doubt very quiet on the trip home. Amelia sat silent beside me, probably having sensed my need for thought. My concentration, though, detracted from my driving ability, so that I was soon aware I had taken a wrong turning somewhere. The last of the streetlights fell far behind us, then the last of the houses, and the road seemed minor, in width and in surface. Our headlights stabbed into the unrelieved darkness, but I was confident we were heading in the right general direction.

'Can you read the stars?' I asked.

'I can't even see any stars.'

It didn't matter. Drive far enough and we would come across a signpost.

By this time, I was certain we had ventured on to the moorland. 'I expect it was somewhere around here that they held the little boy,' I said at last. 'Adrian.'

'You don't know?'

'Nobody ever found out, as far as I'm aware.'

'Hmm!' She was silent for a minute. 'You're still thinking about it, then?'

I grunted. We covered two more miles, and in that distance I had seen no other vehicle. She suddenly said, 'I wonder what he was after, your Chief Superintendent. After all, they did take the three men to court, and convict them. So what did he expect to find out?'

'Oh, I don't know. Where the boy disappeared to, and the girl, and the money.'

'Which?' she demanded. 'That's the important thing, Richard. If he wanted to locate the money — if that was all that interested him — then it wouldn't be difficult for us to forget it. Or was it the boy and the girl?' As I didn't reply, she went on, 'I mean, we know the money's still not turned up, or those three characters would be spending it. And it seems they're not. Perhaps, if your Chief Super was looking for the boy and the girl, we could give him the benefit of the doubt and assume he was simply searching for the truth. Or do we have to reckon that all he wanted was to find the money . . . for himself?'

'No, no. Not George.' I leaned forward. It was the first signpost we'd seen for miles. 'Ah . . . we turn right, I think.'

'What did you mean . . . no, no?'

'The last. Not the money. George would be interested in the people involved.' But, at the time, he'd seemed unduly obsessed with the money.

'As you are, Richard,' she said quietly. 'Always.' Meaning people.

'Damn it, you're inexplicable sometimes, Amelia. Usually you try to persuade me the other way. Now you seem to want me to go on with this.'

She touched my arm. I couldn't see, but I knew she was smiling. 'I was thinking of the parents. All these years, and not knowing! The girl would've had a family too, you know.'

'Her brother was one of the three.'

'Yes — but *he* didn't disappear.'

I was silent, contemplating the agony of not knowing. To be certain your child is dead, as Amelia had been, that would be bad enough. But . . . not to know . . . it was painful even to think about it. Better, surely, for the child to be discovered dead, and given a decent funeral. At least, the distress would then begin to ease. The Spooners and the Craythorpes, an eternity apart as regards their background and wealth, would nevertheless have had to handle the same distress.

At last I was on the road I wanted. Amelia said, 'And it would be very embarrassing, now, to tell Jennie Tate you're not intending to go on with it. Could we face her and tell her that . . . then clear out that dark-room for her? Or do we phone her and ask her to package it up and send it? COD. That's where we're trapped, Richard. And *such* an unpleasant business! A quiet domestic difficulty for you to sort out, and you're in your element. But this . . . yuk!'

Two more miles sped away. Then she said, 'Trapped. How *can* you get out of it?'

There was no need to reply. It had been a decision, not a question. No more was said about it until we were home. Mary was wondering about our evening meal, as usual. She fusses over our welfare. And the two boxers, Sheba and Jake, were worrying about their evening outing. Strangely, I wasn't worrying at all. As far as I was concerned, a decision had been taken. It's so often more difficult to make a decision than to act on it.

That was a fond delusion I used to cherish. I have since changed my mind.

I had brought the Pentax with me. We had a cup of tea, and sat looking at it, the camera on the table between us.

'She said there's a film in it,' I remembered. 'But we don't know if there's anything on it.'

'No,' Amelia agreed. 'We don't. But you can find out very soon. I want to go into town in the morning.' Town being Bridgnorth. She can read my mind.

As it would probably progress the situation a little, this was what we did. While Amelia scouted for what she wanted, I hunted round till I found a camera shop.

'I'm told there's a film in it,' I said, presenting the camera. 'But I don't know how to get it out.'

The young man looked down at it, lying on his counter. 'A Pentax. Nice job. You're not a photographer, then?'

'Completely ignorant,' I admitted. 'But I think I'll have to start learning.'

He picked it up almost reverently, twiddled a knob, and said, 'Yes, there's a film in it, and it seems to have been fully exposed. The counter shows thirty-six. You push this here and it releases the film, then it winds back.' He did that. 'And when it stops winding you open the back like this, and bingo . . . one exposed film.'

'How soon . . . ' I began.

'I can have them back for you early tomorrow afternoon. Black and white, I see. Not so much of that done, these days.'

'You mean the film might have been used ages ago?'

'Oh no. Not necessarily. It's a very fast film. The previous owner might have needed the high speed of this film, in order to work in very poor light.'

My impression was that the previous owner had habitually operated in poor light. I didn't say so.

'It's sticky,' he said, the camera still in his hands, a trace of distaste in his voice. A camera, to him, was a precious thing, and ought to be pristine.

'It could well be,' I agreed. 'There was black sticky tape stuck to it.'

'Was there? Fancy that. Perhaps he forgot his tripod one day, and taped it to a tree. It's been done before. I'll give it a bit of a clean, if you like. Have to be careful with a camera, you know.'

I nodded and smiled, and he disappeared into the rear. Strapped to a tree, I thought. Telephone poles, when alive, used to be trees.

Slowly I wandered round his shop, looking

at his display of books on photography. I was perhaps going to need some help. *Photography for Beginners*. I would certainly need that. And there was a Pentax guide, and a book devoted to the Leica. Only a brochure for the Contax T2, though.

He returned, the Pentax shiny and clean and smelling slightly of surgical spirit.

'It's in perfect condition,' he told me. 'Ah — you want to take these books? Invaluable . . . ' His eyes came up to mine. 'There's a Leica and a Contax, too?'

I smiled at him. 'Somebody's will. I'll have to learn a lot, won't I? There's the three cameras and lots of lenses.'

'If you'd bring them in, I could value them for you. If you're thinking of selling, sir, that is.'

I noticed I'd become a sir. 'No. No thanks.' One didn't sell bequests. It was like gifts. 'Tomorrow afternoon, then.'

I walked out into the October sunlight, suddenly wishing I had a fresh film in the Pentax, and that I knew how to use it. A portion of the young man's enthusiasm had infiltrated my mind.

Amelia was waiting by the old Town Hall. I said, 'You've been quick.'

'It wasn't much. Just looking. I only wanted to come along with you.'

It sounded as though she didn't want me out of her sight. If that was how it affected her, then I'd have to drop this affair, I thought.

'Shall we stroll around?' I suggested. 'It's a lovely morning.'

'Yes. Let's do that.'

So we strolled around, and finished up in the inevitable café — Amelia has her favourite one in Bridgnorth — then went back to collect Amelia's car. Tomorrow afternoon seemed an eternity away. At least, now, I knew that there had been an exposed film in the camera.

But time progresses. After lunch the next day I said I would just pop into town for my photos. Amelia showed no inclination to join me, so I took the two dogs, using my Triumph Stag. They like the Stag, because the rear seat is close to the front ones, and they can sit behind me and pant into my ears. One each. I had them on their leads when I entered the shop.

'I'm sorry, sir, he hasn't been yet.'

I might have expected that. Nothing ever happens as promised, these days. We went out and did some walking round, went back, and yes, they had arrived. I paid for them, and, using great restraint, prevented myself from looking at them there and then. You never

41

know what a window-cleaner's camera might record.

But back in the car I had them out in a flash. Fortunately — and it was not intentional — I kept them in their correct order, though it would have been possible, I supposed, to have restored them to that by checking against the negatives.

The first impression was of disappointment. I had thirty-six photographs apparently the same. Only on a second check did I detect in what way they differed.

They were all of a window. Or rather, of most of a window, a narrow sash window a century old, the side frame visible, and the lower rail. There was a run of bricks beneath the rail, bricks sloping outwards to form a sill. Half of one was broken away. I could barely detect this. The curtains were drawn back. It was night-time, and the lights were on in the room beyond.

The first three photos were of a framed picture on the wall opposite. Then, from number four onwards, there was no picture, but instead the face of a small wall safe. Two similar shots of that face followed, but then there was a change. There was a hand on the dial of the combination lock. The next eighteen all seemed the same, the same hand and the same dial, but differently placed, then the last few were of an open safe. In one, the hand was reaching inside. In the final three the safe door was open, but the interior apparently empty.

I returned them carefully to their packet, and drove home to The Beeches. If the dogs panted at me, I didn't notice.

'Well?' asked Amelia, the moment I set foot inside the door.

'There's something. I'll show you. I just had a quick look through.'

We went through into the sitting-room, followed by Mary with a tea tray set for three. Mary's our friend, and reckons to be in on everything. We go along with that. So the three of us went through the photos, one person at a time, because I had, by then, realized that the sequence was probably important.

'But I don't understand,' said my wife, when she'd gone through them all twice.

'They're pictures of somebody opening a safe, which has a combination lock. From these it might be possible to work out the combination.' It was the only explanation I could offer.

Mary protested. 'And your policeman friend took them! A retired senior man like that, and *he* took them?'

I smiled at her. Mary is impetuous. 'His camera did.'

'I don't understand,' Amelia complained again.

'Put it all together,' I said. 'What have we got? He was supposed to have a window-cleaning round. Perhaps he had — a genuine one. But if so, he was using it for snooping. And then, more recently, there's been the little van and the two ladders, and the camera with the black sticky tape, and the strap — the belt the telephone engineers use.'

'You didn't mention that,' she put in quickly.

'Sorry. I forgot. It was inside the van. And consider this: these are pictures of somebody, assume a man for now, with a light on in his room while he opens his safe — and with the curtains open. He wouldn't do that, surely, unless he knew he was overlooked by no other house. Yet perhaps he *was* overlooked by a telephone pole. But this safe-opening business took place at night. Perhaps George Tate had discovered that the householder went to the safe *only* at night. George had obviously spent a long while on it. But he couldn't go out at night climbing telephone poles. Even in the dark, and there were probably streetlights, it would look suspicious. But he could climb one in daylight, when the owner was absent. That would look natural. And if — when he came down — he left a box-like shape fastened to the pole, who would notice? There are already junction boxes up there, anyway.'

I sat back. My tea was cold. My enthusiasm was warm. They stared at me. In the end, Amelia said, 'Then how did he operate the shutter?'

'I was looking at the books last night. I'll never master all that. But there're things called remote controls. The Pentax winds itself on and resets its shutter. George could have done it from on the ground, perhaps hiding in a hedge.'

She pouted doubtfully and looked across at Mary, who shook her head. Neither would accept it.

'Why didn't he use one of those video cameras, then?' Amelia challenged.

'It would have to be rigged in the daylight, then left until George returned in the evening. An ordinary camera could be mistaken for a junction box, but a video camera would be too obvious.'

She still looked doubtful. 'I still think . . . I mean, a camera . . . how would he know *when* to operate his wonderful remote control?' She was being forceful. 'I mean, how to time it . . . if he was sitting in a hedge.' She nodded. So there.

'He wouldn't know. He would have to guess.'

'Then he was a good guesser.' She gestured towards the set of pictures.

'But we don't know that,' I pointed out. 'Nor how many goes he'd had at it before this one. Perhaps here . . . ' I gestured, 'we've got exactly what he was after.'

'And he kept the previous failures?'

'Hopefully.' It would prove my theory, if nothing else.

Without another word she went to the phone, obtained Jennie's number from Directory Enquiries, and got her at once.

From our end of it I gathered that yes, we'd be welcome to call again the following morning, and no, Jennie hadn't disturbed anything in the dark-room, nor thrown anything away.

Frankly, I felt rather pleased with myself. It had been a tidy bit of reasoning. I carried it on in my mind to include the possibility that George had been killed by the owner of that house *because* he had discovered the combination of the safe. But that was wrong — wasn't it! George hadn't discovered it. He had died before he'd developed and printed this last film.

But I felt we had nearly reached a turning-point, one that had narrowly eluded George Tate.

Such complacency is bound to precede a fall. I had no premonitions on the drive next morning to Jennie's. In fact, Amelia commented on my optimistic mood, and attempted to blunt it.

'I mean,' she expounded, 'even if you find evidence to support your wild ideas, you'll be no further forward. And,' she continued, before I could get a word in, 'I'm still not certain of what your way forward is likely to lead you to, even supposing it leads anywhere.'

'You said it yourself.' I put this lightly. 'I need something to occupy my mind.'

'Yes.' She was silent, silent so long that I glanced sideways at her. Sensing this, she plunged in. 'I'd consider it as something more than an occupation for your mind, when it appears that somebody's already been killed because *he* occupied his mind . . . and on the same thing.'

'George seems to have occupied much more than his mind,' I pointed out. 'His van and his ladders and his cameras — and for months.'

'And look what that got him.' It was her briskly dismissive mood.

47

There had seemed to be some agreement before. To discover what had happened to the little boy and the young girl . . . Amelia would go along with that, if reluctantly. But she appeared to have given it more thought, and now had reservations.

'I intended to occupy only my mind,' I assured her. 'Not a risky thing to do, surely.'

'A bullet is risky.'

'We don't know it's a bullet hole.'

'In the same way, I suppose, that you don't know the boy is dead?'

'Yes. Yes, if you like.'

'And you'd find it interesting — an occupation for your mind — if you could prove the boy is dead?' She sounded disgusted. 'I suppose it would give you pleasure to take your proof, one way or the other, to the parents! There's the girl too, you know. And *her* parents.'

When Amelia gets going like this, you might as well give up and remain silent. In fact, I'd learned, she usually intended it as a monologue. Having made a tentative decision she was not happy with, she would throw objections at her own feet to see whether she could step over them, or even trample them flat. It was a form of self-reassurance. But this time she didn't at once express any more thoughts, and for a mile or more she was silent. Then, having pushed it around a little, she demanded, 'Well? Wouldn't you?'

Experience had taught me to carry in my mind her last previous remarks. 'I wouldn't find it a pleasure — no,' I said. 'A duty, perhaps. For the parents to be certain . . . surely that's something to offer them.'

She relapsed into silence again, but it was a different silence. She had to have time to think it through, but she'd now got a good grasp on it. Fortunately, she hadn't squeezed a conclusion from it by the time I turned the Granada into Primrose Drive.

All was quiet and peaceful. I parked the car out on the street and we walked up to the porch, me reaching for the bell push. The door opened.

Jennie's face was set in an expression I could not analyse. Not stern, not reproving. Cautious, perhaps. She spoke quietly in a dead voice, empty of any emotion.

'Not now, Richard, please,' she said. 'Some other time, perhaps.'

The door began to close. Instinctively, because I had to know the reason for this abruptly disturbing change in attitude, I reached forward with a hand in order to hold the door, but Amelia jerked at my other arm.

'Of course, Jennie, of course,' she said. 'Come along, Richard.'

I have always held the theory that women can speak to each other without words, especially when the communication crackles across a space charged with high emotion. I therefore reacted at once to Amelia's signal, and half turned away.

But a voice from inside the house held me. 'That's Amelia, isn't it? And Richard.'

At this, Jennie couldn't maintain any decisive action. She stepped back, and Tony Brason was standing there at the end of the hall. Jennie looked confused.

'Richard!' he called.

Then he came forward and we shook hands and we thumped each other's shoulders, before he turned to Amelia, at once more serious. He put his hands to her shoulders and kissed her firmly on the cheek, too close to her lips for my liking.

But I was wondering why Jennie should have tried to keep us apart. Did she feel that I, as well as George, must be considered as in opposition to the police?

'You know each other, then?' she asked with uncertainty.

3

'Indeed we do,' I said. Yes, we were friends.

But it hadn't always been so, not by any means. When I'd first met him I'd been a detective inspector and he a country copper, a constable. And at that time I'd used him disgracefully, very nearly wrecking his career. But I'd had a very good reason. I had been fighting to save Amelia from arrest for murder, and only he, naïve and enthusiastic, would have fitted the role I selected for him. Between us — though he wouldn't have seen it in that light — we had saved her.

Since then I'd met him twice, he climbing stubbornly up the ladder of promotion. But the first occasion had been at a bad time for him, as the circumstances had included his wife's tragic death. And once more after that, we had met, in Norfolk, when I'd been trying to help a friend of Amelia's over a difficulty she had.

Oh yes, I knew Tony, knew him so well that I could accept that he had forgotten our original meeting and my initial attack on his personality. If anything, I like to tell myself, I helped him. In any event, he's one of those big, open-hearted people who do not carry grudges very comfortably. But don't imagine him as naïve. Not now. He had an agile mind, and was very perceptive.

If he perceived Jennie's slight embarrassment, he glossed it over, drawing up a chair for Amelia. Jennie darted her eyes from one face to the other, then resumed her own seat.

It seemed that Tony had been on his feet. He was a little restless, and moving around. I stood and watched him.

'This your patch now, Tony?' I asked.

'It is. Inspector. CID. My patch, yes.'

'You certainly cover some territory,' I commented.

'You have to keep moving, these days. Experience. It looks good on your record.'

I nodded, smiling. But he hadn't yet managed to move far enough from his memories. I could see that in his eyes. They didn't meet mine for any period longer than two seconds.

'And what brings you here?' I asked.

'The same as you.' He looked around him. The two women were watching every move. He had a vitality that attracts attention from women. 'We're both beneficiaries in the same will, I believe.'

'Oh?' I asked. 'You mean George Tate's?'

'Of course. You inherited his camera stuff, and I — '

'How d'you know that?' I cut in.

'The solicitor told me.' He raised his eyebrows at my tone.

'I don't think he's supposed to do that.' I wasn't confident on that point, though.

'Oh come on, Richard, you know wills are legally public knowledge. Besides . . . ' He grinned. 'In any event, I know something about Dennis Finch. Nothing spectacular, mind you, but he fell over himself to tell me the lot. It appears you inherited the cameras. That interested me.'

'It would. What d'you know about Finch, Tony?'

'It's trivial.'

'Then it can't matter if you tell me.'

He was annoyed, and glanced at Jennie. But I was slow, and didn't pick it up. I should have realized his reluctance involved Jennie.

'Drop it, will you! It's not why we're here,' he said shortly.

'I know why I am. Why're you? Because of what Finch told you?'

I could sense his reluctance to continue with that, which was why I persisted. But he was moving round the room, still avoiding my eye. He jerked a hand in dismissal. 'Dennis Finch is completely honest.'

'Nevertheless . . . ' I left that hanging as a question.

'For God's sake!' Then he shrugged. 'All right. I happened to be in the bank, one day about three months ago, and saw Finch's clerk paying in £500 in used tenners. You understand . . . ' He glanced again at Jennie, then quickly away. 'Those three kidnappers had been out of prison, on parole, for a few months. You can imagine . . . the whole town knew that tenners in any sort of quantity, in this particular district, had to be looked at a bit warily. So I went to Finch and asked him where he'd got them from. I mean — you'd have expected a solicitor to have told us, without having to be asked. He said a client had paid them to him. I demanded who, and he was sticky on that, then he told me. Guess who.'

'I don't . . . ' Then I understood. 'Don't tell me!'

'Yes. It was George Tate. He'd paid them to Finch, to hold in a special account.'

Jennie made a tiny sound. The blood had drained from her face, and this stifled choke was all she could manage.

'Go on,' I said, almost dreading it.

'It was the proceeds of a blackmail operation. George made a sworn deposition to the solicitor, that he'd extracted that

54

particular £500 from Big Martie Machin, who was supposed to have been the leader of the kidnap gang, as you probably know, Richard. George had done that by issuing threats. People don't usually threaten Big Martie with impunity. But George did it, and was paid off. You can see what he was after.'

Of course I could. At last. It had taken a long while to penetrate. I smiled at Jennie, who looked on the point of either fainting, or launching a violent verbal attack on Tony.

'Yes, I see,' I said quietly. 'Don't you see, Jennie?'

'But he . . . he told me nothing of this. It's the first I've heard about it.'

'He'd have had to play it very carefully,' I told her. 'The kidnap money never turned up, and the assumption had to be that they'd hidden it away, to dig out when they were released. But if they hadn't gone on a spending spree, all three of them, and they'd been on the loose for three or four months, then that would've put a different shade on it.'

Tony seemed to be too tense to take a seat. He flicked a warning glance at me. 'We were all waiting for the first sign, waiting . . . and no big spending was making any sort of appearance. But George . . . Mrs Tate, your husband was a fine man, a most remarkable man. It's now clear he tried something he couldn't have done as a serving police officer. Blackmail. He put Big Martie in a situation where he'd got to produce £500, or else. It was beyond any possibility that our friend Machin could produce £500 by honest employment, and George, I reckon, was counting on that. And it worked. Machin produced the money — in used tens. It was what George had been after, evidence that Big Martie at least had access to cash, though of course he couldn't use it as legal proof, as there was no way the notes could've been traced back. But that appears to be as far as it went. Pity. The Chief Super was getting so close.'

Then at last he took a seat, having talked himself out of his mood of restlessness.

'But he told me nothing,' Jennie whispered again. This was a major issue to her.

'Your husband', said Tony softly, 'would have had to consider the possibility of retaliation from Big Martie. He wouldn't have wanted you to be worried, but he knew he had something that would keep Martie under control. It's more than likely he wouldn't expect you to accept that, you not knowing the people involved. But I assure you, and I know them, what George did, and then used to threaten Martie, could've put Martie into mortal danger.'

This appeared to amuse him. Tony's mood had changed. Now he'd got the worst over, he was prepared to approach it more lightly. His eyes narrowed, but I caught the twinkle in them.

'Are we to be told exactly what George did?' I asked him.

'Well . . . ' He sat back. 'I suppose you could call it indecent exposure.'

Jennie made a tiny eeking sound and flushed scarlet, then the blood ran from her face like a lowered curtain and she was stone white.

'Don't be ridiculous, Tony,' said Amelia, annoyed with him because she had always thought him to be so gentlemanly.

'Sorry.' He looked embarrassed. 'I could've put it better, I suppose. What he did was expose a full spool of film, all of Big Martie doing unspeakable things with Pearlie Stone. Perverted Pearlie, they call her. Or Pearlie the Perv. Then George used those photos to blackmail Martie.'

There was a short silence. I was beginning to see round and through it. 'Big Martie being tough enough to lead a gang of three men and a young girl in snatching a boy of five, but not tough enough to face up to that?'

Tony nodded. 'Exactly.'

Amelia's eyes fastened on me, and they were huge. It was becoming clear that George's activities with his cameras and ladders had been extensive and diverse.

'And what frightened Martie Machin?' I asked.

Tony grinned. 'His wife. You ought to meet her, Richard. It's quite an experience. Martie must've been stupid to go anywhere near Pearlie. His wife would kill him. He'd never have dared to close his eyes in his own home again. 'Bringing her filthy diseases into my house!' I can hear her screaming it at him.' He had managed to sound like a vicious old crone.

'And has she?' I asked. 'Killed him, I mean.'

'No.' Tony smiled beamingly. 'Unfortunately, not to date. She can't have seen the photos. After all, Martie *did* pay out £500 to George, thus proving he had access to it, so George apparently played his hand very close to his chest after that. But Mrs Machin must've heard rumours, because she threw Martie's hat into the street — '

'Hat?' asked Amelia. 'Did you say hat?'

'Yes. Apparently it's a custom round here. The missus tosses your hat in the street, and it's as good as saying, go and join it, buster.

Anyway, he's now staying with Tim Cray-thorpe, another of the gang, and *his* woman. Or perhaps it's the other way round, and they're both living with Pearlie.'

'Craythorpe,' I said. 'He was one of their team. Sylvia was his sister, the girl they had with them on the kidnap.'

'That's the one.'

'The girl who's never been seen since.'

'That's her. So George succeeded with that little plan. He'd got them worrying, if nothing else.'

I thought about that. Tony got to his feet, and again moved around restlessly. He was too tense, too eager to get somewhere with this.

'All right.' I nodded. 'So George had some success with that. He forced Big Martie Machin into producing £500. But if *he'd* got access to the money, why weren't all three of them spending like mad things? I never got the impression they were anything but a group of low-life louts.'

Tony nodded. 'Exactly describes them.'

'So they wouldn't be able to restrain themselves.'

Tony peered at nothing through the french windows. 'Perhaps they left the money with somebody else, to keep and preserve, and *he's* got control of it. Somebody with brains, who'd play it carefully, somebody who'd feed it out only for emergencies.'

'That lot!' I dismissed the idea shortly. 'For them, being in a pub with empty pockets would be considered an emergency.'

Tony stared at me with vacant eyes, his mind a mile away.

'I suppose', I suggested, 'that there was no question that these three *were* guilty of the kidnapping? I mean — these days, no end of convictions are getting quashed.'

He sat down again abruptly, leaning forward with his elbows on his knees, and spoke between raised palms.

'I know what you're thinking. It would explain why the money's never turned up, if an entirely different bunch did it. But no. I've read the file, over and over. Your name's in there, Richard. And believe me, that was a solid case. What about Sylvia, then, the young girl? She fits in with them, through her brother Tim, and *she* hasn't been seen since. No . . . it fits. Three mates . . . they always worked together on the wretched, paltry robberies they did whenever they got hungry or thirsty. All three were missing at the same time — those twenty-three days — not seen at any of their haunts or pubs. And so was the Ford Escort belonging to Ron Phelps, who was always their getaway driver. They were missing, then they turned up again, but not with Sylvia, and they didn't have any reason to lie about her. When they confessed — straight confessions, Richard, every alteration initialled, nothing dicey — when they confessed, they all said the same thing. She'd disappeared. You have to read between the lines on the reports, but I gather they all came out with exactly the same story: that when they got back to the 'place' as they called it, at last with the money, the girl Sylvia and the boy Adrian weren't there. Or something like that.'

Amelia interrupted at that point. She had been very silent, leaning forward with her chin supported in her palm, but silent. Now she saw a point with which a woman's viewpoint might lend credulity to the story.

'It's not so unacceptable,' she said musingly. 'It'd been over three weeks, you say. Three weeks they'd been together, the girl and the little boy. Pretty close, they'd have become. You can't imagine those three men taking much notice of them. And then they got to the third attempt to collect the money, and maybe they were pretty confident that this time they were going to pull it off. If Sylvia had become fond of the lad, and he of her, she'd have realized she was soon going to lose him. She could even . . . ' She paused to clear her throat. ' . . . Even have believed they might harm him, the boy. Adrian. Harm him. And in that case — oh, I don't know. Perhaps she would, in that event, have taken Adrian away, that last day of it all.' She touched her lips. 'Don't you think?' she whispered.

Tony glanced at me, and raised his eyebrows. He'd always admired Amelia. 'Logical, Richard?'

'Very,' I agreed.

'But,' he said, '*how* would she have done it? I mean — they never revealed the location of their place, in fact they seemed confused themselves, and not sure they could find it again. And there's a hell of a lot of wild moorland around there. I haven't had time yet to go checking it.'

'You'd need a lot of time, Tony,' I assured him. 'It's like a wilderness. It'd take you months to cover the lot.'

'Yes. And the place they used would have to be isolated . . . so, how would she have taken the boy away with her? Walking? Never. He wouldn't have been able to walk very far.'

'Their car, perhaps. If she could drive.'

'No,' he said. 'It was that old Ford Escort I mentioned, belonging to Ron Phelps. It was the only vehicle they had, apart from the ones they stole as they needed them, for the job. And when they were arrested, that car was back in town, in the garage Phelps rented.'

None of this sounded very good to me. There was no crack in which I might insert a wedge. 'How long have they been on the streets again?'

'Nearly a year, now.'

'Hmm!'

Nearly a year, and nothing stirring, apart from George Tate's activities.

'And Tim Craythorpe?' I asked. 'What did he have to say about his sister?'

Tony's eyes were bright. One suspended hand slowly clenched into a fist. 'I gather he just shrugged, and said she was old enough to look after herself. He's a moron, that Tim Craythorpe.'

'What about her parents?' Amelia demanded. 'The father and the mother.'

'I'm told he died not long after the kidnap, and the mother's never got over it. She threw Tim out, when he came out of prison. Out on the street.'

'Like Martie's hat?'

'Like that, Richard. That's why he's living with a woman now.'

'With Martie — the woman being this Perverted Pearlie you mentioned?'

'Yes. So I believe. I'm not certain.'

We were all silent. The girl and the boy, that was what I was thinking about. No doubt

63

the others were, too. Excepting, perhaps, Tony, who had already done all the thinking he cared to suffer over.

Jennie had said nothing for a while. She had just sat there with the colour blooming and fading on her cheeks. She tried a weak smile when I turned to her, but she was clearly lost, not knowing which way to think. I smiled back.

'It seems, Jennie,' I said, 'that your husband has been very active since that foul bunch came out of prison. And every move he's made has been with a specific objective. He was working right on the outside edge of the law, but you needn't think any the less of him for that. You ought to be proud of him. Very proud.'

'Oh, I am. I am. I just wish he'd told me.'

'He felt he had to protect you, even from the worry of it. It was like a game of chess to him. Moves and counter-moves. It was a game he had to win, or he'd never rest.'

'He never rested,' she agreed numbly. 'And he didn't win, did he?'

I felt Amelia reaching for my hand. The game wasn't finished. It was simply that I'd taken it over, though with no understanding of his game-plan. Now I was landed with his most recent move, the photographs of the safe door. I had to assume it was the most recent, and his last. The film had been in the camera, fully exposed. And the camera had been in his van when he died. Oh Lord, I thought, what have I inherited? Which reminded me . . .

But Tony got in first, returning to a former conjecture. 'I can't help thinking there's a mastermind behind this, controlling the money, knowing it'd be fatal to allow them a full share all in one go.'

'Nonsense,' I said crisply. 'Can you imagine them going to all that trouble to pick up the money, then calmly handing it over to someone else? More likely, once they'd got their hands on that suitcase of money they'd have headed briskly for the far horizon — and not even gone back to the place, as they called it. Yes. I can see them doing that. And it would explain what happened to Sylvia and Adrian. They just didn't return, and . . . ' I let it tail off; it didn't bear thinking about.

Amelia moaned softly, and whispered, 'Oh no!'

'Go and see her mother,' Tony said icily. 'Ask *her* what she thinks. Ask her if Tim's ever said one word . . . and he's her brother, for heaven's sake.'

'Yes,' I agreed. 'Yes.'

He stared at me bleakly. He hadn't intended it as a suggestion, merely an underlining of the situation. Then he heaved himself to his feet.

'What did I come for?' He slapped his pockets, as though he might have it already. 'Ah yes.'

I prompted, 'Your inheritance.'

'As you have, too?' His lips twitched.

I didn't allow myself to be distracted. 'What did he leave you in his will, Tony?'

He quoted. ' 'To the new officer at the station, DI Brason, who at least took the time to listen to me, I leave my helicopter.' '

'He left . . . what?'

'Here it is.' Tony crossed to the sideboard, on which it was standing. It was not a toy, more a mobile ornament. Tony demonstrated by twirling its rotor. The helicopter rose an inch, it swayed, it pitched, until the rotor slowed and died, when it settled back again. 'I'll take it now, if I may,' he said to Jennie. 'It'll look nice on my desk.'

But Jennie was still a little behind, sifting the gist of our discussion. She could do no more than nod numbly.

He picked it up by its stand and beamed at it, then he turned away. 'His helicopter,' he murmured, as though it meant something. Perhaps it did.

'Tony,' I said. 'We'll need to talk.' I got this in quickly, before he walked out.

'Any time, Richard. Ask for me at the desk.'

'And you'll be out on a job?'

'Leave a message. I've got your phone number. I'll let myself out, Mrs Tate.'

The door closed behind him. There was a long and awkward silence. Then, abruptly, Jennie was on her feet and out of the room as though fleeing. Shortly, we heard a kettle being filled, a pot being clattered.

'She's upset,' Amelia murmured. 'She's doing the only thing she could think to do that doesn't require much thought.'

We sat, and quietly waited. Not silently, but quietly. We whispered together.

'It's obviously not for you, Richard. It's a police job.' She tugged at my arm in emphasis.

'Every action, everything he did, George Tate had a damn good reason.'

'Which is more than you've got.'

'George's death?' I suggested. 'The missing boy? The missing girl?' I touched her cheek with the tips of my fingers. She felt cold. 'Three things I've got.'

'We can drive away from here, and leave it all behind.'

'I wouldn't be leaving any of it, my love. I'd be taking it with me.'

'You're a fool, Richard Patton, and I love you desperately. I couldn't bear it if you . . . if you came to harm.'

'I'll have Tony.'

'It didn't sound to me like it. A voice on a phone — '

'No. You'll see.'

'I don't want to see. I want to go home.'

Fortunately, Jennie came rattling in with a tray of tea things, which she banged down firmly on the small inlaid table between us.

'What an unpleasant young man,' she said, having had time to sort herself out.

I glanced at Amelia, whose lips were set. Tony would be into his thirties now, and Jennie surely not too far in her forties, I guessed. And I'd never thought of Tony as unpleasant.

'You found him so?' I asked, resuming my seat beside Amelia.

'His attitude ... flip and ... and ... graceless. It's hardly a matter to make distasteful jokes about, now is it?'

She was referring to his comment on indecent exposure. But Tony had been nervous. Even now, after such a length of time, he'd been affected by my initial treatment of him. He was still unable to conduct, with any confidence, anything such as a ferreting for information in my presence, feeling that I might trip him up and he'd make, once more, an utter fool of himself. It might have been subconscious, but it was there. And it was my fault, blast it.

'I think he was trying to make light of it,' said Amelia. 'For you, Jennie. I mean, it was a very serious thing your husband did. Blackmail.'

Jennie pouted. Self-disgust silenced me. With my teeth clamped together I could do no more than nod. It was not noticed. As though Amelia's words had been the final tug to the opening lock gates, the words flooded from Jennie, while she occupied her eyes and her hands — clumsily and shakily, but occupied — in pouring tea.

'I think, towards the end, he was a little insane. George was. No — more than a little. And he told me nothing. Nothing! His wife . . . and he made a fool of me. Didn't trust me, as though I might criticize. As though I would! Blackmail, you said.' Then she performed a complete inversion. 'Of course, he knew very well what I'd have said about *that*. Oh yes. He'd have got the sharp edge of my tongue. Deceiving me. Oh . . . you don't have to say anything. I asked for it, letting him have his own way on everything, never asking him . . . him . . . never asking him what the bloody hell he thought he was doing. But no — he had to keep me in the dark. Help yourselves to sugar.'

We did so, while she paused to sip, with lips pursed sourly, at her own tea. I'd found it startling to hear her swear. I didn't dare to catch Amelia's eye, though I could sense she had glanced at me. But we didn't need to say anything.

'Towards the end,' Jennie confided, leaning forward, her eyes bright and, I thought, too unnaturally wild, 'the last six months, d'you know, I was actually afraid of him. Barely aware of me, he was. I was there, put his meals in front of him — when he turned up for them — and if he said a word it was ungracious. The damned fool was driving himself out of his mind. He . . . he set up a bed in the spare bedroom, and got into the habit of going straight there from his dark-room. I can tell you, I started locking my own bedroom door. There! That's how bad it was.' She glanced at her watch. 'Hadn't you better start clearing out that dark-room? You'll have it dark, the way the time's flying. Dark outside, too,' she amplified, and she gave a strange choking sound that could have been a laugh at what might have been intended as a play on words.

'I suppose I had,' I agreed, only too pleased to comply.

'I'll help you, Richard.' Amelia was quick on that.

But I didn't really want her with me, not since I'd heard that George had been taking pictures of Big Martie Machin's activities with Pearlie the Perv. Tony, by using Pearl Stone's nickname so flippantly, had taken some of the sting out of the impact, but I had no doubt that if the photos were still in existence they wouldn't be something Amelia would care to see. So I'd wished to do the job alone. But no, Amelia likes to be in on everything. She was already on her feet.

'You know where it is,' said Jennie, a little listless now that she'd expressed her viewpoint.

We went up to George's dark-room. I knew where it was.

4

I realized at once that Jennie had been in there. Why not? It was her home. But I hoped that she'd not taken away or destroyed any details which, in her reckoning, might have further denigrated her husband's image. No — probably not. It was only now that she was hearing some of the more disturbing facets.

But I was still left with the feeling that Amelia's hands might drop on George's blackmail evidence. Amelia is not a prude, but her experience embraces only the more natural performances. Yet . . . Jennie had been in there. A porcelain tray was further back on the workbench; a drawer was slightly withdrawn. It was a drawer which, previously, I had assumed to be jammed, a shallow one close to the floor and beneath the door of the bench. I crouched and had a look at it. There was a lock to it, and the wood was now broken away where some metal instrument had been used. I slid it open. It was full of manilla envelopes, all bulging with photographs.

Even if Jennie had removed anything, it couldn't have been startling. What was left was quite innocuous. I straightened and quickly scanned through each pack. Amelia took them from my hands as I did so. Nothing but night street shots of men coming out of pubs or going in, or doing likewise at clubs, and similar shots of the same men inside such premises. Nothing wildly exciting there. There was a set taken from outside a restaurant, indistinct because street lighting was reflected back from the windows, and the lights inside were dim and discreet.

I pulled out the drawer and placed it on the working surface. A set of six envelopes was towards the back, strapped together with an elastic band. I removed the bundle — or rather, it fell apart as I touched it. The envelopes were numbered, but strangely not in the normal numerical sequence. Number four was on top, then seven, then six, then five, then eight, and the last bore the number nine. I stared at the numbers, and could make no sense of them. At first, I leapt to the assumption that Jennie had been there and disturbed things — but she couldn't have replaced that rotting rubber band. The numbers weren't even in numerical sequence, nor did they represent dates, I saw. In the top corners there were unmistakable dates: 6 June, 4 July. And so on. *These* were the sequence, the dates. So what did the numbers

4, 7, 6, 5, 8, 9 mean? Inside each envelope was a set of pictures, seemingly copies of the set I already had at home. But they couldn't be. They had to be George's earlier attempts. It was the same window. I recognized the brickwork of the windowsill, and the one broken brick. It was the same safe door, the same combination dial, and the same hand. Yes, the same right hand, blunt fingers, and the signet ring on the third finger.

Amelia said in a choked voice, 'These are the ones that will interest you, Richard.'

I turned, and she was standing there, her hand over her mouth, her eyes huge above it. She thrust a set of prints into my hand.

These were in full colour. I can say this for George (and these were clearly hand-held shots), that they had extraordinary crispness, the colour rendering was superb, and the impression of movement fully but delicately conveyed. Every finest detail was recorded. Clearly, these were copies of the blackmail photos: Pearlie and Big Martie in uninhibited play. George had managed to convey fully the physical and psychological facets of the two performers — and they were gross. With clothes on, they couldn't have been anything you might observe with pleasure. Unclothed, they were flabby and revolting, and pitiably ridiculous.

Then I realized that Amelia's hand was not, as I'd supposed, intended to suppress an attack of nausea. Her eyes were streaming, and she spluttered. I couldn't help it, either. I roared with laughter, and we clung to each other, choking and coughing for a minute.

'Put them away, Richard,' she managed to say eventually. 'They're degrading.' I think she meant to us.

I put them away in my anorak pocket. The rest of the prints I took downstairs in the drawer they'd been in, and tipped them on the back seat of the car. Then we did trip after trip with the rest of my inheritance. He'd meant me to have the lot, I assumed. To use; to use as he had been using it. That part of it I might not be able to carry through, as I couldn't imagine myself ever being able to match his photographic skill. What I *would* do, I hadn't yet decided.

It wasn't until I came to replace the drawers that I realized the bottom one — the shallow one — was less deep than the others. A quick examination revealed that it had been sawn off two inches from the back, and the rear panel nailed on again clumsily. Down on my knees, using my lighter to assist the vision, I could detect something that had filled the gap at the back. My hand would just reach into the enclosed space, and it came out with a roll of paper, again with a rubber band around it, but this band was completely rotted away. It stuck to the paper.

'What is it?' Amelia asked softly.

There were three sheets of A4 typing paper, which had to be held down to remain lying flat. Typing paper — but everything was handwritten. The top sheet read:

Richard,

If you ever read this, it can only be because I shall not be in a position to advise you. I think I can trust you to decide for yourself and make what use you wish of my equipment. You will think this a strange place to hide a letter to you. Far better to leave it with my solicitor, you would say, especially as the hot water pipe runs along the back of my cupboard and the paper may, when you find it, be somewhat toasted. But I reasoned that if you do not find it you will have lost what I remember of your patience and observation, and therefore couldn't put it all together anyway. If you do find it, as you must have done because you are reading it, then perhaps you still possess the qualities I admired, enough to be able to carry it on for me.

There have already been several attempts

on my life. I believe I am getting close to the answers — on both counts. Do not allow this to confuse you. They may or may not be connected.

My best wishes for your success. Tell the parents I did my best.

George Tate.

It was dated three months before.

Amelia had been reading beyond my shoulder. I handed it to her, while I quickly scanned the other pages. They consisted of names and addresses, with several amendments, and tables of dates of movement of the people involved. Big Martie Machin was there, and Ron Phelps, and Tim Craythorpe. Not Pearlie Stone — she was, apparently, unfit to merit entry.

Silently, Amelia handed the letter back to me. I put all the sheets together and thrust them in my inside pocket. I was convinced now that Jennie hadn't seen much of George's work and the evidence of his activities, otherwise she wouldn't have been so upset over Tony's revelations.

But, say what she liked, I was convinced that George had been completely sane, unless he'd deteriorated rapidly during the last three months. There had been clarity and sanity in his letter, even a certain lightness, only his reference to 'both counts' being obscure. George had been sane. He had known exactly what he was doing, and why, and he'd pursued his objectives relentlessly.

The trouble was that he had entrusted me to pick it up and carry it on as far as the finishing line. More than entrusted. He had assumed.

So it was a very silent journey home for both of us, Amelia no doubt worrying that I would comply with George's wishes, me worrying that she was worrying. We were approaching Bridgnorth, very close to home, when Amelia broke the silence.

'I'm not sure she was sincere,' she decided.

'Who?' I asked. 'D'you mean Jennie?'

'Yes. There were times . . . '

'I felt very sorry for her.'

'You're a man. A woman notices other things. Perhaps you were meant to feel sorry.'

I thought about that for a few moments, then, 'I'm not sure I understand.'

'She spoke only to you, Richard, and to Tony, of course. She knew a man would react, but a woman might perhaps see beyond what she was saying.'

'Too subtle for me.'

She nudged my elbow. 'Nonsense. It's your line — interrogating. Seeing beyond what was said.'

I smiled to myself. 'But I wasn't interrogating her, my love. What is it you detected that I missed?'

Women never seem to be able to dissect their impressions. It's always feelings and instincts and intuitions. I wasn't, therefore, taking her very seriously.

'I had the impression, Richard, that she hated her husband. I know . . . she said she thought he was insane at the end. Poor George. But there was no pity in her voice when she said it, no sorrow. And she didn't seem to be mourning him.'

'Because there was no weeping? You can't assume anything from that. He's been dead for over three months.'

'All the same, I felt it was a case of good riddance.'

'Oh . . . come *on*, Amelia love. If there was no regret at his loss, why did she try to persuade me to investigate his death by exhibiting her bullet hole?'

She was silent. I glanced sideways. She was smiling. Noticing my head moving, she said, 'But she didn't. She brought it to your attention. It was almost as though she was saying, 'You see how he's made enemies everywhere! One of them's got fed up with him.' That's what I think.'

'Enemies?'

'Enemies, implying people out there somewhere,' she agreed. 'So that you won't look too close to home.'

We were approaching The Beeches, our home. I slowed.

'Good Lord! You're not pointing a finger at her, surely.'

She said nothing.

'Does she strike you as a woman who would be able to handle a gun — a handgun?'

'Well, no. Certainly not. But she struck me as a woman who would try to make you believe it was a gunshot hole, simply *because* it wouldn't fit her personality.'

I stopped just short of our drive entrance, and turned to her. 'But the police, she told us, wouldn't accept that it was a bullet hole. So why on earth would she bring it to our attention? She would gain nothing. Only — by your reckoning, Amelia — the impression that it was a bullet hole she could never have put there herself.'

'Oh . . . Richard! Don't you see? She knew that whatever George had left you in his will, it would set you off like a fizzing bomb, on the same track as he'd been on. And she doesn't want that. She's had ages of it from her husband, and she wants it to be dropped. Quite simply, Richard, she hoped that the evidence of a bullet hole

80

would frighten you off.'

'Humph!' I said, putting the Granada back into gear.

'Because she doesn't know you.'

'Hah!'

'She's a very devious woman.'

'But not, I feel, as devious as you.'

Strangely, she then allowed me to have the last word on it. But she knew I would go on thinking about it. She's so often right when I'm wrong that I don't dare to argue. I docketed it away in my subconscious and parked the car, turning just in time for the usual frantic welcome. Mary had let them out of the kitchen door on hearing us arrive.

Sheba is a full-grown boxer, has quite a lot of weight to throw around, and she usually throws it at me. Because I'm not keen on being flattened on my back from a standing position I crouch to her, so that the worst I get is a severe rolling and treading on and a frantic cleaning of my face. Jake is not yet full-grown, and is strangely less volatile. He adores Amelia, and is very gentle with her, so that when Amelia crouches she gets the licking without the rolling. Mary disapproves. She says it's not healthy, and you never know where their mouths have been. So far, we've survived.

We went into the kitchen, where Mary was

her usual disapproving self when we've missed a meal.

'I suppose you haven't eaten,' she observed, eyeing us for any perceptible loss of weight. We shook our heads. It was our lunch we'd missed, and we were only a little late.

'It's a good job I put a casserole in the oven, then,' she said.

'Mary, you're a life-saver.' Amelia kissed her cheek. 'I'll just go and clean up a bit . . . ' And off she went.

She hadn't noticed, as I had, the piece of paper lying in the centre of the bare kitchen table.

'What's this?' I asked Mary.

'A man came to see you. I told him you were out and I didn't know when you would be back. I mean — if I *had* known, I'd have been able to prepare a proper meal.'

'Yes, Mary. What sort of a man?'

'An unpleasant one. I don't like men who slouch. There's no excuse . . . ' Noticing my expression, she went on quickly, 'Supercilious and nosy. I didn't like to have him near me. I was worried, I can tell you that. Worried he'd wait around for you, Richard. The sort of man who, if I'd asked him to leave, would've simply sneered, then sat himself down and settled in.'

'So you told him to wait?'

'Outside, yes. He didn't like the dogs, the way they looked at him. 'Good dog,' he said, and Sheba growled. I'd have only needed to say one word — and he knew it. Anyway, he went, and he left you that.' She pointed.

It was a piece of paper she'd torn from a wrapping of something greasy. Mary would feel it to be good enough for him. She had clearly not read what it said; such a thing would have been unladylike and beneath her dignity.

But I read it. 'Patton. Phone me when you get in. Or else. Ron Phelps Esq.' At the bottom he'd added a phone number. Ron Phelps. One of the kidnap trio.

'Or else what?' Amelia asked. She had come quietly to my elbow.

'It's supposed to frighten me. What time was this, Mary?'

'Oh . . . an hour or so ago, when he left.'

'So he passed us on the way. Well, if he's going back to where we've just come from, it'll take him a bit longer yet. So we'll eat first, and I'll phone afterwards.'

'He *has* frightened you,' said Amelia.

'Shall we say: intrigued?'

So we ate without haste, chatting on everyday matters, Amelia reminding me I ought to have tidied our terraced garden for the winter. I took my time going upstairs to change into something more comfortable. Then I took the dogs down to look at the river. The Severn was running high, there having been quite a lot of rain lately, and I warned them not to go in for a swim. They would have been quite safe, but I'd have ended up as soaked as them. Then we made our way sedately back to the house. It was now well over two hours since Ron Phelps had left. If, as was my information, he had always been the driver for that deplorable gang, he wouldn't have taken it slowly. So he would now be there, wherever that was. I went into the living-room and put through the call.

'Blue Boar,' said a gruff voice, with some impatience.

'Have you got a Ron Phelps in the bar?' From the background noise, it would certainly be the bar.

'Yeah,' admitted the voice.

'May I speak to him, please? The name's Patton.'

There was a clatter as he put down the phone. I heard him shout, 'Some la-de-da bugger, Ron. Name of Patton. May I speak to him! Cor!'

In the interval of waiting, I noticed that Amelia had followed me and taken up the extension phone. This was a recent addition.

Previously, she'd listened to similar conversations by putting her ear close to mine. Not convenient. I'd had to crouch in order to reach down far enough. She nodded. She was ready.

'That Patton?' demanded a reedy, slurred voice.

'It is.'

'Ron Phelps. You know who I am.'

It wasn't a question, but I confirmed that I knew.

'Wanta quiet word with ya.'

'Say it then.'

'Not on the phone, y' prat. Here.'

'I assume that by 'here' you mean the Blue Boar at Potterton?'

'Of course. You stoopid or somethin'?'

'Next time I'm around there, I'll call in.'

I heard him take a deep breath. Perhaps the air was thick with smoke. Then he spoke with a heavily controlled patience. 'Next time you're down here better be today. Get it, smart-arse? We'll give y' till six. Six o'clock. Or else.'

Then he hung up. I did too, but slowly. Amelia was still standing there with the phone in her hand. 'I didn't want to go out again,' she said, in a small, meek voice.

'I think I must.'

'You're surely not going to be frightened by

a nasty voice over the phone!' At last she replaced it. 'Richard?'

I didn't want to explain to her that we were dealing, here, with vicious and probably deadly morons. Kidnappers are, by definition, quite heartless. And in their small, tight world of similarly minded gentry they would have a reputation for vicious retaliation and revenge, which would require a constant topping-up of example. Any rebuff would demand retribution, and they would not hesitate to travel to the end of the world in order to extract it. A jaunt of sixty miles back here would be no more than the entrancing interval in which to plan the exact approach needed to make the maximum impact.

It seemed I had stirred something from the bottom of a foul and noisome pool, so that it was clearly a good idea to keep all the action on their own patch. Besides . . .

'But Amelia love,' I said, 'it's a heaven-sent opportunity for me to meet this Ron Phelps face-to-face. There're things I'd like to ask him,' I declared firmly.

'But I thought you weren't going to go on with it.' Her voice wasn't steady. She was poised between a pitiful plea for me to desist, and her disapproval if I did. At the moment, she was lost in the empty space between.

'And who knows,' I said cheerfully, 'I might

even get to meet Perverted Pearlie Stone. That alone's worth the trip.'

'Oh . . . go ahead. Make a joke of it. But it's not funny, and you know it, Richard.'

'Sorry, love. But I can assure you, the fact is that I wasn't given a choice.'

Then she understood. Her hand flew to her mouth. 'He wouldn't . . . '

'He would. *They* would.' I left it at that. She knew what I meant, though I didn't think she appreciated the full tenor of their inclinations.

So off I went again, in my casual clothes. One has to consider the possibility of blood being spilt. I trusted it would be Ron's. It was already after four.

I skirted the ring road and ran through Bridgnorth, where I found a call box. Directory Enquiries gave me the number, and I got through to Tony Brason's station. I asked whether he was in.

'I believe so, sir. Hold on a minute. What name shall I tell him?'

'Richard Patton. I was speaking to him earlier today.'

I got through at once. 'Richard? What's up?'

'Busy?' I asked.

'Just sitting here at my desk, playing with my helicopter. What's the trouble?'

'You always assume trouble.' Then I told him that Ron Phelps had requested my presence at the Blue Boar, and that I was on my way. 'It'll take me about two hours,' I told him.

'And what d'you expect me to do about it?' he asked.

'Just thought you ought to know. If you get word that somebody's wrecking the bar, that'll be me.'

'I've always wanted to arrest you, Richard.'

'Well . . . now's your chance.'

We exchanged facetious formalities and I hung up. I knew he would take it seriously.

The drive was uneventful. I was, by that time, becoming familiar with the route. It wasn't until I was entering the town that I needed directions, but fortunately I spotted a parked patrol car, and they of course knew the Blue Boar.

'Down by the canal, the other side of the old St George's Church. It's a Sainsbury's now. You go down Farend Lane and it's on your left at the bottom.' The officer, leaning against his steering wheel, looked past me. 'That your Granada, sir?'

'It is. My wife's, to be exact.'

'Then I wouldn't take it down there. Leave it in Sainsbury's car-park. It'll be empty now.' In that, he proved to be quite correct.

It was well after six o'clock and the car-park was nearly deserted. The barriers had been left open, and the kiosks were dark and abandoned.

A thin drizzle had welcomed me to the town. It was a miserable and chill evening, with a cold wind cutting through my thin slacks. I reached in the back for my anorak. As I looked round me, a woman walked past rapidly, giving me plenty of spare space. She was aiming for one of the few scattered cars.

'Farend Lane?' I called out.

She waved an arm, glancing at me quickly. 'Over there.' Her steps became almost a run.

I resent that kind of assumption, resent the social climate that makes it necessary for women to walk in fear in our streets.

I hunched my shoulders, and headed down Farend Lane.

It is a fact, which I have often noted, that streets that run parallel to canals are usually, in such districts, decrepit and tawdry terraces, seeming unending, whereas streets that run down to canals, usually being dead-enders, maintain a small amount of seclusion thereby, and thus, at least in the minds of the residents, a slightly more respectable image. Farend Lane was certainly a row, each side, of terraced houses, but the streetlights weren't smashed, the curtains weren't a uniform grey netting, and the front steps were polished, mostly a Cardinal Red.

But all evidence of respectability vanished with the Blue Boar. It had, years before, fronted on the canal, with ten yards of old blue bricks forming a landing stage. It had been a bargees' inn, a resting spot. Probably, stables had once flanked the pub. But at this time the door to the bar opened sideways on to the street, and a large bow window splashed light on the cobbles. The blue-brick yard was now, more likely, where they dumped the drunks, to recover, or to roll into the canal and thereby sober abruptly. This practice no doubt complied with the respectability status of Farend Lane, isolating the disgusting drunk from the sober citizen.

I thrust open the door and walked directly into the bar.

There was no alteration to the massive din that assaulted me, and in no way did my entrance disturb the heavy pall of smoke, which hung from the ceiling almost to my knees. The bar was curved each end. At one end a group was playing darts, which seemed to disappear into a fog as they were thrown. In the centre, tables were fully occupied, and standing room was at a premium. But at the other end there was space. In it, leaning against the bar, stood a gawky, uncoordinated creature, surely a man but not of any set pattern, with a gaunt and scarred face, a long neck, and long dangling arms, one of which took his great flat plate of a hand in an extended tour through the smoke in order to raise a pint glass from bar to lips. I didn't need anybody to tell me. This person was treated with sly respect. No faces turned towards him; no eyes dared to meet his. I saw, when they slowly swivelled to acknowledge an awareness of my presence, that there was a reason for avoiding those eyes. They were a peculiar grey, like a wall-eyed dog's, cold and empty. Teeth showed at his lips, but not because he smiled. It was a sneer of satisfaction. It was not simply that I'd arrived, but that his self-conceit rested on the assumption that I would have to.

This man was accorded respect by the customers, and given space. He was a leading citizen, having spent fifteen years in prison for a kidnap job. They respected him. They didn't want to speak to him, though.

I walked up to him. 'Ron Phelps?'

He jerked his head. 'We'll go in the back.' His voice was thin, almost a whisper, but every word came through, like the darts flying through the fug. It was clear that we were going to speak in the relative silence of the back.

He reached past me and thrust open a door I hadn't noticed. I realized it opened into what might have been called a snug. But there'd been someone standing beside the doorway, and my first and only intimation of that was a blow behind my left ear and a blinding light.

I remember thinking I ought to have worn my hat, then there was nothing, I don't know for how long.

5

I was sitting on a hard stool in a corner, my shoulders supported by both walls. My head throbbed in steady pulses, and my eyes weren't focusing properly. A small, tubby creature with hair drooping on his shoulders, sticking from his ears, and patchily blooming on his chin to circuit the pimples, was slapping my face. He seemed to be enjoying it, judging by his lop-sided grin.

'Y' hit him too 'ard, Martie,' he commented.

'Ain't no such thing, Tim-lad.'

I reached up feebly and managed to catch his wrist. 'I'm awake.'

'Spoilsport.' But Tim Craythorpe, as this must have been, stepped back, allowing himself a final, gentle slap on my cheek, his fingers lingering as he drew his hand away.

I leaned forward, head down between my knees, taking deep breaths. When I straightened I felt better, well enough to reach for my pipe. I wanted to present a relaxed and casual attitude, but my fingers were fumbling when I tried to fill it.

'There was no need for that,' I said. 'I was here.'

'But you was late,' said Big Martie.

· His voice was rough, as though there was something wrong with his vocal cords. This was possible, as everything else about him was wrong. I'd seen him in full colour in the nude, and there had been no indications of his disproportions, other than his vast obesity. The clothes seemed to emphasize much more, his legs being too short for his bulbous body, though perhaps his trousers weren't hitched high enough. He had a thick leather belt anchoring them to his belly, but its bulge reached so far up and so far down that there was no perception of a waist to offer anchorage. The belt dug in fiercely, but well below the plimsoll line. One leg seemed shorter than the other, the left one being bowed but the right one straight and a little shorter. Both arms were too long, fists swinging low, and his hands were distorted, either from using his fists too often on heads too hard, or from arthritis. He would've been around fifty. If it was arthritis, I could hope that he had many years left in which to suffer pain. His neck seemed not to exist, the head being settled stiffly between massive shoulders. The face was a mess. An accident as a child might have had something to do with that. It was likely, and would perhaps explain his character development. As he grew to maturity and saw around him how reasonably normal people turned out when grown, then he might have developed a pathological hatred for humanity.

'All right,' I said. 'So I was late. Now I'm here. So . . . what's it all about?' I fumbled the lighter to my pipe and managed to get it going.

'Y' didn't ask the lady if y' could smoke,' said Martie.

I hadn't realized that there was a lady present. Ron Phelps was there, leaning casually against the door by which we had entered, inspecting his fingernails in a tepid imitation of a thirties film gangster. Martie was there, blocking off a lot of light, and Tim Craythorpe was still with us, sitting on a reversed wooden chair and rocking back and forth as though in a delirium of amusement. From time to time he giggled. There was a small table, which had been thrust away in a corner, a chair behind it, and one more door, probably opening into the yard. One table — then there ought to be four chairs, to allow for a poker session. There were. The other two were in use by the aforementioned lady, sitting on one with her feet up on the other. Pearlie Stone. I knew her face, too. Well now!

'Do you mind if I smoke, Miss Stone?' I asked politely.

She didn't glance in my direction. 'Please yer-bloody-self,' she said without interest. She had a surprisingly youthful and musical voice. Hearing it from such a great heap of flab, I observed her more closely.

'Miss Stone!' said Martie, his voice now tiptoeing as he explored a thought. 'How d'you know who she is?'

In my still slightly fuzzled state, I'd made a mistake. Never reveal your own knowledge, that was the rule, and I'd mentioned Pearlie's name. I got out of it quickly with the truth. 'I've seen the photos.'

But Martie didn't like this sort of truth. 'That bastard!'

And Pearlie laughed, now turning her head to look at me. The laugh revealed a fine set of teeth, and I could see she had a reasonably well proportioned array of features, ruined only by the excessive padding in which they slumped, disheartened and betrayed. She was younger, too, than the photos had depicted her, though now I came to scour my memory it did seem that she had been performing manoeuvres beyond the ability of an older woman. Early or mid-thirties, I now guessed.

'I didn't wish to see those shots,' I assured Martie. 'It was not a pleasant experience.'

'You watch your tongue,' Martie growled.

'Yeah,' agreed Phelps, abandoning his nails.

'And you shurrup!' Martie flared at him in abrupt violence. He was not mentally stable, I reckoned.

Phelps smiled thinly, and looked away. Craythorpe giggled.

'So why am I here?' I asked, getting down to business.

Martie advanced on me, ending up with a thick finger an inch from my nose. His nail was black and cracked. 'You been nosin' into our business.'

'I haven't started yet.'

'Y' been seen visitin' that snooty bitch in Primrose Drive,' he accused me. 'Twice.'

'Her husband left me something in his will.'

'Yeah. Him! Somebody's gonna put a stop to him, if he don't watch it.'

I gave that a second or two. 'He's dead, Martie,' I said at last. 'Somebody *has* put a stop to him.'

'Well yeah.' He rubbed the back of his head, where a neck should have been. 'Yeah. That's right.'

None too bright, was Martie, or the death of George Tate had been of such small significance to him that it hadn't registered in his tiny brain.

'So what did he die of, then?' he demanded.

'His van went off the road.'

'Serve 'im right — nosy bugger.'

'He's been dead three months.'

'So that's why we ain't seen 'im around? There — y' see!' he cried, whirling round and stabbing the same thick finger, first at Phelps and then at Craythorpe. 'Ya told me he'd gone underground.'

'Well, he 'as, ain't he?' Phelps sneered, and tubby Craythorpe whinnied.

'Watch your blood pressure, Martie,' put in Pearlie gently, smiling to herself.

I saw that she was knitting something very voluminous, probably for herself, in a horrible purple colour not really suitable for her bulk, I thought.

'So what did he leave y' then?' Martie demanded.

'Who? Mr Tate? His camera stuff.'

'Oh yeah! Oh, has he, then? An' I suppose y've come round here to try it on us for yerself?'

'Try what?'

'Blackmail. An' it won't work twice, matey. The missus knows now. Won't work. Ha!' He gave a grunted laugh of triumph.

'You've run out of tenners, then?' I tried.

'I told y'!' he shouted. 'Told y', didn't I! It's what you've come for.'

'Martie,' I reminded him, 'I came here at

your request. Remember?'

'Oh yeah. Yeah. My request! That's funny. Request!' He looked round at his two mates. 'That's funny,' he told them.

They obediently laughed, if without enthusiasm. Martie slowly walked across the room. There was a tight, sudden silence, as he looked around. He then turned his attention to me.

'So y' got his camera stuff, then? Well . . . goody for you. But if you think y're gonna be poking the things at us all the time, y've got another think comin'. Clear? Is that clear?'

'Very,' I said. 'I can't say I intended to, but I hadn't quite made up my mind. You've made it up for me, Martie. I shan't be taking any pictures of you, *in flagrante delicto*, or otherwise.'

'In where? We ain't been to any such pub — not any time.'

'It's Latin, Martie. It means: in the act.'

'If y're making your nasty remarks about me'n Pearlie, Patton, y' can just shut your gob, before I shut it for you.'

'It means: in the act of committing an offence, usually an illegal offence.'

'What the bloody hell're you maunderin' about?'

'George Tate. Wasn't that what he was

doing — trying to get pictures of you breaking the law?'

'Come off it. Come *off* it! We ain't been breakin' any laws. On parole, we are. Good boys, we've bin. Ain't we, lads?'

'Sure have. Y're right,' they murmured.

'You've committed an unprovoked attack on me. That's an offence under section . . .'

'If y' don't shurrup, I'll close your trap for y'!' he shouted, thrusting beneath my nose the mangled fist with which he intended to do it.

I was feeling none too secure in that room with the three of them, which was why I was trying to project an image of casual confidence. But it was a balancing act. I wanted to provoke something, but not mayhem. And I couldn't understand what he was getting at, nor why I was there. For the moment, I remained silent.

Martie stood back and stared at me. He'd been trying to interrogate me, but he was hopeless at it. Now he seemed to realize that fact, and went directly to the nub of it.

'What was he after, that Tate character? That's what I wanta know.'

'Ah! Well, that's obvious. There're one or two things about that kidnapping that haven't been answered. He was looking for answers.'

His tiny, dark eyes were bright. 'Such as?'

I chose the one he would understand. 'Where the money disappeared to.'

'Yeah . . . yeah . . . the spondulicks.'

As he hadn't reacted violently, I tried a bit of bluff on him. 'And of course, everybody knows you three have got it tucked away somewhere. If you're waiting to start spending it until after your parole's run out, well, all I can say — '

He was a little late interrupting, but when he did it was violent. Fury seemed to shake the whole of that unwieldy bulk, his face, already red, darkened, and his eyes almost disappeared. 'That's a lie!' he roared. 'A bloody lie!'

'That you've got it? Of *course* you've got it. Who else could have it?'

'Y' keep sayin' that and I'll — '

'And the ex-Chief Super — Mr Tate, to you — conned you into proving it.'

I thought he was about to explode with rage. Certainly, he seemed to swell. But tubby Tim Craythorpe quietly got up from his chair and went over, put his hand on Martie's arm, and said gently, 'Don't let 'im rattle y', Martie. Leave it till after. Let me 'ave him . . . an' you can watch.'

Martie glanced at him. Then he slowly subsided, even tried a tentative grin. 'Y're a good boy, Tim-lad.'

Tim glanced at me, winked, and returned to his chair. He was far from being a boy. Further from being good.

Martie returned his attention to me. 'What d'ya mean? He conned me inta provin' it? What does *that* mean?'

'He blackmailed you into producing some of the tenners that were in that suitcase.'

He stared at me in blank silence, his expression completely wiped clean. Then, 'It don't mean nothin',' he said, his voice low. From his expression, it seemed that he hadn't yet worked out what it might mean.

'It does to me.'

'Then you're bloody stoopid.' He looked round him huntedly, as though searching for sanity and reason. His eyes returned to lock with mine. They narrowed to slits.

'So why d'you think we wanted to see ya?' he demanded forcefully.

To warn me off. To spill a little blood. To break a bone here and there. But I said, 'You haven't told me yet.'

'We want y' to find the money for us, you twat.'

This, I had not expected. It was true that if they had it they wouldn't have been able to resist flashing it around, this seeming to prove that they hadn't. But it was also true that Martie either meant this seriously, or it was a very clever bluff to persuade me, quite simply, that it would be a waste of time investigating them in order to uncover it. In the present company I couldn't imagine that if they pooled all their intellectual resources they would have enough to provoke one clever thought into the open, let alone plan a crafty bluff.

'You mean,' I asked, getting it straight, 'you want me to work on it on your behalf?'

'Y're a private eye, ain't you?'

'No. Just a retired copper.'

'Well then. Y' got nothin' better to do. So do that. Find the money for us. A fair fee. We'll pay y'. Two per cent, the lads agree. Two per cent. That's . . . ' He looked blank.

'Two per cent of half a million is ten thousand.'

'Is it? There y'are then. Ten thousand quid, if y' find it all. How d'you like the sound of that?'

'Well now . . . ' I grinned at him. 'It sounds very equitable, Martie. I mean . . . the answer's yes. I'll try to find your money.'

'There y'are then.' And he beamed a huge smile at me, which wasn't any less evil because he'd intended it to be friendly.

I leaned back into my corner, completely relaxed now, and relit my pipe, stretched out my legs, and blew smoke at the ceiling. There

I'd been, anticipating a protracted and difficult month or two, during which I might have been able to interview all three of them, one at a time, and force them into revealing information. I had not decided on the way in which I would be able to apply that force. Now it was all handed to me, a golden opportunity. They were all here, together, and on my side. No . . . rephrase that. I was on their side.

'I'll need some information, Martie,' I told him chattily. 'You'll understand that. I haven't got much to go on, you might say. Let me explain, first — I was just an ordinary copper, a sergeant, at that time, the time you pulled the kidnap. I was on communications, back at the nerve centre, the operations room. So I wasn't out there on the spot, seeing what went on. Oh, I heard all about it . . . but only from the police side. D'you get me?' I wasn't telling the exact truth, but they didn't deserve it.

Martie turned from me and ambled amiably across the room to Pearlie, pleased with himself for having been able to force me into doing as he wished. He tickled her under one of her chins and picked up the knitting she was working on. He held it up. It was like a bedsheet. 'This the front bit, is it?' And he cackled. She snatched it back. 'It's a cot blanket, you clown.' 'Y' ain't pregnant?' 'No thanks to you.' At this, he cackled again, and turned his head.

'Gerron with it, then,' he said.

'So I need some information,' I told him. 'I can't do it blind.'

'What d'ya wanna know?'

'Pretty well every damned thing. Where was the hide-out, to start with?'

'Don't know,' said Martie. 'Anybody know?'

The other two shook their heads. 'It's just — we found it,' said Phelps.

'But you'd have to travel about, for heaven's sake! You'd get to know the ins and outs.'

'We hadda find a place,' Phelps went on. 'There was lotsa space for lookin' in, around there. So we searched around for a day or two. Found this old dump. Tucked away. Great. Then — if we went anywhere — it'd be easy getting back. Or so we reckoned. Remember the route, sorta thing. Couldn't find it now, though.' He grunted. 'Mosta the time, it was a hell of a job to find it then.'

I sighed. It all sounded so feasible. It was exactly their attitude to what had been a completely botched operation all round.

'All right. We'll leave that for now,' I said. 'Take it from the beginning. You'd found this

105

place. I suppose you'd already got your eyes on the kid — Adrian? You had? It's all right if you just nod.'

Phelps and tubby Tim nodded. Tim said, 'It were a pippin. Out with his nanny, he was, playin' in the drive. Scared the drawers right off her, we did, an' took him away.'

'Sylvia was with you at that time?' I asked casually. 'Your sister,' I reminded him.

'Oh yeah. Sylvie. We reckoned we'd need somebody — a female. He was only a bitty kid. None of us fancied lookin' after 'im.'

'And that arrangement worked?'

Martie turned on me, snarling. 'What y'askin' all this for? Gerron with the job. Find the bleedin' money.'

'Patience, Martie,' I said. 'I need the background story. I can't work with nothing. Was it a success, taking Sylvia along with you?'

Martie waved a hand in angry dismissal, so Phelps, sneering at such a lack of understanding, took it up. After all, Sylvia had been his girl-friend. Supposedly.

'If it matters, they caught on like a house afire. Her an' the kid. Youda thought it was a picnic. We left 'em to it. Sylvie sent Tim off to buy games they could play. In my car . . . '

'The Ford Escort?'

'Yeah.'

'So Sylvia knew nothing about the money, and how difficult it was to collect it. You three ought to have found out first how heavy money is, in bulk.'

'Lotta chance 'f that,' said Phelps. 'Since when'd we seen that sorta money all in one place?'

'All right. So there were two failed pick-ups. You still hadn't got the money. Whose idea was it to use the school bus?'

'Mine,' said Phelps, surprisingly, because he'd seemed as mindless as the other two. 'It was my job, wasn't it? Gettin' it away.'

'Umm!' I said. 'That was clever, Ron. Clever. So you drove that bus to where you'd hidden the Ford, picked up your own car, and hunted out the place again.'

Tim giggled. 'Nearly didn' find it, that time. We was huntin' round for half an hour.'

I said nothing for a whole minute. They had been hunting round for half an hour, with half the county's force searching for them, and they'd become, suddenly, invisible. I stared morosely at my pipe.

'You still had the money?'

'O' course,' said Phelps, frowning.

'Not left it in the bus, by mistake?'

'You know damn well . . . oh, y're bein' clever. Funny. He's bein' funny, Martie.'

Martie came over rapidly. 'We ain't got no

107

time for no funnies. Gerron wi' it.'

'All right, Martie. Just checking,' I assured him. 'So you got back, with the money, to the place. I can't keep calling it a 'place'. What sort of place? An old house, a farm . . . what?'

'If it matters . . . ' said Phelps heavily, his cadaverous face sourly thrust at me, ' . . . it could've bin a house, an' it could've bin a farm. Though who'd build a house in the middle o' nowhere, I dunno.'

'Any outbuildings? Barns or the like.'

'A few wrecks 'f sheds. Could've bin barns, I suppose. The whole lot was in a kinda dip in the ground. Couldn't see it till y' tripped over the doorstep, kinda. Call it a farmhouse.'

Ron Phelps was by far the most intelligent, and, I suspected, the most vicious. He was possibly psychopathic. I wouldn't have wished to dispute anything with him. 'All right,' I agreed. 'A farmhouse.'

It could have been a hill farm, with thousands of sheep roaming the surrounding slopes.

'Well . . . gerron with it,' said Phelps.

'I'm working for you, Ron, not against. Let's have more detail. You managed at last to get back there, with the suitcase. Then what? You took it inside, I suppose. Opened it up, and set about counting it.'

'You crazy?' Phelps demanded. 'So what if

it was a few thou' short? Was we gonna take it back an' complain?' His expression did not change. His eyes remained empty, his lips thin and set. I couldn't guess whether he'd meant it as a joke.

'But you opened it up?' I tried.

'In the hall, yes. We'd wanna *look* at it, y' clown.'

'And it looked good, did it?'

Tubby Tim interrupted. 'It looked bleedin' well lovely.'

'And Sylvia was there at that time? With the boy?'

Tim carried it on, as though it was his right to do so, Sylvia being his sister. 'They both come to 'ave a look.'

'There in the hall?'

'Yeah. We said that. In the hall. So what?'

'Say anything? Did either of them say anything?'

Tim shook his head, his hair flying. 'Who was listenin'? Might've done.'

Martie ambled over and interrupted. 'We're wastin' drinkin' time,' he complained.

Surprisingly, Ron Phelps snapped at him. 'Get 'em in, then. Y've only gotta open the door and holler.'

Martie stood there for a moment, very still, except for his knobby hands, closing to fists, then opening again at his sides. He turned away. I didn't take my eyes off Phelps, who had tensed, but there was a sudden burst of noise as the door opened, and Martie's roar of instructions.

'Did either of them say anything?' I repeated quietly.

Phelps sneered, because female emotion had entered into it. 'Sylvie said somethin' about that bein' the finish, then. And: you'll be going home, Adie.'

'Adie?'

'Her name for him. Adrian's a daft name for a kid.'

'Yes. Did she seem upset?'

'Yes.' He bit it off.

'And the boy?'

Phelps shook his head. 'Said nothin'.'

'Said nothing? Did nothing?'

'Stuck his bottom lip out, then he turned round and run off.'

'From that, I'd guess they'd grown a bit close. The two of them. *She* wasn't much more than a kid, herself.'

'Nearly seventeen,' said Tim.

We were talking about his sister, his younger sister, who hadn't been seen since, but there was nothing in his voice that hinted at sorrow, or even interest.

'A full-grown woman,' said Phelps.

'In what way . . . ' I could have bitten off

110

my tongue, but it was too late to retract it.

Tim got it in a flash. 'You'd bin after her, y' dirty — '

Phelps put two fingers beneath his chin, and seemed to lift him from his feet with them. Tim choked.

'Watch y'r bloody tongue, boy,' whispered Phelps. 'Watch it. It was fifty-fifty.' Then he turned back to me, and I saw only the remnants of his expression, enough, though, to dry my mouth. 'You was sayin'?'

Martie interrupted at that point, blast him, swaying across, rolling because his thighs hadn't enough clearance. 'Anybody thirsty?' He had five pint mugs of draught beer on a tray.

'Put 'em down on the table,' Phelps snapped, not glancing at him. But I reached quickly for my pint.

It was now clear who was in charge here. In the country of the blind . . . Phelps had only half of a normal person's brain, but he outstripped the others. His main shortage — humanity — was his strength here.

'Those two — Sylvia and Adrian — did you get the impression that they'd grown to like each other?' I asked him, because it seemed to me to be an important point. 'Even that they were sorry it was over?'

'Yeah,' he said shortly, his eyes narrowly on Martie's back.

'Right. So there you all were, staring at the money, with the suitcase open on the floor in the hall. Then what?'

'We stuffed a few handfuls into our pockets, an' went out to celebrate.'

'You stuffed . . . ' I stopped, because it answered a little point that had been niggling around in the back of my mind: the origin of the £500 Martie had used to pay off George Tate when he was blackmailed. It was what Martie had had left of the money he'd stuffed into his pockets that night. They'd gone out to the nearest pub to celebrate!

And George Tate had laced the county with patrol cars, while those three guzzled themselves to a near stupor.

'You went out to celebrate?' I asked, just to confirm that I hadn't misheard.

'Didn't I say that?'

'Leaving those two youngsters to guard the money?'

'They could look after their sen.'

I had to assume that somewhere in the house they had set up sleeping facilities for the two, if only sleeping bags, and some means of cooking food — and a reserve. I didn't say so. What I did say was:

'It didn't occur to you that you ought to have spent a little time arranging a hand-over of the boy to his parents?'

Phelps leered. 'There's always termorrer.'

'But it turned out there wasn't. Is that it?'

'We got back . . . '

'Canned to the eyebrows?'

'Will ya listen! We was merry. Got back — round about midnight. Got lost comin' back. In the dark, see. Don't smirk at me like that, Patton, or I'll cut it off y'r face.' This he said with no change of tone.

'It was no smile,' I assured him. 'It was a grimace. The two — '

'No sign of 'em. There was a cellar we'd got arranged, sorta. Couldn't use anythin' but oil-lamps out there in the wild. Anyway, they wasn't down there, an' no lights we could see, so we shouted, an' I got the torches from the car, an' we went out lookin', shoutin' all the time . . . an' there was nothin'. They just wasn't there. Nor the caseful of tenners. All gone.'

'Gone,' I said, trying to find a logical explanation in my mind. 'You were annoyed?'

'Martie went blind crazy.'

'You naturally assumed that Sylvia had hopped it, with the kid and the cash?'

Phelps made angry, violent gestures. 'Nah! Couldna done. She'd never have shifted that case. An' the kid was only a little un. Couldna walked far.'

113

'She could have dragged the suitcase into one of the sheds, and then they hid away.' But, I told myself, that wouldn't have got them far, unless it had been done for a bit of fun.

'D'you think we didn' search for 'em? Martie was snorting, steaming mad. He'd've strangled Sylvie on the spot, if we'd found 'em.'

'But . . . no Sylvia, no Adrian, and no money?'

'Tha's how it was.'

'And eventually you all three drove home — back to here?'

'What else was there to do?'

'You could have phoned the police, anonymous-like, and reported the two of them lost — and they'd have mounted a search.'

'And found us! We hadda get away from there sharpish.'

'They picked you up, anyway, later on.'

'Ya finished?'

'Almost.' I remembered I had a pint of bitter on the floor beside my right foot. I picked it up and downed half of it. 'What do *you* think happened?'

'Ya wanna know? Right. I reckon that little tart, Sylvie, worked hard while we was away. I reckon she killed the kid an' buried him, an' buried the money, an' walked off, got 'erself a lift — an' lost herself in the big wide world. Then she come back an' dug it up, when we was put away, an' she's swannin' it up in a villa in the south of France or somewhere. That's what I think.'

Phelps had thought about it long and deeply. He'd had plenty of time for thinking. The speech poured from him viciously, each word poisoned by the venom that tainted it. There was no rationality in his face now; his eyes were empty, dark reflectors of a void, his mind whirling in chaos behind them.

'An' if you find 'er, Patton,' he said with quiet restraint, 'you let me know fust. Me. An' you hand 'er over to me, so's I can deal with 'er . . . '

I could sense that there was no real sincerity behind this. He was saying what he might be expected to say. I went along with that, testing.

'You're an insane lout,' I said. 'Keep your foul — '

His right hand went back over his left shoulder, ready for a chop with the heel of his hand. I threw the beer in his face and got to my feet, whipping the stool round from behind me. I had it raised high, a nicely balanced weapon, when the yard door opened.

Tony Brason walked in, accompanied by an even bigger colleague, and a good-looking woman, whom I recognized as being the one in the car-park, and who had to be a WPC. She was intended for Pearlie, no doubt, to comfort her when it was all over, though how she would get her arm round those shoulders I couldn't imagine.

'Evenin' all,' said Tony. 'No trouble, I hope.'

'I was just leaving,' I told him.

He stood aside. 'After you.'

I walked over to him, dropping the stool as I went. Martie trailed after me. I thought he was about to try the usual, 'Just a few quiet drinks between friends, officer.'

But no. He put a hand on my shoulder — we were friends, weren't we? Colleagues, anyway.

I hesitated, head bent, my back to him. I wasn't pondering, I was observing the set of his huge feet. I had mine just as I wanted them, left foot a little ahead of the right, right leg slightly bent.

'I owe you one, Martie,' I said, and whipped round, right fist swinging with me, right leg putting power behind it. You aim for the backbone, the instructor used to say, not the belly. I aimed for the backbone, and nearly made it. Martie gave one whoop of surprise and pain, and collapsed on the floor.

'No need for you to have come, Tony,' I said. 'It's all been friendly.'

6

We were standing beside the Granada, Tony and I, in Sainsbury's car-park. The other two officers were sitting quietly in his car, a discreet distance away. They had no doubt guessed that he would have strong words to say to me. He had. He'd already said most of them. The conclusion was uncompromising.

'Of all the bloody stupid things to do . . . you ought to know better, Richard.'

'I had no alternative,' I said. 'He came to the house.'

He knew exactly what I meant. 'We could have given you protection. Discreet surveillance. You know that.'

I tapped out my pipe against my heel. 'Looking back . . . I'm ashamed, Tony. The number of times I've used those same comforting words! Now I know how empty they can sound at the receiving end.'

'If you're at the receiving end, it's your own stupid fault, Richard. Fancy getting tangled up with that revolting crew!'

'I'm not tangled up with them. We're in partnership. If I can find the money, I get two per cent. Isn't that splendid! They're on my side, Tony. I don't need police protection now. If I need any protecting, I've got my own team. You saw them — and if you've ever come across such a stalwart bunch of upstanding — '

'For God's sake!' he snapped. 'It's not funny.'

'I find it amusing. There I was, thinking I'd never be able to frighten any one of them into parting with information — and they heaped it on me, threw it at me. Now I can carry on with what I wanted to do without having to watch my back every second.'

'That was it, was it?' There was a note of contempt in his voice. 'The money. You've got your eye on that. Is that it, Richard? You surprise me.'

He turned away. I touched his arm, and he glanced back over his shoulder. 'I'm trying to find out what happened to the boy and the girl, Tony,' I said quietly.

'Oh sure . . . sure. And how long d'you think they'll wait, these fine friends of yours, while you do that? They'll be at your shoulder, urging you on. You'll see — I know the type. And if you don't get some quick results on the money . . . oh hell! All right. I'll put somebody on to watch out for you.'

'No.'

'No? Why not?'

'They'd spot it. I'd lose their confidence. I want — '

'What you'll get — it strikes me — is an early grave.'

Then he paced away angrily. I stood and watched him go, sorry that I seemed to be losing a friend, and even more sorry that he would probably ignore what I'd asked and put somebody to watch out for me, anyway, and thereby ruin what could be a very fruitful partnership.

'Tony!' I called out.

'What is it?'

His driver put on the headlights. Tony was suddenly a harsh, black silhouette, something of mystery, throwing a long, long shadow. I had wanted his help on one specific aspect, which I didn't wish to share with Martie and his mob. If I was going to attempt to discover the house where the safe-door photos were taken, I was going to need assistance. Bulk assistance. I'd been able to think of nowhere but the police as a source from which I might draw, but it was very clear I'd have difficulty in interesting Tony now. The trouble was that in the matter of the safe, which in any event might not have been connected with the kidnap, any wandering from the path of true probity had been George Tate's.

'Never mind,' I told him. 'Never mind.'

'Richard,' he said, 'there's blood on your neck.'

He got in his car and was driven away.

His remark jerked me back into the unsympathetic maw of reality. I slid on to the driving seat, turned on the interior light, and had a good look at myself. Not too good. There was a box of tissues Amelia kept in reserve. A handful of these, licked well, now came in useful. But I was unable to make a good job of it. There was a distinct bump behind my left ear, and blood on the collar of my shirt. Amelia would notice at once, and there would be recriminations, followed by positive orders that I was not to carry on with it, so that I was on a loser from both directions. I would incur either the cool and destructive disapproval of Amelia, or the hot and destructive fury of Martie's lot. The choice was difficult.

I arrived home to the usual welcome from the dogs. Uncritical affection, that's what you get from animals. With humans it's: does he deserve it? Yes, even with Amelia, who would foresee disaster. I could offer only one detail of possible gain, that I was going to be given two per cent of whatever money I recovered. Was I, in other words, worth £10,000?

On this point, Amelia laughed. She was cleaning the abrasion behind my ear at the time. It was a somewhat shaky laugh. We had had a few drinks, following a hearty and rather late meal, and perhaps we had all three taken just a little too much. *In vino veritas.* We would all have liked to feel that it would have produced a certain amount of truth. But the wine didn't help, and all that we got from it was a feeling of hysteria, and me a throbbing headache.

'But I don't *understand*, Richard!' Amelia cried at one point of my exposition. 'How can they possibly expect you to locate the money, when they've had plenty of time to find it themselves? Or is it that they *have* found it, and it's all a bluff?' And she thumped the arm of the settee with her fist.

'Well, one thing's certain.' I sat back into my chair. 'Whatever George was up to, it must have got them worried. Now it's me they've got to worry about . . . so I'll simply carry on doing what I intended to do, and see what happens.'

'And what was that?' There was a weariness in her voice. 'Are we to be told?' She quelled a yawn by patting her mouth.

Mary was saying nothing, her eyes simply swinging from one face to the other as we spoke. But she was clearly worried.

'Well . . . I've been thinking about the safe-door photos. I mean . . . exactly what was George doing? Clearly, he was trying to penetrate the secret of the combination sequence. So — imagine it. There he'd be, squatting out of sight of the window, shooting off his shutter with a remote control. He couldn't see anything, so he'd have to stick to a programme. He'd have to guess how many seconds there would be between a turn left of the dial and a turn right. *That's* what those numbers on the envelopes were. They were seconds between each photo. What was it . . . four, seven, six, five, eight, nine.'

An interest sparked in Amelia's eyes. 'It wouldn't take many seconds to turn a dial. I mean . . . one or two, perhaps.'

'That's so. And he hadn't tried three seconds. Perhaps this last lot were at three-second intervals, and perhaps he got it right, this time.'

But she was already reaching for that final batch.

First, I numbered them on the backs, as we had to keep them sequential, and with three of us passing them backwards and forwards, that was essential.

I came to know that right hand, the blunt, strong fingers, the square-cut nails, and the signet ring on the third finger.

Slowly, because we had to be certain that the dial had not been moving at the time of each shot, we became more and more certain of the numbers dialled. We had four of the six, then five. But the remaining one was difficult. A knuckle of the bent forefinger just obscured the critical number. My two ladies had by now become quite excited. We were uncertain only of the fifth number in the sequence.

But Amelia was frantically skittering through the rest of the set, and we sat back and watched as she mumbled and muttered to herself. Then she cried out in triumph. She had been able to show that the knuckle intruded at the moment of pause, just before reversal, and from that deduce the missing number. She wrote it all down before she forgot.

We had it! We had cracked the secret of the combination. And . . . what?

It had been an interesting intellectual exercise, and no more. Even if we had a hint as to the manner in which it had attracted George's interest, there was no possible way of discovering the address of the house or the name of the owner.

'Oh hell!' I said. 'Let's get some sleep.'

Always, I find mornings depressing. It's as though the hours of daylight gradually clear my brain, so that it's in the evening that the ideas flood in. Hopefully. That following morning, there were no ideas, and I was restless.

'Surely,' said Amelia, 'you're not thinking of driving there again today! There's nothing you can do.'

If I'd had any concrete intention at all, it was to settle down to a quiet day with my books on photography and my cameras. An interest had been sparked in my mind, and there was a hell of a lot to find out, and memorize.

After breakfast, therefore, I took the dogs down to the river and we went for a long walk along the bank to clear my mind for action, and persuade myself into a receptive mood. If I registered the fact that a car's horn was pipping away at intervals, I certainly didn't imagine it had anything to do with me. Due to the winding nature of the river just below us, and the steepness of the terraced climb up to the house, I was not in sight until I was well up the winding paths. The car horn was even more persistent, and I was able to locate it as coming from our drive, the other side of the house.

And Amelia was waving, then was standing waiting as I climbed. I saw, as I drew closer, that she was clearly disturbed. When I was close enough that her voice would not carry too far, she called out, 'Mary says it's him.'

I was breathing heavily. Out of condition. I ought to have been able to climb that slope faster and without distress.

'Which him?'

'That man. Mary says . . . the same man.'

Hell! I thought. 'All right,' I said. 'I'll see what he wants.'

But I could guess what he wanted. I was both angry and unsettled. I had been too optimistic, imagining that our contract, if that was what it had been, would at least preserve me from their presence in our own district. After all, the action, what there had been originally, had all taken place sixty miles away. There was no *need* for this.

Yes, it was Ron Phelps again, standing beside a smart, new Rover 216 with the window wound down so that he could reach through and keep touching the horn ring. There was a distinct, casual arrogance about this. He was dressed in tatty jeans, but topped by a new anorak with class stamped all over it (somebody else's yesterday) and a peaked cap. He had the appearance of a gentleman farmer who'd just strolled along to watch a point-to-point, because he had a horse running in the third race.

'Come on, come on,' he shouted. 'Don't you know the time? It's nearly ten, and nothing done. Rise an' shine. Let's get crackin'.' He grinned at me evilly.

'Now you look here — '

'No!' It was a gentle word, but his lips had had difficulty with it, fumbling with a single word as though an abrupt stillness had frozen his jaw. Then, the switch abrupt, he raised his eyes past me, lifted his cap, and the smile was smooth, warm, embracing.

'That your wife? We haven't been introduced.'

It had all been done so economically that it was difficult to understand how so little could carry so much menace. At that point the dogs came running to me. I reached down a hand, not taking my eyes from Phelps. Sheba was shuddering. Not Jake; he hadn't grown enough in experience. My fingers calmed Sheba. 'I'll be right with you,' I said quietly, holding his eyes.

He leaned forward. 'We haven't got all day,' he whispered. The more quiet his voice, the more threat he managed to convey.

I turned away. Phelps and I were engaged together in an incident that had happened sixteen years before. We had all the time in the world, but he gave an impression of panic rush.

I spoke rapidly to Amelia. 'I'll have to go with him. I'll need to get an understanding worked out with him. But not here. I'll try to phone you, love, keep you in touch.'

I kissed her quickly on the cheek. She allowed a hand to run down my arm, to linger a moment with my fingers. I was terribly aware that the other two louts could be anywhere, literally anywhere. Ron Phelps knew exactly what he was doing. He was making a point, but it was one I already appreciated: I was to do as I was told. For the moment, I had to go along with it.

He was sitting behind the wheel with the engine running. I slid in beside him on the other seat, and he had the car moving before I had the door slammed. I said nothing as he snaked out of the drive and into the old farm driveway, which was now kept clear for the Ramblers. Fifty yards of this, and we would reach the narrow winding lane, leading out to the main Bridgnorth-Stourport road. It was there, in that deserted lane with its high banks and its ditches, that I made my move, thumping my fist hard down on his knee and banging the gear lever into neutral.

'Stop the car!'

'What the hell . . . '

'Stop the car, or I'll have us in a ditch.' I clutched at the wheel and tried to swing it against his suddenly rigid two-handed grip.

Then he skidded to a halt, cut the engine, and turned on me in fury. 'Ya stupid idiot

. . . what the hell d'ya think you're doin'? All I did's call for y', damn you.'

'Listen to me.' I clutched a handful of sleeve and drew him closer. It wasn't a pleasant experience. His irises were brown, but with a milky white rim round them. It frosted them with a distinct chill. And he smiled such a smile of menace that it would've frightened me off if he'd been the aggressor. But for the moment, I was.

'Now you just get a few things straight, Mr Ron Phelps. We've got an agreement. Right? An agreement that I'd try to find out what happened on that one evening, sixteen years ago, when a suitcase full of money and a young woman and a boy all disappeared. Phut! I don't stand much chance. Next to none. But I will not have your unsavoury bunch interfering in how I do it. Get it? And . . . '

He gave a short bark of dismissal. 'Y' must think we're daft. Trust you! You're outa your tiny mind, Patton. We're payin' you. Employin' you. Get it straight, matey. And I'm here to help. Help you, Patton. Get it? Y' said it y'self; you was a clerk, back at the shack an' takin' down messages. Ain't that so? Ain't it?'

I had to agree that in the main it was true. My involvement had been mainly clerical.

But I didn't say that.

'I want to get something very clear, Phelps. I'm as interested as you are in finding out what happened. But I don't think we've got a ghost of a chance doing it like this. Oh, get the damned car moving, if we're going anywhere.'

I waited until he'd got out on the main road. There was no need for instructions; he knew where he was going. We headed for Potterton and its moors.

'You know how I've become involved,' I said in a reasonable voice. 'I've kind of inherited it from George Tate. But I don't know where *he* was heading and I don't know how to take it along. All right . . . you've told me more than I ever knew. And I don't believe a good part of it. But I've got to do it in my own way.'

Phelps was being strangely silent. His attitude was all wrong for what he purported to be doing. I would have expected him to force me into doing the driving, because this would have given him more control, as I'd already demonstrated. But no. He seemed content to drive, though he had, after all, been their getaway driver. Maybe he simply liked driving. Certainly, when we got on to more open roads, and later on the motorway, he began to strip away the miles at speeds I

130

would not have attempted, and well over prevailing speed limits. And he was strangely silent.

But fortune seemed to favour him — as it did the whole group. Look at the absurd luck that had enabled them to escape capture when they finally had the money, and to escape notice when they went on their celebratory booze-up! In any event, he had us in the operative area a good half an hour before I could have done it. And he hadn't taken me up on it when I'd virtually called him a liar.

Eventually, I realized we were entering the moorlands. He turned on to a minor road, with a confidence that indicated he still knew what he was doing. Dwellings were soon behind us, and in all directions the moors spread out all round us. There was nothing but the heaving flanks of hills and the mist-laden valleys between. It was not an ideal day to go searching for their 'place', if that was what we were doing.

And in the middle of all that open space he drew up at a pub. An insignificant building, it was, against its vast backdrop of grey and green. The Saracen's Head. We got out, and went in for a drink.

'I'll get 'em in,' he said.

'Draught bitter,' I said. 'If they've got it.'

'Some of the best,' he assured me.

We took our drinks to a table in the corner, the bar being empty apart from us. We gurgled a little down, and I said, 'You seemed to know.'

He raised his eyebrows.

'That the beer's good,' I explained.

'Sure I do.' He shrugged. This was a changed Ron Phelps. Gone was the evil assertiveness, the impression of a poised viciousness about to explode. He wouldn't meet my eyes, probably being ashamed of what he would consider to be a weakness. But he simply wasn't prepared to make the effort to preserve his reputation. Not with me. I wasn't worth it.

'I reckon', he said, 'I know every pub within a radius of twenty miles. We're bang in the middle here. The middle o' the moors. We've bin out of the nick getting on for a year now. The others . . . rubbish, filth, that's what they are. Useless. They always left it t' me. Ron'll find it. Ron'll do this, do t'other. So that's what I bin doing, the past few months. Lookin' for it.'

'The place?'

'Yeah — the place. Y'see . . . an' I told you this . . . we always 'ad a job getting back to it. Findin' it. Oh sure, I'd got maps. We hunted it out, before we planned the job. Stuck a cross on the map.'

He was silent, staring past my ear with a bitter intensity. His voice had seemed simply to fade away.

'Well then,' I said in the end, because the silence was becoming chill and external, as though pressed on us. 'Well then — one cross, and that ought to have done it.'

'Yeah. Sure.' He was disgusted.

'Get you another?' I asked, staring at his empty glass in preference to his abruptly empty eyes.

'Nah!' he said. 'I'm drivin'.'

This he said quite solemnly, as though he cherished a serious respect for the law, but then I realized that his respect was for his own driving ability and his reactions.

'That one cross?' I asked. 'Didn't it do it?'

'They must've moved the soddin' thing.'

'The cross or the building?'

A corner of his lips moved, flicked, and retreated to sourness. 'Both — it strikes me.'

'Witches and warlocks on the trail, huh? Riding, riding . . . '

'I tell y',' he said. 'Not once did we manage to drive straight back to it. It never *was* where the cross was, so we put another, an' next time it wasn't *there*, an' in the end the whole bloody map was covered in the stupid crosses.'

He stared morosely into his empty glass. It seemed to me that the answer was quite simple — they had started off with the cross in the wrong place, and each subsequent cross had been orientated from the first, so that they'd never been anywhere near the correct location with their magic markers.

'An' what d'you think I've been doing the past months?' he demanded. 'I bin going over and over it again — an' I can't find the damned place at all.'

I was taking my time filling my pipe, now feeling more optimistic. There was not going to be any wild and violent outbreak from Ron Phelps. He needed me. For what, I wasn't yet clear, but it had something to do with his authority. My previous guess that he, and not Martie Machin, was the boss of their little gang, was probably correct. Ron just didn't make it obvious. But they must have relied on him deeply, and his physical pressure would have been a major element in it. He could be more vicious than Tim Craythorpe, more physically violent than Martie, and he could run rings round them when it came to assembling two consecutive thoughts. So they had trusted him. And that trust had extended to the location of the 'place', and possibly, by some miracle, the money. They had trusted him in that, and he hadn't yet succeeded.

But, more important than that, he was losing faith in himself and his own abilities. Maybe, even, he'd succumbed to the tempting idea that magic *was* involved, and the whole set-up had been spirited away.

'Let's get outside,' he said abruptly, and we went out into the lowering late-afternoon sunlight. It was well after noon.

'I don't know what you expect from me,' I said, standing beside him and staring at the distant hills, grey and blue in the hovering ground-mist, heaving up their flanks in one direction, languorously extending their shrub-capped slopes apparently for miles in another.

'What you was gonna do all on your tod, and that's find out what happened.'

'I'd have come at it from another angle,' I told him.

'Such as? Give us a f'rinstance.'

I shrugged. 'What I was trained for: questioning, evaluating, cross-questioning. Trying to get a lot of pieces that fit together and make a bit of sense. I already know it from the police point of view. And now I've heard another story from you lot.'

'What d'ya mean — story?'

'Statement, then. You said . . . correct me if I'm wrong . . . you said you dumped the school bus — right, we found it — and you drove off in the Ford Escort with the suitcase of money. Even *then* you got lost, and it took you half an hour to find the place! That's pure farce, Phelps. You hunting for the place, and the county's finest hunting for you. And neither of you got one sight of the others.'

'We wasn't looking.'

'No. Of course you weren't. What you ought to have been doing, once you *had* found the place, was leaving that kid somewhere and giving the parents a ring on the phone, then loading the lot, money, Sylvia and the three of you, all into your car . . . and off home. But no. You had to go out and celebrate.'

'Not my idea.' He seemed to be on the defensive now. If he'd had any authority at that time, he ought to have controlled them better.

'You could say that about anything,' I said with disgust. 'Load the responsibility on the others. But you don't fool me, Ron Phelps. You can sit back and watch that great ape, Martie, doing his muscle-man act, and sneer at Tim with his nasty little suggestive gestures and nods and winks, and his lascivious drooling . . . '

'His what?'

'Lustful . . . perverted . . . snide.'

'Oh sure. That's Tim, spot on.'

'And you could sit back and watch all that

136

going on, and smile to yourself and get your own little bit of jollies just by watching. But you ought to have controlled them when it came to the serious stuff.'

'What're you on about?'

I stood, an empty glass in my left hand, looking around me. The visibility was now crisply clear, the ground mist having lifted. There was hardly a twig moving and the valley was holding its breath. Weak sunlight now wanly spread behind a limpid cloud layer, barely casting shadows. The minor road on which the pub was situated crawled along the shallow flank of the hillside, and behind us, dense woodland mounted to the skyline. I saw, taking more notice of details now, that the trees were massed rhododendrons, the buds already on them for next year. Below us the valley was bare, rocky, negative, no character to it at all. A stream trickled along, but half-heartedly. In both directions the terrain seemed the same, small belts of trees, a bit of scrub here and there, the odd scattering of gorse. The meagre sunlight cut swathes of shadow down the flanks behind us. It was impossible to trace the line of the road in either direction.

'You could have organized it better,' I told him. 'I bet you left Martie to plan the thing. Tcha! To start with — why pick a location which was virtually local to you? Of *course* you'd be missed from your usual haunts. You *were* missed. Damn it all, the arresting officers could have sat on your dustbin lids and waited for you to come home. You'd lost before you'd even started.'

I glanced sideways at him. He was smiling thinly. I couldn't see why.

'No protests?' I asked. 'No comments?'

'Say it.'

'Describe the place you found.'

'What?'

'Describe it.'

His shoulders lifted. 'A buildin'. I dunno. Like any other, I suppose. Tucked into a hill, sort of no back yard — y' get what I mean. Roof half off, or fallin' down, but one end of it sorta waterproof. Front door an' a hall, stairs at the side, your left goin' in. But the roof'd fallen in on one side. Long hall. On one side 'f that, a bit of a room, no winderframe. An' at the end of the hall, stairs down to a cellar, on the left. That's where we kep' him. The boy. Laid it on all snug, we did. Lotsa food in tins and stuff, jus' needed warmin' up. A paraffin stove, we got one o' them, an' a heater. Whatever. Cosy.'

'Hmm!' I lit my pipe. 'But from outside, a crumbling dump?'

'If y' like.'

138

I walked a few paces, back and forth, and finally settled again. 'I was in charge of the police map, Ronnie-lad. The operations map. Large scale. D'you know, these moors cover an area of twenty miles by nearly thirty. Near as damn it six hundred square miles. And barely a road in all that wide open space. Tracks . . . that's all. Tracks and what'd been farms. And there was room for a lot of those old farms. Oh . . . a great number, believe me. And you can reckon they'd all have been built to much the same design and with the same materials. D'you get what I'm trying to get across, Ronnie? Do you understand?'

He didn't. It irritated him. In his circle of friends, he was probably regarded with respect for his intelligence. It's a matter of relativity. In the bar of the Blue Boar, Einstein would have been lost and confused. Effluvium = Mass × Cigarettes squared.

'Say it!' he snapped.

'Don't you see! You lot went off boozing that last evening, your pockets full of tenners. You wouldn't have been able to find your own fly zips, when you left the pub. And you got back and there was no money, no Sylvia, no Adrian. Of *course* there wasn't, you incompetent clod! You'd probably gone back to the wrong bloody place!'

I felt him go rigid, glanced at him, and watched the blood run from his face. His cheeks seemed to sink inwards, his eyes to darken. Then he raised a fist in the air and shouted, 'No! No! No!'

7

I knew in that moment that we had breached a barrier. In the far reaches of his murky subconscious mind he had been carrying around much the same idea, afraid to bring it out into the light for a careful examination. My simple words had flushed it out into full view, along with its implications.

From somewhere in the undergrowth a bird or an animal screamed in response. Three times.

I said nothing, waiting. He stood very still, his face set. Then he put his fingertips together, forming a cage, raised it and blew gently into it, as though the fingers needed warming — as though the breath needed trapping before it formed itself into words he might regret. An archaic ritual.

Then I'd waited long enough. 'It's a distinct possibility,' I said softly.

But his mind had already rejected it. 'No.' His lack of emphasis lent confidence to the word. 'It doesn't fit.' He had recovered his self-possession.

But I got the impression he'd thought about it, over and over, but delicately.

141

'In what way doesn't it fit?' I asked.

'It was the proper place.' He nodded. 'The cellar, where we'd fixed up for Sylvie an' the kid . . . all the stuff we'd brought was still there.'

'Are you sure of that?' Silence. I glanced at him. His eyes were on the far distant hills. 'Did you check that yourself?'

'No. You wouldn't have got me down there for anythin'. Can't stand bein' shut in — all close.'

Was that why he was more human, out here in the wilds? I wondered how he had fared in prison.

'Then what *did* you do?'

His breath made a small juddering sound as he drew it in. 'I sent Tim, with a torch, down into the cellar to 'ave a look.'

'And he said?' I was having to drag it from him.

'He comes back and says the cookin' stuff was all there, an' the food an' the stove, an' the water. But no money . . . no kid . . . and no sign . . . ' He stopped.

'No sign of his sister, Sylvia?'

'Nothin'.'

'And you took his word for that?' I asked softly.

He turned then and looked me directly in the eyes. It seemed that the ice-rim around his irises had invaded them completely. They were cold, expressionless, empty. 'Why not? She was *his* sister.'

'Yes,' I said. But from me it was a condemnation.

His hand jerked out and gripped my shoulder. I tensed myself for action. But he only wanted to hold me there, so that I couldn't evade his voice.

'She was his sister — yeah! Christ — I've been dumb. That nasty little slob, he's made a mug outa me!'

'It doesn't follow,' I said. 'Cool down, Ronnie. He could've been telling the truth. The cellar was empty, but it was the right place.'

But he wasn't listening any more. He launched into a long and rambling replay of that evening. That night, rather. It had been almost midnight when they'd returned to the farmhouse — when they at last located it.

'The little bastard could've been lyin',' Phelps said, glowering around. 'Could've had it fixed with his sister. Somethin' like that. P'raps she'd managed to get all that money down into the cellar, while we was off an' away. Could've bin done. You gotta admit — it could've bin done. Yeah . . . I can just see Sylvie doin' it. She'd have made it a game, her an' the kid, takin' it down in bundles or plastic bags. But not much at a time. Then at the end the empty suitcase. Sure. Then they'd lie quiet in the dark, an' when we all got back, him, that bleedin' Tim, he'd say they wasn't there. Nor the money. All gone.'

I shook my head, pursing my lips in doubt. 'He wouldn't have dared risk it. You'd have checked. You wouldn't have trusted him — you would have checked for yourself. He would have thought that. And if he'd been caught out lying, you'd have killed him. There and then.'

'He knew I couldn't stand the thought of goin' down there.'

'You wouldn't need to. Stand at the top with a torch, and you'd be able to see in one glance. The camping equipment would've been there. It had to be the right place, Ronnie. Admit it.'

'The stuff had *gone!*' he cried out. 'The money — all gone. So all right . . . he didn't have to risk anythin'. He'd brought us back to the wrong place — as you said. It was him driving.'

'But he wouldn't have dared to risk that, either. One quick look into a derelict and empty cellar, and you'd have known.'

He looked at me with a wild light in his eyes, then he ran both hands up the back of

144

his neck. 'However it was.' He wagged his head around, hunting for the truth.

'So . . . how was it? Make up your mind.'

'He was lyin' either way,' he decided furiously. 'That bleedin' Tim. I'll screw it outa him.'

'In what way was he lying?' I persisted. 'Either way, you said.'

'If it was the wrong place, he was lyin', and if it was the right place, an' they was there all the time — '

'We've been over all that,' I cut in. 'So where does it get you?'

'Whatsamarrer wi' you!' he cried out, frustration flushing his cheeks. 'Say somethin' useful, for a change.'

'All right. If Tim was lying, what had he got in mind? How did he intend to carry it on?'

He stared at me as though I was insane. 'Ain't it bloody obvious?'

'To me, it is. After a few minutes of thought, it's obvious. You've had sixteen years to think in, Ronnie, and it's only now you've seen it.'

'I could kick myself.'

'Sure you could,' I said comfortingly. 'So . . . *now* what do you think happened?'

He started to walk away towards the car. I put the glass down on an outside table and went after him.

'Well? What *do* you think?' I was deliberately pushing him.

He stood there with a hand on the car door, looking back at the pub. 'Too long we was here.'

'Here? This was the pub?'

'Sure was.'

'Your local, so to speak?'

'Call it that.' He opened the door.

'So . . . in daylight . . . you ought to be able to find your way from here to the place.'

He slid in behind the wheel and slammed the door viciously. I got inside quickly in case his anger prompted him into accelerating away furiously. But he sat a moment, his hand on the ignition key. Then he said, 'Nah! Tried it, ain't I! Couldn't find the blasted place. No way, I couldn't.'

'Then we'll give it another try.'

He allowed the car to drift away slowly. 'Don't even know which way to go,' he complained.

'Then it doesn't matter. Just drive. Try along that track there.'

'I suppose it's as good as any.'

He seemed repressed, abruptly reluctant to proceed in any direction. I knew what he was thinking, and allowed him to get on with it for a while. However he tossed it, heads or tails, it was blank both sides.

146

We were driving along what might have been called a track, as we'd headed directly away from the road. No surface had ever been laid because the sub-terrain was rock, frost-broken and uneven rock, thrusting through the skimpy grass layer. It stretched ahead as twin, foot-wide wheel tracks of greyish-reddish rock against the green, ambling with apparent lack of purpose along the flanks of shallow hills. From time to time other, even less distinct double tracks headed off in either direction, upwards or downwards, apparently heading nowhere. Sparse sheep scattered the slopes. No buildings or parts of buildings lent artificial design or pattern to the landscape. No red bricks lent life to a drab and uninspiring view. In any event — it seemed to me — any construction would have been undertaken with the materials immediately available, that ubiquitous grey rock. This meant that such a construction, now derelict, would not be distinct against a background of rock outcrop of the same colour.

It seemed that our success rested on a considerable amount of luck.

'Have you thought of this?' I said, after a long interval when there'd been nothing worth saying.

'Thought of what?'

'Tim. If he *was* lying.'

'Must've bin.' His knuckles were white on the steering wheel. 'So what?'

'He would've had to have a reason. Whatever he was doing, he perhaps wanted to persuade you and Martie that the money and the rest had gone. Whatever lie he chose. Why would he do that?'

'Obvious — ain't it? He was gonna come back the next day — the day after that, p'raps. Come back on his own to collect the money for hisself.'

'And the others — Sylvia and Adrian — what would he do about them?'

'I don't know,' he snapped.

'I mean . . . he wouldn't dare let 'em free to roam around in amongst other people, ordinary people, Ronnie, who'd ask them questions — and they'd get answers. What would Tim have to do?'

He was silent. Then he abruptly stopped the car, got out, and looked round. But I was at his shoulder.

'Well . . . what would he — '

'Shurrup!' he cut in. He was staring into the distance

'Something?'

'That chunk of rock. Funny-shaped. Thought I remembered it, but there ain't no side track, no nothin'.'

148

'Could have grown over,' I suggested.

'Nah! Reckon I was wrong.'

We got back in the car, and he drove a little further.

'But he didn't do that, did he?' I persisted. 'Tim. He didn't come back. And you know why, as well as I do, Ronnie. You'd been away from your usual haunts for three weeks. All three of you. You turned up just after the hand-over, so you were picked up and held for questioning. You never did get the chance to come back here, any single one of you. Isn't that how it was?'

His palm thumped the steering wheel. 'That's how it was.'

'So if we find the place, the real and genuine place, and Tim *was* lying, then it ought to be there, still. Waiting for us. And I'll have earned my two per cent.'

'You keep goin' on about that, and it'll get you a flat nose, Patton.'

'On about what?'

'The money.'

'Isn't that what it's all about?' I asked innocently.

'Shut y'r mouth.'

I did — for two whole minutes. Then, 'How long', I asked, 'after you got back to civilization was it before you were picked up?'

'Next day.' He clipped the words.

'All three of you?'

Silence.

'All of you?'

'Tim', he said with chill quietness, 'was picked up two days later.'

'So he'd have had time,' I commented equably.

'I told y'. Shut your bloody mouth,' he shouted savagely.

I was silent. It was getting to be well past lunchtime, and I was hungry. The landscape was unchanging, unfolding itself in undulating and barely varying slopes, the same copses of trees clinging to sheltered hollows, the same gorse, the same scrub. And heaven knew how many miles from anywhere we could eat.

'Don't you remember anything, damn it?' I demanded. 'A blasted oak or a ruined barn to guide you, or a bit of a tower . . .'

'No.'

'There must be something.'

'Patton,' he said, 'I could dump you here, on the side o' the track. Dump you. If you don't shut y'r mouth.'

'You'd leave me to starve?'

'Hah!' He laughed in evil disgust.

I was silent for two minutes. Then, 'Anything you recognize around here?'

'No.'

150

'Perhaps I ought to drive, and you'd have more chance to look around.'

'I'm doin' the driving.'

'Don't go so fast, then. There's plenty of time. Sixteen years've gone by. No hurry now.'

He shook his head. Shook it, looking down at his lap. 'Won't anythin' shut you up?'

'I was asked for my assistance. What else can I do? You won't let me say anything — '

'Shut your trap — will y'!'

I was silent. The track or road, or whatever it could be called, had drifted down into the bottom of the valley. It might or might not have been the same valley as the one in which we had started. Everything looked the same, and if the track wound it didn't follow the course of the paltry stream that trickled along beside us. Sometimes it was there, the stream, sometimes not. We parted company and it hid itself away. Then suddenly, there it was again, but now the other side of the track. As we had seen no bridges or culverts, the assumption had to be that it was not the same stream. So perhaps we were tracking from one valley to another.

We saw no sign of any other vehicles. In practice, the car we were using was not really suitable for the terrain. A Rover, but their Landrover would have served us better.

And still the slopes folded and unfolded, revealing their flanks, their bands of trees. Then, two blinks later, they were not the same flanks, not the same trees. There seemed to be little life around. The sheep, yes, but they appeared to be forlorn, wild descendants of former domestic stock. We raised no grouse or pheasants, saw no circling predators, no scurrying rats or other small animals. We bounced along, rattling like a pebble in a large, empty bucket.

Any track that led sideways from the one we were using seemed to peter out at the first hint of a rise facing it. Even the tracks hadn't the incentive to pursue that direction, or the energy to climb. There was no point in exploring them.

After a long period of silence, sullen I thought on his part, I said, if only to lighten the mood, 'You should've nicked a different vehicle.'

'It was the first one with the keys left in.'

I stared sideways at his set profile. 'They left the keys in? It's nearly new! You must be joking.'

'Please yerself. You'll never believe a soddin' word.'

'No. Really. I wouldn't have thought — '

'Walk round any car-park. Any time. Quietly — just looking. Try the doors, an' I'll

152

bet you anythin' you like that for every fifty you try, at least two'll have the doors unlocked. An' if they're unlocked, it's a fair bet it's because the driver got out without the keys in his hand. It's God's truth. Try it, some day.'

'So you'll just dump it?' I asked, wondering how that would leave me, wondering whether I'd have to inform the police where it'd been left. But of course . . . I wouldn't know that.

'Dump it? Nah!' He shrugged. 'I'll leave it where I picked it up. Top up the tank first. Only fair.'

Fair! Ron Phelps, talking about fairness! He seemed to sense my surprise. 'I ain't in the market for nickin' cars,' he said, with contempt for those who were. 'You keepin' your eyes around?'

'I am, Ronnie. But there's nothing to look at. Nothing but country.'

'Told you . . . didn't I!'

I didn't know what that meant, unless he was demonstrating how easy it was to get lost around there. I already understood that completely. It was necessary to assure myself that if we kept going long enough we would eventually find ourselves back in civilization. And yet . . .

It had been an uninspiring day, the sun barely forcing its way through low cloud, for the past few minutes. But I'd been orientating myself by the sun, when it had appeared, having regard for the hour hand on my watch. And it did seem, though I hoped I might be wrong there, that we had almost doubled back on ourselves several times, and that, though the track seemed to head away in a fairly straight line along a fairly straight valley, I had only to turn round and look back the way we had come to discover that our track had completely disappeared, as though it had been rolled up the moment we had finished with it.

'We're not going to get anywhere like this,' I said.

'So what d'you want to do?' he demanded in fury. He was growing increasingly impatient with me.

'Try something else. It's useless just driving along here. If the blasted house was visible from here, you wouldn't have had difficulty finding it when you were here last.'

'So what d'you want me to *do*?' he shouted.

'Turn off on the first decent-looking track that heads anywhere.'

'Lotta good that'll do.'

'It's something to try.'

'Y've seen for yerself,' he said, almost snarling. 'The side tracks go nowhere.'

I sighed. 'All right. Stop the car, Ronnie. We've got to talk.'

'We've had nothin' but talk all the way.' But he allowed the car to drift to a halt. Then he sat, staring ahead, tapping his fingers on the wheel. 'Now what?'

'You know what, as well as I do. This is hopeless. A dead waste of time. You haven't got a clue on how to go about it — '

He jerked his head round, cutting in angrily. 'It's what y're here for, Patton. What we're payin' y' for.'

I allowed that to ride. 'What *you* are doing,' I told him, 'is stupid. You ought to have had large-scale Ordnance Survey maps of the area, one to twenty-five thousand, and a compass, and you ought to mark exactly where you've been. Coded colours, so that you know which days, too, and crosses where you come across any old ruin or sign of a building. What you ought — '

'Then we'll bloody well do it. All right? *You* can get the soddin' maps and the compass an' your pretty coloured pens. Me — I'll drive. We'll do that, if it'll make y' happy. Okay?'

'No. It's not okay.'

'We're payin' y' to do what you're bleedin' well told.'

I half turned, so that I could tap him with a

forefinger on the shoulder. Just so that he wouldn't forget I was there.

'You're *not* paying me. I agreed to look for the money, and if I found it I'd get two per cent. But doing it my way, on my own. Coming at it from another angle.'

'You'll do what you're told. We've got a contract.'

I laughed, trying to sound amused, but probably sounding merely derisive.

'Oh sure — we've got a contract. A verbal contract, though that's legal enough. It's a contract that leaves you free to get on with this stupid game you've been playing — but you can do that on your own. Me . . . I'm intending to go along a different route altogether . . . '

'You've gotta do what you're told. It's a contract.'

'What sort of contract?' I asked amiably.

'A . . . bloody . . . contract.'

'Legally, there're two sorts of contract,' I told him. 'No . . . listen. There's a contract *of* service, and a contract *for* services. Now . . . if you were employing me under a contract of service, then you'd be the boss. You'd be able to tell me what to do and when and how to do it, and sack me when you felt like it.'

'That's the one for me.' His voice was

uncertain, and a tiny smile tried to cling to his lips. I had the impression he was humouring me, not feeling too safe with a madman, and with all that bare space around.

'But *is* it?' I asked. 'Think. You'll have all those rights, including a right of control and of termination, and the rest. But you'd have the responsibilities. I'd have to be paid at regular intervals, and you'd need to learn how to deduct income tax and National Insurance — '

'Will you soddin' well drop it!' he shouted.

'All right. So assume we've got the other sort of contract, a contract for services. I find the money for you, and that's the service. Then I get paid. Is *that* how you want it?'

He got out of the car, stuck his hands in his anorak pockets, and walked up and down for a few minutes. Then he stood still and gazed into the middle distance. I put my head out of the window.

'Is *that* what you want?' I shouted.

'Yes, damn you, yes.'

'Then you've got no right to tell me how to do my part of it.'

He didn't reply. He stood with his chin raised, staring up the facing slope, far to my left as I sat there.

'C'm here!' he called, waving his arm.

I got out. It was a good idea to stretch my

legs, anyway. He was standing at the edge of the track we were taking, looking over a shallow valley. A hundred yards from us the stream — *a* stream — ran parallel to the track, a poor and paltry stream, maybe four feet across. It was ten feet or so below our level, and beyond it, mistily, the hillside rose, as a hundred other hillsides had risen, the dimly defined double tracks of a driveway from the distant past heading away towards a promontory, and apparently skirting it. Visible signs of it disappeared long before it reached a scattered curtain of trees.

'Looka that,' he said.

'I've seen it all before.'

'*That*,' he said, jerking a forefinger.

What he was pointing at was a rudimentary bridge spanning the stream. It seemed to consist of two flat slabs of rock, each around eight feet long, which had simply been laid down. They could have been there a couple of hundred years, and become part of the growth. They lived there . . . but they had not grown there. They had been brought, probably at a large expense in manpower and horsepower.

And so much effort would not have been expended unless a certain amount of permanency had been intended. Such as when a house, a farm, a dwelling of some sort, had been built, and access to it over the stream had been required.

I glanced at him. 'Shall we try it?'

His eyes were bright when he looked at me. A lock of lank hair had fallen over his left eye, but it shone through.

'I seem to remember a bridge,' he said quietly. 'Dimly, I remember.'

'So we try it,' I agreed.

We got back into the car. There was a fresh jauntiness to his movements. He turned the car off the main track and bumped it over the bridge.

'Straight ahead,' he said.

This minor track was visible only when it led directly away from us. The smallest amount of bend in it seemed to wipe it clean, then there it was again, sweeping round a jutting snarl of naked rock, or skirting the lower edge of a belt of conifers. We were rising steadily. I turned and glanced back, and there was no sign of the little bridge, no sign of the major track.

'It'll soon be getting dark,' I said.

Clouds were massing to our left. The west. The sun decided to give a last flick of a glance around its territory, then the clouds pounced in. Yes, the west.

I was hungry, emptily, painfully hungry. But we were heaven knew how many miles from any supply of food, and every minute travelling further away. Nothing I said now would have persuaded Ron Phelps to stop, turn around, and head back towards that isolated pub, and hopefully an isolated cheese sandwich.

He had put on the car's headlights. The sun, which had been to our left, the far side of the flat valley, was now suddenly behind clouds on our right, which didn't seem reasonable as the whole hillside, tatty trees, tangled gorse, naked rock, all this was suddenly on the wrong side of us.

We must have skirted a bluff. The sun suddenly fought its way free and painted the grey outcrops a blood red, and now the exposed rock was a cliff, which rose up into the sky, the track running closer and closer beneath it until it towered above us, waiting it seemed for the slightest disturbance in the air to crumble it down, such as from a car's engine revving fast in second gear, as Ronnie fought the steering wheel and we scrabbled round, the sun directly behind and sinking into a black cloud, the track now directly against the near-vertical face of the rock.

Ron Phelps was tense, nervous, leaning forward over the wheel, his eyes darting this way, that. Then we left the sun behind altogether, and we were round the bluff to where the grassland ran softly into a cleft, and here, protected from north and east against the winter's ferocity, a building had stood.

It didn't stand now. It was not beaten down by storms, but was rotted away by time and neglect; not fallen nobly with an outcry of protest and a rising of dust, but crumbled gently into dissolution. The roof was tilted, that part of it still attached. A large section had fallen through, leaving fangs like rotten teeth in aged gums. Windows were now gaps, and the front steps were hidden beneath piles of fallen rubble. Tiles hung drunkenly to rotted slats. Wooden splinters indicated where a door and window frames had been.

Ronnie sat with the engine running, as though he didn't realize he'd not yet switched it off. The full headlights cut the shapes into jagged silhouette. He seemed not to be breathing,

'Is this it?' I asked.

He drew air in noisily, but said nothing.

'Is it?'

'I think so,' he whispered.

'Only think?'

'Almost certain.'

'Make up your mind.'

He switched off lights and engine. In the sudden silence the remains of the building disappeared. What sun was still above the horizon was way round the other side of the bluff. The shadows were black and solid.

'Did you bring a torch?' I asked.

'Yeah.'

'Then let's go and have a closer look.'

Now that we seemed to have found it, he was suddenly reluctant to take it any further. Superstition? If he didn't count to seventy-three in threes, it would lie hidden for ever.

'Where's the torch?'

'Two of 'em. On the back seat.'

I hadn't noticed them. I got out. My eyes were now adapting; the building was again taking shape. But it was repressive. A soft wind now moaned through the trees, which, to one side, had so far encroached as to be part, now, of the destructive force deployed against the existence of the building. Shadows moved and swayed. I opened the car's rear door and fetched out the two torches, and tried them. They were bright, the batteries fresh.

'Aren't you getting out?' I asked.

'I suppose.'

He climbed out awkwardly and I thrust one of the torches at him. 'Here. You'd better lead. You know the place and I don't.'

Then he said something strange. 'I don't know that I know it.'

I thought about that. 'You mean you're still not sure?'

'It's . . . changed. Seems smaller, somehow.'

'Of course it does. It's falling down.'

Slowly, our torchlights darting this way and that, trying to trap a retreating, fleeing shadow, trying to check that it was a rat, or a . . . what? Person? Stop it, Richard. You're becoming fanciful.

'Take it very carefully,' I said. 'With all this brick and stone down, another pound or two might take us through the floor.' And heaven knew how much more on top of us if we did.

The front wall had collapsed outwards, spreading slates and bricks in sprawling heaps on what had been the entrance steps. A length of fluted column lay on its side; the house had been built with pride. At one time, neighbours had driven here in their curricles and phaetons, to be welcomed at the graceful porch.

We scrambled over what had been the entrance, scrambled gently and tenderly, hearing the whole structure groan at our pitiful addition to the weight it was already supporting.

'Careful,' I said, as he stumbled. 'Recognize it yet?'

'No.'

We would have been standing just inside the hall, though now it was open to the sky, which was dark enough to display stars.

'Is this the same hall?'

'Could be.'

'Where you opened the suitcase?'

'There was a roof on. Then, there was a roof on.' He seemed not to have anticipated any change.

'Imagine a roof. Would this have been — '

'Don't be so bloody daft!' he burst out. 'How can I tell?'

'I suppose you can't. All right — try another check. If this was *your* hall, where was the cellar entrance from here?'

'What?'

I didn't repeat it, simply waited.

'Further along,' he said reluctantly. 'Stairs was on the left.' He waved his torch beam. Yes — there were the remains of a staircase, cascaded with tiles, only the lower few stairs intact. 'Jus' past the stairs, a door. On the left. Steps down. Stone steps. Into the cellar.'

'The cellar you fixed up for Sylvia and the kid?'

'Tha's it. What we fixed up.'

'Not you, Ron. You wouldn't go down, you said. And I'd reckon Martie was too fat to risk the steps. In other words — the cellar Tim fixed up.'

'All right . . . all right.'

'Where Tim went when you managed to find your way back from the pub, and he came back and said the stuff was still there — but not the money, not Sylvia, and not the boy, Adrian?'

'You stoopid or summat? Yes, yes, yes!'

'So now's your chance to check it for yourself.'

'What?'

'Go down yourself, and see what's still there.'

'No!'

'No, Ronnie? You don't want to check? What d'you want to do, then? Drive away from here, and come back when there's bags of daylight left? If you could ever find it again! Ah, there's the rub.'

'What're you talkin' like that for?'

'I'm talking in this way because this is what we came for — and you're too scared to go down there in the dark. It's your chance to check — for yourself — what the position is now. Don't you *see* that?'

'I can see it.'

'Well then.'

'You can do it.' He shrugged and the torchlight danced. 'You do it.'

'What?' I stared at him, his face in shadow so that I could detect no expression. It was

165

fascinating. Put him in the middle of a bar brawl, and he would wade in, with no fear of a knife between the ribs, no consideration for a set of brass knuckles caving in his skull. But . . . a dark cellar, and he was terrified!

It was only then that I realized he'd already decided what would be there, if he ever found the place, and I understood why he'd wanted me with him. Now, I wasn't too keen, myself.

'All right,' I said. 'So I'll go. But listen, Ronnie. You stand well back. Not one foot inside the hall when I'm down there. And don't shout. The vibration could do the trick. I'll go down, but very slowly and carefully. If anything collapses, and I don't shout that I'm all right, you're not to come after me with rescue in mind. Get that?'

'I won't come after you,' he promised, his voice empty of everything but certainty.

'You'd have to drive away as fast as you can push it, and get back to that pub. Then phone for help. All right? If I get stuck down there, that is.'

'Sure.'

'You're certain you don't want to go down there yourself?'

'Dead certain.'

'When I get back, I might lie to you about what's down there.'

'I'll risk that.'

166

'I'm glad to find something you'll risk. Very well,' I said, trying to sound as though I did this sort of thing all the while. 'Stand back.'

Carefully, so very gently, he stepped back out of the debris and stood on basic rock outside.

I advanced slowly down what had been the hall, picking my way between the loose debris. It was encouraging to observe that further back there was not too much of this, so that the stress on the flooring was less, where it mattered. To be sure, it creaked, but that was to be expected.

The remains of the staircase were to my left, coming down from above my left shoulder. I grasped the vertical banister post at the foot of the stairs and tried to move it. But it was reassuringly solid. The bottom six feet of the staircase also appeared sound, and the oak panelling closing it in on the hall side was uncracked. Considerably more encouraged now, I moved onwards on sliding feet, beyond the foot of the stairs.

The door to the cellar was where Phelps had said it should be. Indeed, it did seem that this was the correct building. But the cellar door itself hung raggedly on one hinge. I eased it fully open, creaking and grinding, and splashed torchlight down the stairs.

Blessedly, they were stone, as Phelps had

said. In fact, when I got to a closer examination it seemed that the complete cellar had been hacked out of the solid rock. Now I felt much better about venturing below.

It was a small cellar, for what had been the size of the house. Its smell was that of a dry mustiness rather than of damp. The steps clung to the side wall. I walked down slowly, carefully, my palm sliding down the wall surface, dry, dry, to the very bottom, and chillingly cold.

Animals had been down there. With the door flapping open, it would have presented a precious winter hide. Animals. Foxes, squirrels — no, not squirrels. Perhaps stoats, weasels, even sheep and wild cats. In any event, I knew from the smell that animals had been there, and therefore I didn't expect to find a trace of food. And there was none.

But the containers were there, the tins, surprisingly very little rusted, and the plastic boxes. The little stove was there, a tin kettle, a teapot on its side in a corner. As my torchlight flicked over it, a rat's head popped out of the teapot, and popped back. There were plates, broken now, and two straw mattresses, torn to shreds and housing several families of mice. A five-gallon plastic bucket lay on its side, its lid at the far end of the cellar. It was packed with straw, which seemed to be seething with the life that had carried it there. Possibly more mice. And there were the scattered portions of what could have been half a dozen jigsaw puzzles, and the chewed remains of several paperback books. But no chewed bits of tenners.

There was nothing else. No remains of a suitcase, no money, and none of what I had been dreading — human skeletons.

After one last glance around, I climbed slowly to the hall again, resting a moment with my hand on the banister post, unable to understand why I seemed to be so exhausted.

Outside, in what was now solid darkness, I saw Ron's torch flicker. He had seen me. He called out in a breathless whisper, 'Anything?'

'It's the correct place,' I replied, managing a reasonably normal voice. 'Signs of occupation, but no money and no suitcase.'

'So it's a wash-out?'

He now appeared in what had been the main entrance, balancing precariously on the loose masonry. 'Nowhere else to look?' he asked tentatively.

'It's not here, Ronnie.'

'Hah!' he said in disgust.

But there was one more hiding place. Beneath the foot of the staircase there was the small door to a cupboard. I'd been subconsciously looking for one, as a similar cupboard had recently figured in an enquiry I was then making. But that had been a reasonably large one. This . . . and I had no more than the sight of a half-inset brass ring handle to indicate its presence . . . was very much smaller, tucked into the bottom corner and no more than three feet high at its taller end, where the hinges would be. It sloped down to a foot in depth, where the catch was located.

'There's a small cupboard here,' I said.

'So what?'

'Big enough for a suitcase.'

'Oh. Oh yes!'

'Stay where you are,' I told him, and I crouched to it.

The door was such a good fit that I could barely detect the line around it where the opening would be. I lifted the brass catch, which was stiff, and could turn it only with the greatest effort. The door naturally opened outwards, but did so with a considerable amount of creaking against its surrounding frame. It drew open reluctantly, groaning at the disturbance.

It was dry in there. Dry and air-proof, and the smell was of a pungent dust. So this, I thought in that first second, was how stale and tinder-dry money smelt. I cast the torchlight inside. It wasn't money, though. There was no suitcase.

At first, my thought was that she was alive, that my torch might waken her and she would lift her head. She was sitting with her back against the deeper of the walls, her toes against the far edge, which would be the back of the lowest stair riser. Because of the restricted space, this meant that her legs had to be bent, and it was on her arms, hanging forward over the knees, that her cheek rested. Her face was turned directly towards me, as though waiting for me and about to smile at her release.

But it was a dead face, though the hair was mostly intact, hanging forward like a tatty veil, and the skin, what I could see of it, was shrunk over the bone structure, and showed patches of grey. The face of an old woman. She was wearing jeans and a T-shirt. The material was intact, but looked as though it would disintegrate if I touched it. It was not difficult to realize that this was a young person, had not reached seventeen, but had not changed radically in sixteen years.

All this I registered in the few seconds of shock whilst I levelled the torchlight inside. Then I flicked it aside, and with my other hand fumbled the door shut. Shut to, but not pushed into place. Shut. Just shut. Close it to, don't fasten it . . .

And I realized I was instructing myself over and over on this, as my hands didn't seem to be doing it gently enough. I forced myself to my feet and stumbled towards the open air.

'Any joy?' asked Ronnie.

'Not joy. But I think we've found Sylvia,' I said, ridiculously, for an experienced copper, finding it difficult to say. 'Found Sylvia.'

8

Eventually we managed to sort things out between us: what had to be done and who was to do it. One of us had to get back to the Saracen's Head, and call the police. The other had to stay behind, with the two hand torches, in order to make signals. Any failure to relocate it would be dangerous.

'We might never find the place again, if we both go,' I explained.

I was being very careful with him, as his mind stubbornly refused to accept the truth, but it was clear that he couldn't wait to get away from there, and that he had no desire ever to see it again. So that settled one point.

'Right,' I said. 'You drive back to the pub. It should be easy enough if you follow the track back to the stone bridge, cross it, and turn right. Then just keep going.'

'Yeah,' he said doubtfully.

We were sitting in the car with the interior light on. He seemed listless, his brain not functioning.

'And don't rush it,' I instructed him. 'You don't want a busted suspension. Are you listening, Ronnie?'

'I'm listenin'.'

'Get to the pub and dial 999, and ask for the police. No, be more specific. Ask for Detective Inspector Brason. It'll save a lot of wasted time on explanations.'

'I suppose.' A pause. 'What about you?'

'I'll climb up the hill behind the house and look out for car headlights. Then I'll signal with the torches, sort of guide you in. Do you understand what you've got to do?' I waited for his head to nod. 'Right. Then do it.'

I had the passenger's door open. He made no move to start the engine. I asked, 'What's up? Why're you just sitting there?'

He turned to look directly at me at last. The light, being inset in the roof, wasn't ideal. It cast harsh shadows beneath his eyebrows. His eyes were tiny reflections of the light, pin-points in the corners. Lines ran down from his nose, cut deeply, dragging down the corners of his mouth.

'How d'you know it's Sylvia?' Somewhere behind that gruff and impersonal enquiry there was a desperate need to know. Pride prevented him from revealing any emotional involvement; pride betrayed him, the effort it took controlling it producing the words as one toneless slur.

'It's got to be her. How many girls in their teens could it possibly be?'

'How d'you know . . . ' Stubborn, he was. He moistened his lips. 'How d'you know, after all this time . . . know it's a girl?'

'It's girl-shaped. Now . . . get moving.'

'No . . . ' His hand reached across, groping for me. 'How could it be? She must've been dead sixteen years.'

I got out and slammed the door. 'Get moving,' I shouted. 'Leave it. Later.'

He started the engine. I stood back. There was room to circle away from me, but no, his mood dictated that he should vent his tight anger on me in some way. Violently, trying to spin the tyres on naked rock that wouldn't accept it, he circled me tightly, nearly running over my toes. I shouted after him, but got no reaction. His tail-lights retreated into the night.

I was none too pleased to find myself alone out there with two torches and a corpse for company. But my explanation to Ronnie — that we would never find it again if we both went — though valid, was not the mainspring of my decision.

I wanted time on my own to assimilate the implications. I wanted to check what I had seen, because otherwise it would become a nightmare, a wide-awake nightmare that could follow me into sleep. I wanted to confirm the fact that I could still force myself into doing it, and that retirement had not softened my ability to be completely objective when necessary. And there was something that I had to check.

On the rock surface outside the front entrance, I put down one of the torches, switched off. That was so that I'd have a reserve, in case I slipped and dropped the other, breaking the bulb. Then, stepping now with more confidence because it had taken my weight before, I moved slowly down the hall, and to the cupboard. It was comforting to be able to glance upwards at the crisp stars in a black sky.

As I had already handled the door, and had a good reason for having done so, I was not now concerned about fingerprints. Such matters, after this length of time, would be irrelevant, anyway. I edged the door open, beyond my left shoulder, so that I had a clear and unobstructed view inside.

With some relief I saw that nothing had changed. After the initial shock, it had been easy to persuade myself that I had coloured the picture with imagination, clothed a skeleton with flesh. But it was not so. The complete shape was real. This was a young woman, undoubtedly. The hair, even now, had a softness and a flow that was feminine. I did not dare to touch, in fact I could not have brought myself to touching, but I could see that the skin clung to the bones. The age of the face was seventy, of the figure seventeen.

I noted, now that I was able to concentrate, that she was wearing a bracelet on her right wrist. It was barely tarnished. And though the left hand was further from me, it was clutched around her shinbone, and I could see she had a ring on the third finger of that hand. Had she been engaged? I'd heard no mention of that. But it was a plain signet ring, with no stone. Around her neck hung a cheap string of blue beads. I forced myself to turn my attention elsewhere.

It was vital to remember that the catch, when I had first touched it, had been fastened. It was simple enough, a straight-forward rotating catch in the corner of the door, just beyond the figure's toes. But the plate into which the tongue rotated was inset into the stairway, into the banister post in fact. From inside, she could not have reached down to there without effort, and then would have found nothing to grasp. Assuming she had been alive, that is. And, as the hinges were to my left, they were opposite her shoulders, so that it would have been impossible for her to exert enough force to break open a door catch that was opposite her toes.

This all explained the condition of the body. I had heard about it. In fact, it was mentioned in police training manuals. I had even come across it. This was mummification due to a dry atmosphere and lack of air movement.

There were recorded cases, either accidental or criminal, where bodies had been similarly mummified. The Rhyl mummy had been a strangled woman, shut away for years while her pension had continued to be claimed — I remembered that one. Heaven knows how many unwanted and self-delivered babies had been summarily killed and the body hidden in a box in the loft. I'd had one of those myself — had been involved in it — when I was a constable.

And now . . . poor Sylvia.

I was mildly pleased that I could still be so detached. The trick is to dissociate yourself completely from the fact that this had been a person. It was now a forensic specimen, and I could do nothing but sigh, and leave it to the specialists.

But there was one more thing that I had to do, and I had reached the stage where I could do it. Of course, I dared not move the body, but I could put my face very close, now holding my breath and balancing precariously on my knees. I raised the torch to a position just above my right shoulder. There was a small space the far side of her body. Only a very small space . . .

But the portion I could see was empty. I sighed again, with relief. One of these bodies was one too many.

Then I retreated from the hall and into the clean and wide spaces, took a torch in each hand, and slowly climbed the steep slope behind the house until there was no more climbing to be done.

I was unable to say, having regard to the winding nature of the approach track, exactly from which direction they would arrive. I had to hope that I would see headlights eventually. I sat on a knoll of rock, slowly filled my pipe, then lit it and drew in smoke luxuriously.

And waited.

That was my intention, to allow the tension to ease, and my lungs be filled with clean air, although heavily modified with tobacco smoke. But it wasn't like that. I hadn't realized it was so cold. The chill entered my bones. It seemed that it rose around me, though cool air must theoretically fall. But this was a special air because it rose from the tattered remains of the house below me, as though the shell of it still breathed. And the still night, clear as crystal and now with not a

179

hint of breeze, seemed gently and sombrely to moan. I turned, and it was in my face, turned again, and it was out there in the night, a soft sigh that moved gently over the scrub grass, slid smoothly over the exposed rock. And below me the house waited. There was no impatience. Indeed, it was a companionable, welcoming feeling, reaching up to me. The house was my friend. Or I was its friend. I had come there and released its burden. It whispered that it perhaps had other secrets to offer me.

And I knew they were secrets I didn't wish to penetrate, yet they were offered to me alone. Perhaps I ought to have been warmed by this knowledge. The chosen one. But I felt that I was chosen more as a sacrifice than as a beneficiary. The house wanted to free itself of all its secrets, so that it could rest. I was to lift them from those weary and collapsing shoulders, and on to my own.

Impatiently, aware that my pipe was cold and that I was stiff from the chill in my bones — yet what else could a dead house offer but chills? — I got to my feet and walked around restlessly. The platform at the top, the section on which it was possible to walk on the level, was no more than ten feet in any direction. Back and forth, round and round, I walked. The impulse was to abandon my post. Ron

Phelps must surely now be able to find his way back, having driven it twice. But if he couldn't, and I wasn't in a position to signal him in, they might prowl the district all night and not find me. And would I dare to set off on foot in any direction with any hope of fighting free of that treacherous moorland?

Fanciful. Think logically, Richard, I told myself. Logically, they might show at any time now. I looked at my watch. It was luminous, and yet strangely I saw nothing, and had to use a torch. Phelps had been gone for forty minutes now. Would they never . . .

I saw them on that instant, saw them not as a blaze of distant headlights but as blue spurts of light against the horizon. This I ought to have expected, although on the open moorland there would be little or no traffic to warn. But there was no wailing of distant sirens; the wailing was here, in the air around me. I extended my arms, both torches switched on, and waved in two reaching arcs. Then at last headlights speared in my direction. Four sets I counted, and two overlapping splashes of blue light. Even when it was clear that they were headed directly towards me, I found myself unable to abandon my position, in case, if I took my eyes from them for a second, they would melt into the night and disappear.

Only when they drew to a halt below me did I lower the torches and begin to bound down the treacherous slope. There was Phelps in the Rover he had borrowed, a police patrol car, a plain dark car, and an ambulance. And Tony Brason standing waiting for me with feet apart and his shoulders square, and with his voice flat and empty when he greeted me.

'Richard . . . you've been busy, I hear.'

'Some success,' I protested, still short of breath.

'What I've been hearing doesn't make sense.'

Phelps was climbing out of the Rover. There were four officers in the patrol car. The ambulance sat there silently, with nobody rushing to open the rear doors and slide out a stretcher. A tall, slim man was getting out of the car I assumed to be Tony's.

'You took your time,' I said.

Tony shrugged. 'No hurry, was there? I had to make some sense of the story. It all sounded wild . . . fantastic. But I decided to bring along the hospital pathologist. It sounded . . . sort of . . . as though it wasn't a simple matter of certifying death. I mean — an expert on it straightaway. I don't know . . .'

I felt I had to sit down. There was nowhere

except the cars. The tall, slim man was now at Tony's shoulder. 'Professor Atkinson,' Tony introduced him. 'This is Richard Patton, doctor.'

I nodded. 'Can we sit down?' I asked.

Tony looked at me sharply. 'My car.' He gestured.

So I got into the back with Atkinson, Tony in the front, twisted round so that he could keep his eyes on me. I glanced at my watch, completely confused as to where we were in the time-scale. It was nine o'clock. Twelve hours since I had eaten, since either Phelps or I had eaten. And Amelia . . .

'Have you got a radio phone I can use?' I asked.

'I've done it,' said Tony. 'I thought you wouldn't mind. Rang Amelia and told her you were stuck out here.'

'Mind!' I flicked him a quick smile of gratitude.

'She's driving down. I told her to go straight to the station. They'll look after her.'

I nodded. Amelia hated night driving. 'I'm sure they will.'

He turned away, and brought out a vacuum flask and a packet of sandwiches. 'Phelps said neither of you had had anything to eat since breakfast. He's had his. This is yours. Now . . . let's hear it, before we make a move.'

So, past a mouthful of cheese and tomato and a cupful of hot coffee, I told him — how we'd found the place by sheer luck, and what I'd uncovered. Beside me, I was aware, Atkinson sat with his eyes not leaving my face for a second. Tony had only the dashlights on. It was weirdly shadowed. Nobody interrupted.

'I've come across something like it before,' I explained. 'It's a young woman, I'd say dead for sixteen years. You'll find her tucked away in the cupboard beneath the foot of the stairs. It was latched. I unlatched it, expecting something else, frankly.'

'Something else?' Tony murmured.

'A suitcase full of money.'

'But it was — '

'Sylvia Craythorpe,' I said. 'Must be, though I never saw her alive, of course. Can't be anybody else.'

'And the boy?'

'No.' Then I qualified it. 'I think not. It doesn't seem so.'

'Go on.'

I spoke now directly to Atkinson. 'It's not going to be easy. The hall floor may not be sound. It creaked with only me on it, and there's a lot of bricks and rock . . . '

'We'll shift those for a start,' Tony said.

'Yes. Good idea. But even then . . . I don't

184

see how you'll be able to remove her.'

'Leave that to me,' said Atkinson.

'There's a six-inch sill. Remove that, and you might be able to slide — '

'I'll decide,' said Atkinson softly. 'Inspector . . . can you get somebody started on shifting the stuff in the hall?'

'Right.' Tony got out of the car.

I could just detect that Atkinson was smiling gently, his eyes on my face. 'It's shaken you, hasn't it?' He didn't wait for a reply. 'And there's something else, isn't there?'

I was wiping my fingers with my handkerchief. 'Possibly. I tried to check, but . . . There was a boy, five to six years old. He and the girl disappeared together. I mean — at the same time. There's a small space at the back of the cupboard . . . I tried to look, and I'm almost certain there's nothing but space. But there's just a possibility. I think you ought to be prepared . . . in case.'

'Yes. Yes, don't worry.'

'I shan't rest until I know for sure.'

'Of course not. Now . . . ah, here's the DI back.'

Tony opened the rear door. 'It'll take a few minutes. The hall floor doesn't seem too bad to me. I think you might — '

'I'll come and look.'

185

Tony tried to stop me when I moved to follow them, but I shook my head. I went no further than the foot of what had been the steps. They'd rigged a small spotlight, directly dog-clipped to the battery of the patrol car. Its engine was running. Already, with four constables working on it, they had most of the hall cleared of rubble. I stood outside in the dark as the doctor carefully made his way down the hall, Tony at his shoulder with a hand torch, because the floodlight cast heavy shadows into the cupboard.

There now seemed to be no sound from anywhere. Nobody whispered; everybody either sat or stood silently. I couldn't see what the pathologist was doing. Didn't want to. After two or three minutes he took the torch from Tony's fingers. I saw it moving around. Then he sat up straight and turned his head. 'No,' he called out.

'Nothing?' I asked.

'Nothing.'

Slowly I walked back to Tony's car, but I didn't get inside, just stood there by it, until Tony said at my shoulder, 'I'll have you driven back in the patrol car, Richard.'

Unfortunately, he didn't mean back home, which was where I wanted to be, only back to Potterton. Where Amelia would eventually arrive.

'Fine. Yes. Thanks.'

'Can I go now, Mr Brason?' asked Phelps, suddenly at his elbow.

We turned and stared at him. Somehow I'd discounted him from the proceedings, had forgotten he was there.

'I'll know where to find you,' Tony agreed. 'You can go in the same car.'

'The Rover . . . '

'Which has no doubt been stolen,' said Tony flatly, 'and which will be returned to its rightful owner. One of my men will drive it.'

'It wasn't nicked,' Phelps protested. 'Borrowed. I was gonna return it.'

'Ha!' growled Tony with disgust.

'I think that's so,' I put in quietly, but I was too tired to make an issue of it. The legal point about borrowing didn't apply to cars, anyway.

'All the same, he'll go back in the patrol car. I'll be in touch, Richard.'

'Yes. Thanks.'

As we drove away, the official photographer had begun taking his flash photos of the scene. What is normally a blinding light was a series of tiny sparks in that vast open space. I think, then, I must have fallen asleep, as I had no impression of the passage of time. My next awareness was of being ushered through a doorway directly leading from the police

187

car-park, so that we entered the reception lobby from the rear.

Amelia was sitting on a bench at the side, her eyes fixed on the swing doors out to the street. She had both dogs with her, sprawled behind her legs with their noses on their paws, apparently asleep. But it was they who sensed my presence, whose heads came up, who began such a frantic barking, whose sudden lunges took the leads from her fingers as they pounced at me. Boxers have perhaps the most miserable-looking faces of all dogs, except to those who know them. Their delight was overpowering.

Laughing, crouching, my arms round them, I looked beyond them at Amelia, now on her feet. She was one intense frown, five feet six inches of concentrated frown.

'Richard,' she said softly.

Then she smiled as I stood up, leaving one hand dangling for the dogs to slop at.

'Thank you for coming, love,' I said. I had a free arm, so I put it round her shoulders. She raised her face. I kissed her lips. They tasted salty.

'It's been bad, hasn't it?' she asked, still very quietly.

'It's been bad,' I agreed. 'Shall we go home now?'

'Yes please.'

I smiled at her, released her, and went over to the desk. 'Inspector Brason knows where to find me,' I said.

'Yes sir. He's called in.'

I turned. Ron Phelps was at my shoulder. 'Drop me off, Mr Patton?' he asked.

I almost laughed at his cheek. 'The dogs wouldn't let you get in the car.'

'They would if you told 'em.'

'I'm not about to tell them, Ronnie. Take a bus, take a taxi. This is your home town, but we're sixty miles from ours. In any event . . . '

'In any event,' said the duty sergeant, leaning heavily over his counter, 'Mr Brason wants a word with you. Take a seat, Mr Phelps. If you please.'

We left by the same door into the car-park. The Granada was parked in a dark corner. Amelia headed for the driver's side.

'I'll drive, love,' I said.

'No. You've had a long day. I'll drive.'

'Yes,' I said, 'it's been a long day. But, d'you know, I haven't driven one yard. It's all right. I can cope.'

And it would concentrate my mind on thoughts I could handle.

She conceded, but I could see she wasn't happy about it. As I took us out of the town, confidently because I was getting to know the route, I could feel her eyes on me. When we were well clear of the late-night traffic, she asked, 'Is it true, Richard, what I heard?'

'That depends what it is.'

'That you've found . . . something.'

'Yes,' I said. 'Something. I'm sorry to have to say it, but I found the body of the girl, Sylvia.'

There was silence as she thought about it. Then, 'You're sure?'

'I'm sure.'

'After all these years?'

'I'm sure.'

I felt her glance at me. She didn't push it, but allowed it to rest for a couple of miles. I found, though I'd been confident of my reserves, that I was desperately tired. Twice, I realized I'd reached the far side of small towns without any recollection of driving through. That worried me. I was driving by instinct.

'So you've done what you set out to do?' she said at last, tentatively.

'Partly.'

'Isn't it enough?'

'The boy wasn't there.'

'You can't expect to find everything!'

'The money wasn't there, either.'

'To hell with the money!' she said violently.

To hear Amelia swearing was unusual; to hear her doing it with such emphasis was unprecedented.

'My attitude completely,' I said gently, to balance her anger. 'But you see, my love, unless I at least pretend to be searching for the money, I shall lose the support of Ron Phelps and his two unpleasant mates. And they have no neutrality in their mean little souls: it's either for or against. I'd prefer it to be for.'

'Richard!' she muttered sadly.

'And I've developed a very useful relationship with Ron Phelps.'

'I can hardly believe that.'

'But I assure you . . . I know his limitations and weaknesses. And he knows I know. That's very important.'

She was unconvinced. It was quite clear that she believed I had done enough to clear the dust from an old tragedy, and it could be left to others to polish it. But I was caught in a conviction that I'd barely touched its surface. There were too many layers to be explored; I had brushed only the first.

There was naturally a hot meal awaiting me at home. Theoretically, with that inside me, I ought to have been ready for bed, and in fact I felt exhausted. But I was still winding down. The tension wouldn't let go. I could have sworn I would lie awake, twitching and turning, if I stretched out on a bed, but somehow I got there without even noticing it.

I cannot remember dreaming, but there was a background impression of noise, and twice I awoke to the sound of the phone ringing. That much could well have been a dream, I told myself, sitting on the edge of the bed in the morning and waiting for my mind to clear.

Unfortunately, it had been only too real.

9

They had allowed me a lie-in until nine instead of my usual seven thirty. I took a quick shower, threw on old grey slacks and a black roll-neck sweater and went down to breakfast, to be greeted with:

'Richard, the phone's been ringing all morning. Literally *everybody's* been trying — '

'Oh Lord!' I hadn't realized.

Amelia stared at me, large-eyed and pursed-lipped. She nodded. 'Yes. The press are waiting out at the front, and a TV group who want to interview you for — '

'No!' I said flatly. 'Let 'em pester the police.'

'They've done that, apparently. Tony phoned.'

I sat at the kitchen table. Mary, her expression one of disapproval of everything and everybody, put a breakfast plate in front of me.

'If you're going to speak to them,' she said, 'you'd better have a shave first. Stubble looks simply terrible on the screen. And Amelia, don't you think he ought to wear something a bit smarter . . . '

'I do not intend to speak to anybody,' I said. 'What d'you think they'll ask? Mr Patton, how did you feel when you found the girl's body!' I mimicked this horribly.

'Not even speak to anybody on the phone?' asked Amelia. I couldn't tell whether this disapproval was for my attitude or for the press.

I sighed. 'Who's been on the phone, then?'

She sat opposite to me at the kitchen table, leaning forward and speaking quietly, reasonably.

'Richard, you can't expect to escape entirely. You'll have to speak to somebody, you know. I told you . . . Tony called.'

'I'll call him back.'

'And there's a Mrs Craythorpe, who's asked you to go and see her.'

'Craythorpe?' For a second the name didn't register.

'The girl's mother.'

'Yes,' I said. 'Her mother. Yes . . . I'd better see her.'

I hadn't expected all this. In fact, I hadn't thought anything through properly. But now I had to turn my mind to it, and urgently. Who, for instance, was going to identify the body? Surely they wouldn't inflict that on her mother! Intolerable. Perhaps Ron Phelps would do it. Or her brother, Tim. Or maybe

194

— and Tony would surely try this first — it would be possible to lay the facts before the coroner, who, if he was reasonable, would accept identification from the background evidence. It could not be anybody else. Yes — that would probably be done. But I couldn't see how they would be able to hold an inquest with any chance of reaching a verdict on the cause of her death. Accident or deliberate? Suicide was ruled out, for starters. Death, then, by misadventure?

And yet — though I'm not a pathologist and have very little forensic knowledge — I had managed to pick up a few things during my period of service in the CID. If any bones were fractured — skull or hyoid, for instance — the evidence would point to murder. But whether or not a pathologist, after a sixteen-year interval, could pin-point any organic cause of death, I didn't know. One point was very clear though: the catch to that cupboard door had been fastened, and from the outside.

And her mother wanted to speak to me!

Oh yes, and Tony would certainly be wanting a statement from me. I was the only person capable of a definite deposition that the catch had been fastened. I was, therefore, the only person whose evidence would indicate that an inquest verdict of murder might be appropriate.

'I'll phone Tony,' I said, and I must have been a long while thinking about it, because when I looked up they were both staring at me with concern. 'This morning,' I explained.

'And Mrs Craythorpe?' Amelia asked. The mother would naturally be her prime concern.

'Tony will be able to give me her address.'

'I've got her address. Are you going to see her?'

'I must.'

'Yes,' she murmured. 'You must. We must,' she clarified.

I smiled at her. 'Any more tea?' I asked, and Mary had it on the table before I'd said the last word.

'And there's somebody called Rennie. Julian, I think he said. Julian Rennie, personal secretary to Marcus Spooner. *He* wants you to go and see him. To see Mr Spooner. Isn't he the . . . ' She glanced at Mary for her assistance. I'm afraid my expression might not have been encouraging.

'Yes,' I said. 'Marcus Spooner is the father of young Adrian.' I might have guessed. I *would* have guessed, given time, that he'd want to see me. 'Of course, I'll have to go. *He* wanted to see me? Not his wife? Surely she . . . '

Amelia shook her head. 'There was no mention of a wife. Perhaps she's dead. It's been sixteen years, after all.' She touched her lips with her fingers. 'Perhaps of a broken heart.'

'Yes,' I agreed, not wanting to think about that. I got up from the table abruptly. 'I'll take the dogs down to the river.'

They were there in a flash.

'There're people out at the front, waiting.'

'Let 'em wait. I've got to clear my head, love. Coming?'

'No, Richard. Think it out for yourself.'

I nodded, held the door open for Sheba and Jake, and paused. I thought she ought to know.

'Not of a broken heart, love. When I was there they'd got Mrs Spooner under heavy sedation. Drugs. If they eased them off, she was in hysterics. No . . . I'd say they probably became a permanent prop — the drugs. She more likely died of an overdose. Though perhaps you're right . . . of a broken heart.' This I conceded, observing her expression.

Without looking back, I went out after the dogs.

Our kitchen door opens directly on to a paved terrace, and within ten yards the ground level suddenly plunges down the steep slope to the Severn, where the river turns in a sweep around the foot of our terraced garden. Even with the winding path down to the water, the grades are still steep. But the steepness of the rise is a godsend when the river floods. The highest it has come at those times, since we've lived there, has been ten feet above the bank, which did no more than rob us of a couple of dozen roses. But the main delight is the peace and seclusion this offers us. We can walk the river path in both directions, thus trespassing into our neighbours' properties, as they can ours. We have good neighbours, so everybody is happy.

Except at times like these, and I was not happy at all. The dogs loved it. I prowled the riverside moodily.

It seemed that I had inherited nothing but trouble from George Tate. That, I could handle. But it was proliferating wildly, and my control over the course of events was fragile. In fact — look at it sombrely — I had very little control at all. Events were controlling me. But worst of all was the fact that it was taking place at a distance of sixty miles. On the face of it, that was a good thing. It kept my womenfolk well away from it. But already there were indications that it was moving in our direction, and there'd been a firm hint that Amelia, after the events of the

198

previous day, was not going to allow me too far from her sight again. Nor did I wish to be separated from her. But could I drag her into the unpleasantness that I could see looming ahead?

I was the only one who could give evidence that the cupboard door was latched.

It was impossible for me to join in the abandoned joy of the dogs. I think they felt this. After a few minutes they contented themselves with prowling, one each side of me, almost treading on my heels. I decided to go back to the house.

Up on the terrace, they were waiting for me, about a dozen of them, complete with cameras that clashed and whined, recorders, video cameras, and out-thrust mikes. I stopped. The dogs were uneasy. I snapped my fingers at them and they leaned, one each side, against my legs.

'I've nothing to say,' I said. 'You'll have to see the police.'

'Mr Patton . . . it was you who found her.'

'Nothing to say.'

Then the inevitable question: 'What were your thoughts when you found her?'

'Almost as disgusted as I am feeling right now.'

'Can you tell us . . . '

'What do you intend . . . '

'If you'll excuse me,' I said, and advanced. They held their positions stolidly.

I put a hand on each of the dog's heads, and said, 'The dogs're uneasy. You're on their territory. Will you please let me through before I lose control of them.'

For a moment their faces were blank. Sheba's ears went back. The deep growl in her throat sounded menacing. They stood back. I said thank you, and we walked into the kitchen.

'Did you get phone numbers?' I asked Amelia. My voice wasn't steady. I was surprised to find that I was shaking with anger.

'An address for Mrs Craythorpe,' she assured me patiently. 'A number for Mr Spooner's secretary. What are you going to do, Richard?'

'Phone first, then decide. I think we ought to see Mrs Craythorpe first, then Tony at the station. He'll want a statement. Then Spooner, I suppose.' I had been to his home, but couldn't remember where it was.

'You said 'we'.'

But I'd made up my mind. We had to stay together. 'Yes love, we.' I tilted my head at her. 'Isn't that what you want?'

She relaxed. She grinned; not a smile, a full and triumphant grin. 'I was going to come with you anyway.'

On the pad on the phone table in the living-room she had written down Mrs Craythorpe's address and a phone number, with the bracketed name: Julian Rennie. Where had I heard that name? But of course . . . Renee. Or Renée. Yes. When I'd visited the Spooners, with George Tate, arranging the cash situation, he had called his wife Renée, though pronouncing it Reenee. I had assumed this to be his wife, the stiff and contained and apparently voiceless woman who had stood beside him. At that first visit, she had still been able to stand.

'Hello. Julian Rennie speaking.'

'It's Richard Patton. I believe you wanted a word.'

His voice was cultured, Oxbridge, with a touch of the Counties, and loaded with contained confidence. 'My employer wishes to see you. Marcus Spooner. You will understand, and I'm sure I don't need to explain the importance.' There was a touch of condescension there. 'He wishes to see you today, as soon as you can get here.'

It was very close to a royal command.

'I'll come when I can. What's the address?'

Calmly, he gave me the address. Cumberland House. 'It's just outside the village of Cumberland Cross.' And then, still in the same uninflected voice, he added, 'He will expect you this morning.'

'I can't promise.'

'Mr Spooner is a busy man.'

'Me too, sonny.' I hung up.

'Richard,' said Amelia, replacing the extension phone, 'you were not polite.'

'Nor was he. We see Mrs Craythorpe first, I think.'

The living-room window overlooks our entrance drive. They were still there, waiting. They would wait for ever, dying to hear how I'd felt.

I said, 'We'll take both cars, and do a switch in Bridgnorth. I'll drive up to High Town, and if you'll head for Low Town, and park by the bottom of the Cliff Railway, I think I can drop 'em. Okay?'

She gave me a weak smile. 'It sounds fun.'

Oh yes, great fun, until we got where we were heading, then it wasn't going to be fun at all. And it would all be a waste of time, because they would know very well exactly where we were going.

Before we started out, I phoned Tony. He was put through at once.

'Richard — where are you?'

'At home.'

'I need to see you.'

'We were just about to jump into a car or two and head your way. All right if I drop in?'

'If you don't,' he said flatly, 'I'll be applying for a warrant for your arrest.' He hung up.

I had to assume he was joking, but nevertheless his attitude so occupied my mind that I forgot to shave and change. It seemed urgent to get going. I was annoyed that the necessity — or so it seemed to me — of evading the media mob would delay our arrival at the other end.

In the event, it worked perfectly. I parked the Stag in High Town, Bridgnorth, and fed enough cash into the ticket machine to last a day, and already they were in trouble. The car-park was packed; I seemed to have found one of the last slots. They couldn't hang around there, as it was a restricted zone. So the cars went away to seek sanctuary, while the bulk of them trod on my heels, went so far as walking backwards in front of me, and generally made a public exhibition of themselves. It's all narrow streets around there, with minimum widths of pavement. They occupied more than their recognized allowance of space.

I made a great show of nonchalance, ignoring their shouts for information. Very childish, I was being. I'd have shaken free of them if I'd been a little more forthcoming. But I had to make a show of my personal feelings. When I felt myself weakening, I was asked the forbidden question, as far as I was concerned. 'How did she look when you found her?' That did it. 'Grr!' I said, and pretended to be interested in the shops.

At last, with my pipe going well, I cut down the side turning at the end of High Street, strolled round the corner that looks so innocent, and there was the top of the Cliff Railway. A stranger wouldn't have suspected its presence.

Here I could lean over the railing that ran along the cliff top, and calmly, placidly, survey the view over the Severn. The drop from High Town to Low Town is a sheer 200 feet of sandstone cliff, down which the Cliff Railway operates, as near vertical as damn it. They used to run water into the tanks of the top cabin until its weight overcame the weight of the one below — and down one went and up came the other. Now, I've heard, it's electric. Romance is dead. I casually slipped on at the last possible moment, and slowly descended to Low Town, where Amelia in the Granada was parked only forty yards away. She was in the passenger's seat. The engine was ticking over, and in two seconds we were away. It would take the crowd I'd left behind several minutes to organize themselves and find their way round by road.

'I hope', she said, 'that you're satisfied with

yourself. You've gained nothing. They'll know very well where we're heading . . . so what was the point?'

I shrugged. 'I gained a little time.'

But what I'd really gained was infinitely more important, though I didn't realize it. If it hadn't been for the delay and the obstruction, I would have managed to make my visits in a different order, and the truth might never have appeared. My intention was to see Mrs Craythorpe first; she had a prior claim. Then Tony — he would want his statement. And finally, time permitting, there was a visit to Cumberland House to see Marcus Spooner. His interest in the situation was as vital as anybody's, but I had nothing to say to him that was relevant to his son's fate.

Yet one glance along Lock Lane, when I'd found it, deflected me. This was Mrs Craythorpe's address: 37 Lock Lane. The lane was long, it wound, and it seemed endless, but it was not closely built on, being on the outskirts of Potterton, and our view along it was extensive. I didn't need to be told which cottage was Mrs Craythorpe's. The media were there already, and in force. They would not be the same group, but the threat was the same, as it appeared to me.

Lock Lane leads down to a basin on the same canal as the Blue Boar shares, but a full mile from the pub. This is the basin where two canals meet, and the lock referred to is in fact a series of locks, necessary for the negotiation of the junction, on three levels. The lane was a dead end, Mrs Craythorpe's cottage being a hundred yards short of the nearest lock. Down there I would be trapped, I decided. It was an instant decision, based on my mood, when I'd have done better to resign myself to it, flannel my way through a sticky interview, and be free of it. But no — I had to be morosely stupid, slam on the brakes, perform a rapid three-point turn, and get away from there smartly.

Thereby, I failed to prevent a further tragedy, or so I am convinced.

The obvious course, once I was committed to leaving Mrs Craythorpe until later, was to visit Tony. This was more straightforward. Although the media were naturally besieging the station, they were doing so at the front, and thronging the reception area. I thought I was entitled to use the police car-park at the rear. In this way, Amelia and I penetrated the more private areas of the station, and from one or two enquiries addressed to wandering officers, found our way up to Tony's office.

'About time, too,' was his greeting. 'What's kept you?'

I snapped to attention, using two fingers in a mock salute. He remained grim.

'I've come to make a statement, officer,' I said.

'Stop playing the fool, Richard, and find a chair for Amelia.'

'I have one, Tony,' she said, and I found one for myself in a corner, drawing it forward to face his desk.

He made a tent with his fingers and peered at me above it. 'If you're prepared to listen seriously, Richard, let me impress on you that you've got yourself into a right mess, here, and you've got *us* into a right mess, and it's touch-and-go whether or not the Chief Super tosses you in a cell.'

'But I've done nothing illegal. I've even found a body for you — and that was no damned pleasure, I can assure you.'

He sighed. It was closer to a groan. 'You've associated yourself with a gang of convicted kidnappers. You were actually working *with* Phelps when you found the house and . . . the rest. Now, how d'you think that's going to read, splashed on the front page of tomorrow's papers? Police Officer In League With Crooks. Lovely. Discovers Body Of Young Girl. Splendid!'

'I'm not a police officer.'

'You've been one.'

'Only a lowly inspector. Nothing to boast about.'

'Thank you. But you're not going to distract me, Richard. They've interviewed Phelps. He's told 'em the lot, slanted in his direction, of course. It's going to stink to high heaven. He's told them you and he were searching for the money. He says you actually thought that the stair-cupboard was big enough to have taken the suitcase. And you were *with* the team that worked on the kidnap. For Chrissake, Richard, can't you imagine the way it's going to sound?'

'I know how it *was*.'

'I don't think you do. I really don't think you realize what you've done.'

'All right, Tony. All right. I am packed full of contrition. But it's done, and I've come to make an official statement of my part in it. Shall we record it? Have you got a tapedeck?'

'Richard . . . '

'I'm not being facetious. I've operated within the law. Now I want to make my statement. May we do that? And while it's being typed, we'll have a cup of tea and talk about it. Quietly, informally.'

He stared at me blankly for a few seconds, then he slapped his desk top with his palms and reached down to open a drawer. He brought out a tapedeck and rigged a mike on its stand, pointing at me.

'Talk,' he said pushing a button.

'But first, let me say . . . '

'Oh no!'

'First, Tony, I'm aching for news. Have they done a post-mortem examination? If so, any news on that?'

He switched off his deck and put it into rewind. 'I'm not sure that Amelia . . . ' He raised his eyebrows at her.

'For pity's sake!' she said in exasperation. 'I get tired of being treated like a delicate piece of porcelain. What makes you big, complacent men think you can face the horrible things, and women can't? I'm tired of it. Say it, Tony. I'm not going to swoon away.'

He looked at me, shrugged, smiled, and said, 'Right. Yes. There's been a post-mortem. I was there. And strangely, it wasn't as bad as I'd expected. She was mummified, and the pathologist said he doubted there'd be enough evidence to be certain about the cause of death. There'd been no violence. If there was poison involved — which is very doubtful, you'll admit — he didn't think the forensic lab would be able to detect it after all this time. It has to go down as probable asphyxiation. Sylvia Craythorpe got herself shut in there . . . and died.'

He stopped. He'd omitted a lot of detail, I guessed.

'You've got formal identification?' I asked.

'Yes. We held Phelps, under a charge of stealing a car — '

'I'm certain he was intending to return it, and with a full tank. That would probably clear him of any charge.'

Tony gave an empty laugh. 'You don't believe that!'

'I'm certain of it. Car theft would be beneath Phelps's contempt.'

'Oh Lord! They *have* undermined you, Richard.'

'I'm not a beginner, you know. Was the identification positive?'

'Yes. He didn't hesitate. The ring, the bracelet, even the cheap necklace — he'd given those to her himself.'

I raised my eyebrows at that. 'Did I tell you the cupboard door was latched? From the outside.'

'You did. What're you getting at, Richard?'

I shook my head. 'I don't know. I'm suggesting murder, perhaps.'

'Hmm!'

'Anything else?' I asked.

'A detail. Sylvia was pregnant. Three months, the pathologist thought.'

There was a silence. I heard Amelia draw a

shuddering breath.

I said quietly, 'Phelps didn't hesitate, you said.'

'Took one glance, and said it's Sylvia. What're you thinking, Richard?'

'I'm not sure. But it'd be one way of terminating an inconvenient pregnancy.'

'Richard!' murmured Amelia, in protest.

'Just a thought.'

I said no more on the subject. I couldn't remove from my memory the fact that those three louts had returned drunk to the house — and it might not have been the correct one. And that Tim Craythorpe was the one who'd said it was — and could have been lying. And also that he might have returned to the correct one, the following day, for the money. It might, therefore, follow from that . . . and oh hell, I didn't want to take it any further.

'Let's get this statement done,' I said.

Without a word, Tony reached forward and switched on his deck. I made my statement.

10

After I'd finished dictating, and the typist had collected it, Tony sat back and was silent for a minute or two. He hadn't once interrupted. He knew I was capable of making a crisp and precise report without any prompting. But he'd said nothing about a cup of tea while we waited. At last he spoke.

'I take it you've realized that Phelps is probably the brains of that outfit, and perhaps even more clever than you've allowed for. Don't you think, Richard?'

'I've taken that into account.'

'But you do realize he might have been leading you by the nose all the while? I mean, he *did* find the house. It was he who noticed the stone-slab bridge. Perhaps he knew exactly where it was. Perhaps he led you there. Perhaps he simply wanted . . . oh hell, I don't know.'

'Exactly. So I suggest that, for now, we take it as it appears on the surface.'

'Yes,' he agreed. 'Care to come down to our new canteen for a cuppa? Class, this is. They call it a restaurant. Isn't that grand?'

We went down with him. It was certainly

much more classy than the canteens I'd been used to, but you still had to serve yourself. We three sat in a little huddle in a remote corner.

'The Chief Super will have made a short statement to the press by now,' said Tony. 'I suppose you realize you'll have to speak to them? After all, you'll want the chance to put it from your own point of view, if only to keep the record straight.'

'I suppose so. But they'll bend it, anyway.'

'And you'd better just say you were pressured into helping them. Under threat.'

'I'll say no such thing. I was invited, and it suited me.'

'Richard — are you forcing me into locking you up! Talk sense.'

'I'll tell the truth.'

'Hah!' It was a sarcastic comment on the various shades of truth. 'And tell 'em you've inherited George Tate's investigation? Come off it, Richard. You can't do that. Not the truth.'

'No,' said Amelia. 'You can't.'

'All right. All right. I'll be good. They pressured me. I just went along with it. How would that be?'

'Fine. You do that, then. Because — you see — we don't want any idea leaking out that you've inherited George's photos. Whatever *they* were.' He paused, hoping I would tell

213

him. I said nothing.

'I suppose there *were* photos?'

'Yes.'

'Any use?' He was fishing.

'To you, no. To me, perhaps. I don't know, Tony. I haven't examined every one in detail.'

'Then I suggest you do. You never know. He could well have been on to something.'

'That's so.' I was now certain he had been. George, in his letter left for me to find, had mentioned two 'somethings'. Two counts, he had called them. But, he'd commented, they might not have been connected. I ought to have examined his photographic efforts in more detail.

'Ah!' said Tony. 'It's ready.' Somebody had signalled to him. He gestured back. 'Your statement, Richard.'

Back in his office, Tony stood at his window, staring out, Amelia sat quietly, and I, placidly smoking now, carefully read through the five pages of typed statement, signed each page, and read the usual declaration at the end as to the fact that it contained five pages, etc., etc. The familiar procedure. I then read through it again, changed a word here and there, crossing the original one through and initialling the amendment, and finally signed the last page. Tony looked it through, and added the time and date, the location, and his signature, rank and number.

At that moment, as though by some secret signal I could not detect, the door opened behind me. I turned my head. He was a large and bluff man with ginger hair and blue eyes and a bellicose attitude. He slammed the door behind him. I got to my feet politely, expecting to shake hands.

'Detective Chief Superintendent Barker, Richard,' Tony introduced him quietly. 'This is Richard Patton, sir.'

He did not offer to shake hands. I stuck my right hand inside my trouser pocket, used my left to remove the pipe from my teeth, and said, 'Pleased to meet you.'

He grunted. 'That your statement? Let me see.'

Tony handed it over. Barker took my chair, leaned it back, put his feet on Tony's desk, with the ankles crossed, and read my statement. Then he read it again.

'Right,' he said, not looking round. 'Now I'll tell you what you're going to do. You'll go down and face that mob in reception and tell them you did not do any of this voluntarily. That you were forced to go along with Phelps, and by chance found the body. You will say no more, and you will, from now on, avoid any contact whatsoever with this case or these people, and you will not . . . I say

215

not . . . interfere with police enquiries. Understood?'

He didn't even glance over his shoulder, so I reckoned he required no answer. I gave him none. I took Amelia's arm, opened the door with my other hand, used the same hand to wave to Tony, then quietly closed the door behind us. We silently walked down the stairs.

'You can't talk to them now,' Amelia whispered, when we were one flight from reception.

'Why not?'

'You're shaking, Richard. I can feel it. You're furious. You'll say something you'll regret.'

'Oh no, my love. Now, I *want* to speak to them, and that makes it so much easier. But I shan't regret one word.'

So — there in the duty office, with the desk sergeant looking very anxious — I informed the ladies and gentlemen of the press that I had entered into a verbal agreement with Machin, Phelps and Craythorpe, to help find the house they had used, the money they hadn't got, the girl they'd had with them, and the kidnapped boy.

'It's worked so far,' I said. 'We've found two of the four, the girl and the house. Now all we need to do is find the money and the little boy. Which we will do. Thank you.'

Then I put an arm round Amelia's shoulders, put my head down and my other shoulder forward, and ploughed through the opening they silently allowed us. They loved it. The cameras clashed madly. I didn't look round.

But in the car-park, opening the Granada's door, I looked up, and there was Barker, scowling down at me from Tony's window. The duty sergeant would have phoned up. That scowl of Barker's ought to have petrified me.

'Now you've done it,' said Amelia, as I drove away.

'I don't regret it. I told you I wouldn't.'

'Certainly not.' She rested her head on my left shoulder for a moment. 'Have I told you lately that I love you?'

'I seem to remember you mentioned it.'

'Now you know why.'

'I'm blowed if I do.' I glanced sideways at her. 'I'll never understand women.'

'We like to remain slightly mysterious.'

'Oh, you do. You do,' I assured her. 'It's why I love you, plus about a thousand other reasons I can't go into now.'

'Why not, Richard? I'd like to know.'

'I'm driving, my pet. Let me concentrate, please.'

'Sometimes', she said, 'you're absolutely

217

maddening. And where do you propose to go now?'

'It's after one o'clock. If we go to Mrs Craythorpe's at this time, she might feel she ought to feed us, and if we head for Spooner's place, you can bet he won't even offer. So I suggest we get a bit of lunch while we're in town, and then decide what to do.'

What I did decide to do first, after a quick snack, was to have a word with Dennis Finch, George Tate's solicitor. It was a matter of luck, of course, that he wouldn't be inundated with appointments. I was lucky. He was not engaged, and in fact seemed quite pleased to see us. I suspected he had recognized George's intention that I should pick up where he had left off, and Finch approved — quietly and unofficially.

'That £500 in tenners,' I said. 'I've heard about it. It was blackmail money, wasn't it?'

'It was.'

'You knew that, and where George had got it from?'

'Oh yes.'

'Then weren't you conniving in an illegal action?'

'Oh yes.'

'And you're not worried about it?'

'Not a bit.'

'Hmm! And would you mind telling me

218

where that money is now?'

'I don't mind at all. He left instructions. It's in a deposit account, gathering interest. At the end of the month I shall send it to the RSPCA. George's idea, that was. He rather liked animals, though he was unfair to them by describing Machin as an animal. Perhaps he had Machin in mind when he said he preferred animals to people.'

I was aware that Amelia was smiling. She could go along with that.

'He met a lot of unpleasant people, in his job,' I suggested.

'True. But outside that, he was very undiscerning.' He looked down at his blotter. 'Particularly where women were concerned.'

'Oh,' I said, wondering whether to pursue that. Amelia decided we should not.

'But men always are,' she burst out.

He got to his feet. 'I'm sorry — I have an appointment.' He held out his hand. 'I'll wish you luck, Mr Patton.'

'Thank you.'

He turned, smiling, to Amelia. 'Your husband clearly isn't,' he remarked, obliquely I thought.

But she understood, taking my arm when we were out on the street. 'What a very pleasant man,' she said.

I glanced sideways at her. A tiny smile was

tweaking the corners of her mouth.

We were now becoming more conversant with the centre of the town, so that there was no difficulty in finding our car-park.

'Where to now?' she asked.

'Mrs Craythorpe. I've made my statement to the press, so there'll be no difficulties.'

In practice, the main difficulty was parking. Lock Lane was still thronged with cars, and as there was no pavement, only grass verges, they were causing congestion. Not, I supposed, that it mattered. There was only one more cottage beyond Mrs Craythorpe's, and that was the old lock gatekeeper's, which was now a neat and compact residence, and the lane ended there. Beyond the locks, where there was a humpbacked bridge, there was nothing but fields, these rising steeply towards the top of a hill. Horses were grazing there, and certainly there was no throughway. So any press obstruction was irrelevant to possible through traffic.

We had to weave our way round the press vehicles, and go almost as far as the lock in order to park. I slid in behind a nearly new silver Mercedes Benz 190.

We got out and I locked the doors, pretending to pay no attention to the man leaning against the Merc. He was looking into the distance and placidly smoking a cigarette.

A Merc is not the kind of car used by the press, and indeed he carried no camera, and there was no evidence of so much as a notebook. I nodded to him. He nodded back. If it hadn't been a Merc he was using, I would have guessed he might be a CID officer. But that did not fit the car's image, either. In any event, he would barely have met the height regulations, and, seeming to be well into his forties, he wasn't going to grow any more. He was stocky, dark, with a rough face that gave the impression he had been around, and in many strange places. A strong face, craggy, large hands, though he handled the cigarette delicately. After the first glance, he paid me no attention. His gaze was not directly levelled at Mrs Craythorpe's cottage, but there seemed no other objective for his interest.

It occurred to me, as we walked back to No.37, that this was a typical area in which telephone poles would be in use. But there was none. In fact, as we drew closer, it was apparent that the cottage was small, and its appearance ramshackle. She was probably existing on her widow's pension, meagrely supplemented by occasional contributions from Tim's ill-gotten gains.

I asked Amelia, 'Was it Mrs Craythorpe who phoned?'

'No. Oh no. Didn't I say? It was your friend, that Phelps creature.'

'Ah!' I said. 'Yes.' Not her son Tim, then.

They had seen us arrive, and advanced as though about to devour us. I held up both palms, as they shouted out my name. 'Mr Patton, Mr Patton.'

'I've made my statement,' I called out. Didn't those cameras ever run out of film? 'Nothing more to say, and I'm sure Mrs Craythorpe won't want to speak to you.'

'Ask her. Ask her.'

We edged through. 'I'll ask.' I knocked on the door and called out, 'It's Richard Patton, Mrs Craythorpe.'

'Come in. It's open.' The voice seemed weak, distant.

I opened the door with a thumb latch. There was no lock to it, but there were rusty bolts, top and bottom. The door led directly into a tiny, square hall, from which an open door on our left led into her sitting-room. It was in there that she was sitting in a basketwork armchair and a profusion of cushions, too close I'd have thought to a large, roaring coal fire. Wasn't this a smoke-restricted zone? A coal bucket beside the old stone fireplace was piled high with coal. There was no sign of Tim, for which I was thankful.

She turned her head and stared at us, her grey eyes seeming to be unfocused, her small mouth pursed, her mass of grey hair untidy and uncombed. Her neck was long, channelled with folding flesh. Her face was a mass of wrinkles. In her hands, which seemed distorted by arthritis, she was holding a round embroidery frame. As I approached closer I saw that she was using cottons or silks, not wool, and that the design she was working on was minutely detailed, and involved very fine stitching. Would this be *petit point*, I wondered. Certainly the canvas she was working on had a very close weave.

Then I saw that her glasses were perched high in her hair. The needle was in her fingers, seemingly held at a strange angle. She blinked at us; she was obviously very near-sighted. Her eyes were dry.

'You wanted to see me,' I said, leading in delicately. 'I'm Richard Patton, and this is my wife, Amelia.'

For ten more seconds she stared, as though not being able to see me. Then I realized that quietly, undemonstratively, she had begun to weep. It was gentle, but abrupt, as though she'd been unable to accept the death of Sylvia until she saw me in the flesh. I was her reality.

Still the tears flowed. She seemed unaware

of them. The small window was at her far shoulder, and her face was heavily cast in side-lighting. She made a gesture. It indicated a single upright wooden chair, thrust against a table at the rear. I fetched it for Amelia. Against that far wall there was a noble old grandfather clock. I glanced at my watch. We disagreed by only one minute. My watch must have been wrong.

Amelia took the chair from my hands and carefully placed it on the far side of Mrs Craythorpe, but close to her. It left me free to stand beside the fireplace, and thus face the old woman without her having to turn her head.

She made no attempt to wipe away her tears, as though unaware of them. Her eyes were considering me, measuring me.

Then suddenly she said, 'You was the one as found her, wasn't y'.' A statement, not a question.

'I was.'

'A copper.'

'Ex-copper. I was an inspector.'

'Hmm! So what was y' doing with that Ron Phelps?'

'We were kind of working together, trying to locate the house. D'you mind if I smoke?' The unflinching eyes were making me nervous.

She sniffed, then whipped the back of her right hand across her eyes. I flinched, because that hand still held the needle, and in fact she had drawn it off a thread of crimson silk.

'Now look what you've made me do,' she complained.

'Let me.' Amelia reached forward, intending, I thought, to rethread the needle for her. But Mrs Craythorpe clung possessively to her independence.

'I can do it. I can do it.'

And she could, and without her glasses, which must have been for distances beyond three feet. She hadn't used them for looking at me. Perhaps she didn't care what I looked like; her interest was in what I had to say. Considering that she was threading a needle so fine I could barely see it, she managed it better than I could. Then, with the needle poised again and her eyes still on it, she said, 'Tell me about it.'

That was difficult. I fumbled my way into it. 'I suppose Ron Phelps has told you. There's really not much more to say. We were looking for the house, we found it, and we were also looking for the suitcase full of money. By sheer chance, I found your daughter, Sylvia, shut in a cupboard.'

'How was she killed? Who done it?'

Now she had her eyes directly on the

needle, which was reaching through, was drawn down from beneath, and popped up again about half a millimetre from the previous thread. I could never have done that, but a few million stitches had probably preceded that one.

'You can't assume she was killed,' I said quietly. 'The experts aren't committing themselves.'

'Tcha!' she said. 'I knew she'd come to a sticky end, that girl. Wild, she was, man mad. And her only sixteen! It's shocking. In my day, they'd have dipped her in the canal. Cooled her down.' She abruptly made a sound that could have been a senile chuckle. 'Bert did it to me, one time. That was my man. Bert. Caught me with another feller down by the lock. That was before we was wed. Now *there* was a jealous man, my Bert. One glance at me from another bloke, an' he was in there with his fists flyin'. Oh — a fine man, was my Bert. Chucked me in the canal, he did. An' the other feller. Me in the canal, an' I could climb outa there. The other feller in the lock, an' he couldn't. Water was right down low, it was, an' he couldn't swim! Laugh! I nearly split me corsets. Bert had to open the gate an' fill it up. Like a flounder, he was, when we pulled him out. Nearly a gonner. Laugh!'

She stopped abruptly, raising her face to me, the tears flowing still. 'We *did* have a time, me an' Bert.' But the tears weren't from joy.

'It certainly sounds like it,' I agreed.

'That was his job, see. The locks. All his life. Born at the gatehouse, he was. This place here was where I was born. Always on the gates, was Bert. Had wages at fust, then that packed in when the longboats stopped comin' through, till it got to be this holiday lot we got now. Then he was on the gates agin. Hadda be an expert, 'cause of the basin. Three locks. No amateurs. So from then on it was tips. Tips! We got by, God alone knows how. *Now* look what we've come to. Tim an' Sylvia — and her gone now. Wouldn't 'ave mattered if it'd been him. Tim. He's never been any good. Useless. He was me fust, see. Had five kids, we did, but only two of 'em thrived. Somethin' terrible, it was, the way they went. A judgement, I reckon. For Tim.'

I didn't know what she meant. I was glad only that she was steering clear of Sylvia, skating round the subject. 'Tim?' I asked gently.

'He was the fust. Not Bert's. Dunno. Take y' choice outa half a dozen, but he wasn't Bert's. But it got us married. A useless tyke, that's what our Tim's always bin. Useless.

Bert said from the first sight of 'im we oughta chuck him back.'

'Chuck him back,' I murmured.

'In the cut, he meant. The cut. It's what we called the canal. Chuck him in the cut, said my Bert. Best place for him. Reckon he guessed Tim wasn't 'is'n.'

I glanced at Amelia for help. There didn't seem to be anything I could say.

She murmured, 'So they didn't get on, your Bert and young Tim?'

'Nah! Tim soon got inta the habit of keepin' outa his way.' She sighed, knotted her thread, and cut it off. She then searched through a tangle of colours before selecting another. She seemed not to be working to a printed pattern, but making it up as she went along. I could detect that it was going to be an arrangement of roses. Mrs Craythorpe had gone silent. We waited. Then she got going with green — a leaf, I assumed.

'I get paid for this,' she told us. 'A man puts 'em in frames wi' glass over, and the shop in town sells 'em. But paid, I get.' It was her quiet, personal pride. 'Then two years later, along come Sylvia,' she continued, without any change of tone. 'No arguin' that she was Bert's. He'd've killed me if I'd even looked at another chap. Tim hated her from the very start. Hated her. Couldn't blame him. A clip over the ear for Tim, an' a cuddle for Sylvia, that's what they got from Bert. Hated her. Tim wouldn't even *look* at her. Then, later — an' I can't understand this, worry over it as I might — they got to be friends. The two kids. Reckon she was the age for a bitta devilment, an' he knew where she could find it. You'd never believe — that last time, the last time I set eyes on Sylvia — they was giggling away like a coupla dafties about somethin'. Whispering. An' that Ron Phelps — he was hangin' round her like a randy tom cat. An' her only sixteen! Disgraceful!' She stopped. She held up her needle as though staring at it, but I was certain she was seeing nothing but her memories. 'Mind y',' she said at last. 'Be fair. I was only seventeen when I married Bert.'

She was, therefore, not as old as I'd thought. If Tim had been only eighteen at the time of the kidnap, and Mrs Craythorpe therefore, at that time, around thirty-five, she would be in her fifties now. But she'd had a wearing life. It had aged her.

'An' then,' she went on, 'they said they'd be away for a bit. Tim and Sylvia. Away. Oh . . . not a murmur on the where and the why. But away. But we know now, don't we? We know. They was off on that nasty kidnap lark. Typical. Typical of Sylvia, that was. Mad on kids, she was. An' her only sixteen. Wouldna been surprised if she'd started one of her own, any time. Daft little thing. But off they goes, and I don't see 'em for ages. Didn't see Sylvia at all, after that. Not hide nor hair of her, I didn't see.'

She was silent for a moment. I wondered whether to say something, but she seemed to be doing all right without encouragement. Eventually, she sighed, and went on.

'But Tim turned up. You could reckon on that. And oh — all strange, he was. Couldn't stand still. Half excited, half worried. Said he'd lost her. *Lost* her! How could he lose Sylvia? Said he didn't know where she'd got to. An' I'd told him, before they went, I'd laid it on the line for him . . . he was gonna look after her. But no — he comes back wi' nothing. No Sylvia.' She smiled grimly to herself. 'Bert near as damn it killed him. Here in the parlour. Laid inta him, he did, and it was all Tim could do t' crawl outa the door. But it were my Bert as it killed, when they didn't find Sylvia. Drunk every night, he was, an' most of the days. Fell in his canal, he did. Comin' from the pub. Musta bin blind — walked past his own house. Ain't that daft! Musta headed back to his old home, the gatehouse. Anyway, they fished him outa the lock the next day. Dead as a door-nail. Still

230

. . . it was the way he'd wanna go. His precious cut.'

Yet perhaps it had not been a mistake. Without Sylvia, Bert hadn't wanted to live.

'D'you know what happened?' she demanded abruptly, her voice crisp.

'With Sylvia?' I asked. 'No. I'm sorry, but no. It's a mystery. Ron Phelps told me they went off on a booze-up, to celebrate, the evening they got hold of the money. And when they got back to the house, there was no money and no boy and no Sylvia. He thought that he and his two mates might've got lost, being puddled, you see, and they'd found the wrong house. But no. We found the same place yesterday, and the camping stuff they'd taken along was still there in the cellar.'

She was silent. The needle made two more explorations. Then she looked up. 'That's what Ron told me.'

I thought about it. 'When did he tell you that?'

'Today. This mornin'.' Then, thoughtfully, she said, 'He wouldna have dared tell me that, before he was certain she was dead.'

'I don't understand you, Mrs Craythorpe.'

'If he'd told me then — at *that* time — I'd have shopped the lot of 'em, and to hell with Tim, an' the police would've found her.'

231

But not in time. By a long way, not in time.

'But . . . ' I protested quietly. 'But you said — the way you spoke — Ron Phelps is a friend.'

'He certainly is. Brings me coal, does me shoppin'. He's my friend. Because of Sylvia, y' see. We both loved Sylvia.'

And then, shockingly, because she had seemed so calm and contained, she dropped the embroidery ring in her lap and plunged her face into her hands, and at last genuinely wept with her shoulders shaking, and wails only inadequately restrained by her fingers.

Amelia slid the chair closer, her hand to Mrs Craythorpe's arm, then around her shoulders. Women can do this competently. I'm no good at it at all. After a few moments, at a nod from Amelia, I wandered off to find the kitchen, lit the gas ring, boiled water in the tin kettle, brewed tea in the old chipped and brown teapot, and brought it back, a bit at a time because there was no tray, with milk in the bottle and sugar in the bag, and three not-very-clean mugs.

Later, when she was calm and rational, I explained exactly how it had been, how I'd found Sylvia locked in a cupboard (without telling her the condition in which I'd found her) and at least she could now accept that her daughter, dear Bert's daughter, was really and undisputably dead, and she need no longer listen for her footsteps at the door and her voice crying out, 'I'm back, ma,' as the latch was lifted.

When we eventually turned to leave, Mrs Craythorpe said, 'D'you think I oughta go and see the others? Bein' in the same boat, sorta, with the little boy not been found.' She nodded. 'Ron'd take me.'

I shook my head. 'I really don't think it would be a good idea, Mrs Craythorpe.'

She at the Spooners', offering her unrefined and down-to-earth comfort!

'P'raps not. P'raps they'll come here.'

'I wouldn't count on it.'

We said our goodbyes. I stood outside and told the press she had nothing to say, but was of course distressed, and they made reluctant movements of dispersal.

Slowly, silently, Amelia clutching my arm closely, we walked down the lane to the Granada. The Merc was still there. The man, in a brown leather bomber jacket and grey slacks, still leaned casually against it, and still slowly smoked a cigarette. He'd had time for a dozen. We nodded to each other again.

I said, 'If you're waiting to have a word with Mrs Craythorpe, I'm afraid you're out of luck. She's rather distressed.'

'Sure. Reckon she would be.' He looked me

up and down. 'Your name Patton?'

'It is.' I prodded for his name, hesitating with my hand.

He didn't offer his, hand or name, simply stared at his cigarette. 'It was you found her body, wasn't it?'

'The girl? Yes.' I was curious about him, as he was clearly not a member of the press.

'How did she die?'

I hesitated. 'Who're you?'

'It doesn't matter who. Can you just tell me how they say she died?'

'I don't know. The experts can't be positive. It'll be in all the papers, I expect.'

'Guess,' he suggested.

I was irritated, but his interest captured me. 'At a guess, asphyxiation. She was shut in a cupboard.'

His face had been set, expressionless. It didn't change, even when he came out with something quite appalling.

'Take long, would it? For her to die, I mean.'

'What the hell's the matter with you?' I demanded angrily. 'You a nutter, or something?'

He shook his head. 'I'm sorry. It must've sounded awful — but it does matter. I can't tell you how much it matters.' He threw away his cigarette and tramped on it, then glanced at me, ashamedly I thought. 'It matters to me.'

'Care to tell me why?' I asked, pushing him.

'I can't tell you. All right!' His anger was suddenly explosive. 'All right — forget I asked.' He moved towards the driver's door.

I said quietly, 'At a guess — if it really was shortage of air — a quarter of an hour. Perhaps half an hour.' He was very still. I added, 'If that makes you happy.'

'Happy!' He darted one more glance at me, and it was loaded with distress. 'Oh sure . . . happy!'

Then he was inside, had started the engine, and was round in one tyre-screaming sweep that involved the grass verge the other side.

It was only as he'd grasped the steering wheel that I'd noticed the signet ring on his third finger. It was gold, in the photos black and white.

11

We sat in the Granada. I had found time, while in town, to nip into Smith's to buy one or two maps. One to 25,000, as I'd explained to Ron Phelps. These we now spread out across the steering wheel, until I settled on the map that included the village of Cumberland Cross, and in a far corner what seemed to be the pub at which the celebrating trio had got themselves severely drunk on the night of the pick-up. The Saracen's Head, that was the pub. When I linked this map with the adjoining one my guess was confirmed, as Potterton covered a good part of it, the map also covering the route out to the pub, which I now recalled clearly.

Houses and streets were recorded, but none of the possible dozens of ruined farms out on the moors. They would not be considered as dwellings.

'Look,' I said. 'There's Cumberland Cross, so this large building here's probably Cumberland House. And this must be the minor road across the moors, because that's the pub, the Saracen's Head. And they've even got the track Phelps and I took, on our

236

way to the house or farm, or whatever you'd like to call it.'

'Yes,' said Amelia. 'How interesting.'

'I *told* Phelps he ought to have had large-scale maps.'

'What a pity you weren't in charge of the kidnap, Richard.'

I glanced at her. Her lips were puckered. 'At least, nobody would've died.'

'You've got something in mind.' She nodded to herself.

'Well . . . we want to get to Cumberland House. We really ought to see Mr Spooner today, and we can do it easily by taking this main road . . . ' I indicated it. A ten-mile run. 'But we could also do it by heading for the Saracen's Head, and taking a quick look at the place on the way.'

She pouted. 'Must we? That wretched place of yours!'

'It's just a thought. Something niggling at me, and I can't tie it down. There might be something I missed in the dark, and I'd like a quick look round in daylight. That's all.'

'As long as we're not there when it gets dark,' she conceded, but with no show of enthusiasm. 'But it's one place I didn't ever want to see.'

'You can stay in the car, love.'

So that's what we did, easily finding the

pub, easily locating the track that led off into the wilds.

'What a dreadfully depressing district,' said Amelia.

'It's probably beautiful in the summer.'

What I had to look for was the stone-slab bridge. As I knew it was there, and was keeping an eye open for it, this wasn't difficult.

'It gets worse,' she said. 'Desolate. I don't think I want to see your farm or house, or whatever it was.'

I noted that it was now mine, because she was losing all her remaining dregs of patience.

It would have been difficult to explain what I hoped to gain by this diversion. Vaguely, it had occurred to me that there ought to be some way of checking Tim's statement, that on the night they returned from the pub they had truly found the correct ruin. There ought surely to have been something unique to that particular place, which would have confirmed that they had, or had not, located their own dilapidated pile of masonry. I couldn't entirely dismiss from my mind the possibility that they had returned to the wrong place, and that Tim had realized it from one glance into its cellar, and had realized how he might profit from it. That he had lied.

Yet this assumed a mental alertness that seemed particularly absent in Tim. It also assumed he would have been willing to take a risk. For half a million pounds, though, he might well have been prepared to take on a whole bundle of risks.

But the scent was stale, by a matter of sixteen years. I was being optimistic.

We rounded the rock bluff, and there it was. I stopped the car. We sat with the engine silent and stared at it.

'Here?' Amelia whispered.

'This is it.'

'You went inside there?'

'Yes'

'Into the cellar?'

'Yes.'

'How *could* you?'

'It's a matter, I suppose, of training and sheer stupidity.'

'You're surely not intending — '

'I am not,' I assured her. 'I just want a look round outside.'

I got out of the car and did that. There was not going to be all that much light left, but I didn't think I would need it. There just wasn't anything that might have distinguished this pile of rubble from other piles of similar dissolution that were no doubt scattered across the moors. Even the fact that it had been built against a protecting bluff would no doubt have been a universal adoption by the other farms.

Nevertheless I walked around, not now expecting anything, merely satisfying myself that I had done it. But there was no strangely shaped tree that couldn't have been missed; there was no unusual outcrop of rock; there was no stream or noisy waterfall.

It might have been the shallow cast of the sun, precisely right to catch a reflection, or the warm colour of its lowering light darkening the green of the sparse grass to grey but lending itself to a similarly warm colour in the spectrum. But there was a wink of yellow light that caught my eye. I stopped, searching more intently for what it was, until the glint was again there. I crouched down.

It was a much-tarnished but still recognizable brass tube, the shell case of a thirty-eight calibre cartridge. My interest revived, I spread my area of search, moving around in a crab-like attitude, and found two more. I straightened, and returned to the car, smiling. This was because I could now justify this diversion, and not from any pleasure raised by the discovery. I slid in behind the wheel, reached for a handkerchief, and tried to clean them.

'Three,' I said. 'Thirty-eight calibre cartridge cases. I'd say they were fired from an automatic pistol. Yes. Look there, that's the mark the extractor makes.'

'They carried guns?' she asked. 'It's the first I've heard about guns.' She frowned heavily.

'No. They're not the type for guns. Knuckledusters and coshes and knives ... those probably. Guns, no. That's what makes it rather interesting.'

'Can we get away from here, Richard?' she suggested in a small voice. 'The light's going.'

I dropped the cartridges in my trouser pocket, started the car, swung in a wide circle, and headed back towards the Saracen's Head.

But when, I was thinking, had shots been fired? And by whom, at whom?

From the pub we had an easy run to Cumberland Cross. The minor road led us on to a major one inside ten miles, and, only a mile from the junction, there was the village. I got out and enquired. The shops were closing, but everybody knew the House. Out the other end of the High Street for half a mile, then it was on our left.

It was a pity it was dark when I turned in between the two stone gateposts, which had no gates. In daylight we would have gained a better idea of the size of the property, and of its importance in the community. But now, all I could see was a drive disappearing between mature trees. As we turned in, the headlights swung across the face of a gatehouse, looking rather seedy and curtainless and, I thought, not occupied. This gave me the wrong impression, as there was another, larger, house a hundred yards further on, and at first I mistook it for the House itself. If so, it was smaller than I would have expected, set back from the drive, but this place was clearly in use. Curtains hung at these windows, and there was light behind one set of them, downstairs. A dark shape, clearly a car, crouched beside it. There could have been a garage, but I didn't see one. Then we were past. This would probably have been what they used to call a dower house, in which a widow would be segregated in order to keep her away from the main household when another mistress had taken over, the wife of an elder son. They knew what they were about in those days. It tended towards harmony.

From then on the drive wound. Just beyond the dower house the surface dipped down a short slope, we crossed over a narrow wooden bridge, then swept up again into more twists and turns. In the daylight this would have been visually effective, as the drive suddenly swung out of the trees, revealing the vast expanse of Cumberland House. As it was, our headlights swept across its noble front, but did not penetrate to the far corners.

I doused the lights, removed the keys (in case Ron was around) and we stood beside the car for a moment. Beyond the dark bulk I could now detect distant lights. The house was set on a rise, and probably enjoyed a magnificent view at the rear.

'Your Mr Spooner', said Amelia, 'could've paid out half a million without noticing it.'

I grunted. 'He could also be existing on debt. You never know. At *that* time, he might have had to squeeze his reserves. He would miss it then.'

We mounted wide and somewhat slippy steps to the front porch. There was a tiny white, illuminated button in the centre of an ornate brass plate. I pressed the button, but heard no response. We waited two minutes, then the heavy door swung open with the ponderous weight of a strongroom door.

The property was large enough to have utilized the services of a butler, but I think these have gone out of fashion. The short, slim man who stood there was dressed in much the same style, but the trousers were not pin-striped. Yet he was neat, poised, and somewhat deprecating. Were my black sweater, my old slacks, and my no doubt flamboyantly unshaven chin so off-putting? He certainly could not have faulted Amelia, though he clearly faulted something. And he revealed a shade of annoyance.

'If you are Richard Patton, you were expected hours ago,' he said with distant disapproval.

'Richard Patton, yes. And my wife, Amelia.' I was being meticulously polite.

'You'd better come in. I'll see if he can see you . . . at this time.'

With a tiny gesture, he left us standing in the vast hall. Really, it needed more furnishings to absorb such a volume of unused space. Armour should have been guarding the walls, a refectory table somewhere near the centre would not have looked out of place, and carpets or rugs might have warmed the mosaic floor, the walls were bare, actually bare stone, apart from oblong shapes, high up, which must have been paintings. But chandeliers had been hung low, tinkling gently in drifting draughts, and the shadows were deep higher up. You could have thrown a party in the vast, empty and cold chimney-piece.

We looked at each other. We raised our

eyebrows. We didn't dare to speak in case the echoes rocketed around and came back at us in a scrambled roar.

'If you'll come this way . . . '

The young man . . . no, perhaps not young, as his thin face was gaunt and his forehead receded so far that it threatened to become a definite baldness . . . the man, clearly the secretary, Julian Rennie, led the way to an oak door beyond the foot of the grand staircase, in the far right corner. I had referred to him, after our original phone call, as sonny. Now that I'd met him, I'd have found it absurd to say this to his face.

Marcus Spooner stood waiting for us, his back to an open fire in what seemed a cosy room, after the chill of the hall, but was still very spacious. Dark walnut panelling to shoulder height all round the room seemed to close in the walls a little. This fact and a luxurious three-piece . . . no, eight-piece when I'd got round to counting it . . . the eight-piece suite, then, covered a lot of floor. There was a table, but small, bearing nothing, not even flowers. No woman now in the family, then. The desk across one corner was huge. This must have been Spooner's office, his working room, his lounge. It could accommodate all these variations.

He himself was taller than his secretary, but

equally slim, though his face was gaunt in a different way. He had aged considerably since I had seen him last. This was from worry, decisions, pressures, and the unrelenting weight of supporting an empire on his narrow shoulders. All these had carved the passage of the years into his face. His eyes were bleak and half buried beneath heavy eyebrows, his mouth was wide, the lips just at that time sourly twisted.

'Will you take a seat?' he asked. This was a deep and ponderous voice, carrying the weight of responsibility at a measured and authoritative pace. His suggestion was addressed to Amelia, as he himself made no move to sit, so I had to remain on my feet.

'I expected you earlier,' he went on, his attention now concentrated on me. It was a reprimand — it demanded an excuse.

I didn't intend to offer him one. 'We're here now. I'm Richard Patton, and this is my wife, Amelia.'

It could have been anger that caught flickers in his eyes. Or even wry amusement. He was a man whose emotions would always be hard to decipher. He gave little away. He gestured, not looking away from me. 'My secretary, Julian Rennie. No . . . don't leave us, Julian.'

I thought at first that the intention was to

have notes taken. But Rennie sat casually sideways on the over-stuffed arm of a plump easy chair, one toe just reaching the luxurious carpeting. Of course, if he'd wanted a record of our talk, Spooner could have had hidden microphones and a fortune in recording equipment.

I had difficulty tearing my attention away from Rennie. Only once had I encountered such a lack of expression, and that on the face of a mass killer. But Rennie looked too fragile, too effete, to offer violence to a fly. Simply, Spooner wanted him there. For a moment I had the wild idea that he might have felt in need of support. But not Spooner. When he next spoke, all shades of politeness had disappeared. His voice was flat, condemnatory; he was the man in charge.

'My secretary contacted you early this morning. I can see no reason for this delay, when you must surely have realized I would be deeply interested.'

No more than interested? I do not enjoy being addressed like a servant at fault. I hoped my voice was toneless when I replied.

'I realized, of course, that I'd have to see you. You were on my list.'

'List?' He seemed not to understand. 'Your duty was obviously to contact me at once, when you found . . . what you did find.'

247

'Clearly the police — '

'She'd been dead sixteen years.' This was supposed to dismiss all my excuses. 'My son . . . ' His voice tailed off. His hand moved in a gesture, unfulfilled. It was in control at once. It had been slightly theatrical.

'I'm afraid there was no sign of your son, Mr Spooner. The police would've ransacked the house and the surroundings. You would have been informed of anything significant.'

He shook his head angrily. 'You seem not to understand — though I'd have thought it was obvious. I meant, of course, any evidence of what . . . of any possible explanation . . . of what happened to him. I'd have expected you to contact me at once.'

I didn't dare to look at Amelia for assistance. She, too, would have been lost. With Mrs Craythorpe, she had known exactly what to do and say. With Spooner . . . there was no sign of grief, however delayed. If there had been initial mourning, there had been sixteen years in which it might have faded. Perhaps this incident had aroused it, warmed it to life.

'I'm sorry,' I said. 'My duty was to contact the police first. I *am* an ex-inspector of police, you know, and I was fully aware they would get in touch with you. But there was nothing to tell you. There was no indication of what might have happened to Adrian. I've been back there, today, in daylight — '

'Today?' he cut in.

'Yes. To see it better in daylight. But there was still . . . nothing.'

There, I admit, I lied a little. But what inferences could be drawn from three old cartridge cases?

'I cannot believe — '

He had interrupted me. I responded. 'There was nothing relevant to your son's disappearance. But surely, after all this time, we have to assume he can't be alive.' I saw his jaw about to move, and pressed ahead, raising my voice. 'I can appreciate, truly I can, that what you want is something positive, one way or the other. And I wish I could offer it. But, as of this moment there's nothing.'

He pounced on that. He was not a man to miss one word or intonation.

'As of this moment?' His hand jerked; a finger very nearly got pointed at my face. 'You mean you're intending to continue pursuing it?' His frown was heavy. It was from a lack of comprehension, I assumed.

'That was my intention,' I admitted, keeping it flatly formal.

'I will pay you,' he shot out, using his harsh and overriding boardroom voice. Was this room possibly his boardroom? Did he call the members in from afar, imperiously? 'Whatever you ask,' he added.

I flashed a quick glance at Amelia, whose lower lip was protruding with disapproval.

'I'm not asking you for money.' I certainly didn't want to dance to his tune. 'That wasn't what I — '

'I will pay you . . . handsomely.' That was his premier ability, being able to pay. Then he added, offering it as an honour, 'You would work for me.'

I managed to smile. 'I think you ought to know that I'm already under contract — as you might put it. The three kidnappers have engaged me to find the ransom money for them. That also disappeared, you know. I'm to receive two per cent of all I help them to find. That was what we were doing, Phelps and I, when we discovered the dead girl. So you can see — there would be a conflict of interests if I were to take you on.'

I was surprised he hadn't interrupted. Blood had drained from his face, but now flooded back.

'You're in league with crooks!' His voice was not under complete control.

'It doesn't prevent me from combining the one job with the other. Quite frankly, Mr Spooner, if I ever find what happened to the half a million pounds, it'll no doubt also reveal what happened to your son. Then I would tell you, freely, with no payment expected. After all . . . ' I tried to smile at him, but it no doubt came out rather twisted. 'After all, I'll have done well — with two per cent of their money.'

'Of *my* money!' he snapped.

I'd been wondering how often I had to mention the money before he produced that remark.

'Well yes, I suppose so,' I said thoughtfully, raising a palm to calm him. 'Yes, come to think of it, it's yours. Legally it's yours. You paid it for a consideration that failed. You paid for the return of your son, safe and well, and you didn't get him. The money is undisputedly yours. The difficulty is that when — and if — I ever locate it, I would have a certain amount of difficulty bringing it to you. They'd cut my throat first.' I smiled then, making light of the possibility. 'And I'm fond of my throat.'

'Damn it!' he shouted. 'This is . . . is insufferable.'

'I agree. But after all, it's only your money we're talking about here. Insufferable, yes, to lose that. But surely you've had to endure much worse than that, over the past sixteen years. Not knowing. Not knowing about

251

Adrian, I mean,' I amplified, in case he'd missed the point.

He was silent, his throat working, but to no good effect.

'But I assure you,' I went on, 'that anything bearing any connection with your affairs, which I might come across, I'll let you know. I only wanted to explain why I can't allow myself to be employed by you. Now . . . if you'll excuse us . . . '

I held out a hand to Amelia. Rising to her feet with her usual grace, she took it.

Spooner recovered his manners after an enormous effort. 'Julian. Show them out.'

He might have worded it, 'Remove this creature from my sight.' That was what his eyes told me.

Julian Rennie swung himself to his feet, almost languidly. But then I realized, as he went before us, that he was having difficulty controlling his legs. He was actually shaking, perhaps at the thought of the fury he would face on his return.

'Good-night,' he said, his hand holding open the door. His voice, too, was not completely under control. 'Oh . . . Mr Patton.' He advanced towards me, out to the porch. 'A word of advice, if I may. Don't cross him. You went too far — and he doesn't forget.'

'Thank you,' I said. Out there, in the dark and not able to see his face clearly, I once again nearly added, sonny. Spooner had treated him as no more than a tool to be wielded, to respond, to do its job.

We sat in the car. Rennie, watching us safely inside, now swung the front door shut. I started the engine and put on the lights.

'You didn't manage *that* very well, Richard, did you?' said my wife severely.

Slowly I turned the car on the drive. 'I thought I had. I was trying to discover what he valued most, his money or his son. The son lost.'

'I knew what you were doing, it's just that I don't think you were very subtle about it.'

'But people like Spooner don't appreciate subtlety.'

'And I don't appreciate having to worry about your welfare, Richard. On one side, now, you've got those three appalling bullies, and on the other, Spooner. If he could've killed you, there and then, he'd have enjoyed doing it.'

I laughed, easing the car to a walking pace for the little bridge. 'But he'd have to find somebody he could pay to kill me. Julian? Never. So . . . we've got time to get clear.'

'You're surely not suggesting he's on the phone this very minute?'

'I was joking, love. Spooner's not a killer, not even a crook. No, I'll qualify that: he could well be operating illegally, but that sort of thing doesn't come to light in the high finance business until some huge combine or some investment fund or some stockmarket certainty crashes. And ruins a few thousand lives. On that, perhaps, he could be called a crook — even a killer if the ruin brings about a suicide or two. But he juggles, and if he keeps his eye in, and his hands busy, he need never drop one of his precious golden balls. Oh . . . I don't know! Where does crookery begin and where does it end? It's so much easier to recognize Phelps and Machin and Tim Craythorpe for what they are.'

We breasted the rise beyond the bridge, my headlights raking the sky. I turned out of the drive, past the dark and silent gatehouse and on to the main road. It was now a straightforward run home, which was little more than forty-five miles away.

A hundred yards past the gatehouse I drew in at the side of the road, then, noting that the grass verge was wide, turned on to it.

'Now what?' asked Amelia, a little wearily I thought.

With the lights off and the dashboard dark, the night now seemed impenetrable. Nothing stirred. If we went straight home we would be nicely in time for the meal Mary would no doubt have prepared, and be worrying over. But you have to take events as they are offered.

'Didn't you notice?' I asked. 'No — obviously you didn't. As we came up from that bit of a rise from the bridge the lights caught the top of the telephone pole, outside what was probably a dower house. And d'you know what . . . there was a length of black adhesive tape fluttering about, right near the top.'

'And what', she asked in a cold and unencouraging voice, 'do you propose to do about it?'

'It's a heaven-sent opportunity,' I explained. There was no point in telling her that of late I'd cultivated a telephone pole fetish, keeping my eyes open for them and automatically looking for black, sticky tape. 'Didn't you notice — there're no lights on in the house now.'

'But the car was still there.' She nodded. I wasn't the only one to keep a look-out.

'Yes. Probably so. But Amelia, love, just imagine for a moment that our joking on the subject might have been a little too near the truth. You said Spooner would be on the phone as soon as we'd left. Perhaps he was. Perhaps he's got someone at the dower house, *his* man, waiting for orders. And he's been summoned to the boss-man for instructions. That would fit. And now's the chance — we know where he is.'

'Richard — no. Really . . . it's too risky.'

'You just sit here — and I'll be quick. Where's that bit of paper you wrote the combination on?'

'I left it at home.' Too quickly, that was. She's a rotten liar. She calls them fibs.

'Amelia!'

Sighing, she reached into a pocket of her two-piece. 'You won't be able to get in. You can't *break* in! Surely not!'

'If he's only gone up to the big house, he'll probably have left the door unlatched.'

'Small chance of that.' But she was hopeful on that issue.

'If it's not open, I'll come straight back.'

She sighed heavily, making sure I heard it. I slipped quietly out of the car, not slamming the door. Now I was pleased that I hadn't been particular about my appearance that morning. I was in mainly dark clothes, and the stubble on my chin would blur the usually revealing lighter patch of a face. I moved very carefully and quietly — I hoped.

I hadn't brought the torch from the car because we were too close to the big house and it could easily be noticed from there. But the sky was clear, and already there was a nip in the air. The stars offered a little light, and there was a half-moon, just rising.

Outside on the driveway, I stood beside the pole that had attracted my interest, and looked up at the house. There it was, the same window. There, too, I could swear, was the same broken brick in the sill. More confident now, I moved along the side of the house. This was where the main door was. He could step straight out of his car on to his front doorstep. In this light, I couldn't see what colour the car was, but it was certainly something light, such as silver. And it seemed, from its shape, to be a Mercedes. I touched the house door. It was unlocked, and swung open. Everything was in my favour. I stood in the hall to orientate myself. Up the stairs ahead, turn left on the landing, and it ought to be the end door, straight ahead.

I went up slowly, two at a time. It's quieter, and you get half as many creaks. There were no creaks at all, nor along the landing. I opened the door I had selected, and saw at once that I'd calculated correctly. Even the moon; aware that I would need a little help, fought its way free of leafy trees and offered me light just when I needed it.

On the wall to my left was the window, the curtains drawn back, and directly opposite to it was the picture on the wall. I even recognized it — a print of a Renoir — so good had George's photography been. I went straight to it.

For a few moments it seemed that I was going to be defeated by the picture. I hadn't noticed, from George's photographs, how it opened from the wall. Then I discovered that it hinged outwards, and had a little catch. It swung open gently. I took the piece of paper from my pocket, and by turning it about was just able to decipher the six numbers. I put it away, and applied myself to the task, my fingers on the dial.

The lights came on. I whirled round. My acquaintance from Lock Lane was standing there in the doorway, in jeans and a short canvas jacket with an elasticated waist. He was just returning to his pocket the hand he'd used on the light switch. Both hands were now casually thrust in the jacket pockets. There was no telling what they might be grasping.

'You were just about to open my safe,' he said, equably enough.

I nodded. There seemed to be nothing I could say.

'So George Tate was finally successful.' He smiled. It was more a beam of triumph, as though the accomplishment had been his own. 'All right, go ahead. Let's see if he got it right.'

I was at first reluctant to turn my back on him, but he nodded encouragingly. 'Go on. Give it a whirl.'

What else could I have done? I turned back to the safe and dialled the combination, then operated the handle. The small steel door swung open.

12

At first it seemed that the safe was empty. It was a twelve-inch cube, with a one-inch ledge all round. I was about to reach inside when his right hand, stretched beyond my shoulder, beat me to it, and emerged grasping an automatic pistol. He stood back quickly, well clear of me. His hand lowered the pistol loosely to his side, but I could see that he was not unused to handling it. He smiled.

'One of my duties is to act as a guard for Mr Spooner,' he explained. 'And as an outside guard for the house.'

'With a pistol? That's illegal.'

'Tut, tut. Illegal, is it? I've got a licence for this. I joined a club, just to get that licence. The police have approved my security arrangements, so I'm covered.'

He meant the security of the pistol, not its use on the occasional burglar. 'I'd hardly say that,' I told him. 'You're not allowed to shoot burglars. You'd even be in trouble shooting back at a burglar. Put the damned thing away.'

He laughed. 'It's not loaded.'

For a moment I couldn't think what to say.

Then, 'A thirty-eight, is it?' I asked, being interested in that particular calibre.

'Yes. Smith & Wesson. At the club, they consider me to be a good shot. It wouldn't be necessary to kill you, anyway.'

Although his smile was now complacent, I realized he would not be safe to tackle, even if he'd been unarmed. He looked as though he had been a commando, or something like that, even perhaps a mercenary. A dangerous man, poised, in control.

'You could put holes in me,' I agreed. 'Carefully not lethal, but painful.'

'I could. Mr Spooner phoned me. I was told to see you off the premises. Lovely phrase, that. It covers anything. To see you off. But he instructs and I obey. It would never occur to him that I have my own life, and might have a personal interest in what's going on.'

There was no smile to accompany this. His own personal interest might also have been to see me off. Yet he seemed prepared to chat. I felt, even, that he might be fishing for information.

I moved from one foot to the other. 'But you say the gun's not loaded, so you can't expect me to be impressed.'

Smiling, he removed his left hand from his pocket. It held a magazine. Smoothly, his eyes not leaving my face, and as though he'd practised doing it in the dark, he slapped it into the butt, jerked back the slide, and said, 'It is now.'

I watched it warily. 'One of your duties, you said . . . to guard the grounds. There are others? May I make a guess? Chauffeur? You drive him to work?'

'He works here. They come to him.'

'Come here? It's a bit out of the way.' Yet I'd imagined they might.

'They fly in. There's a helicopter pad, out at the back.' He was now completely relaxed.

'But you're his chauffeur?' I persisted.

'Sometimes. I like driving his Corniche.'

'A man of all duties?'

'Well yes.'

'And other times?'

At last I detected in him a shortening of his patience, but perhaps he was merely annoyed with himself for failing to see where I was heading. Yet I felt that he wanted to know more.

'What other times?' he demanded.

'Surely he needs to visit the city, from time to time. Or one of the other cities.'

'Oh . . . that! I fly him in. We've got our own chopper.'

'Well . . . good for you.' I felt it was time to stop chatting idly. 'And now . . . ' I made it sound like a challenge.

He shrugged. 'Now you've found out what George Tate was trying to get at. He wanted to see what was in my safe. Stupid man. Don't you think he was stupid? Over-persistent, anyway. Obsessed . . . say. He wanted to know what and who I was. Cunning bastard, wasn't he, but not as clever as he thought he was. As though I didn't notice what he was up to! That ridiculous trick with the camera . . . of *course* I noticed. I used to come in here just in order to open the safe, to give him a bit of practice. It was all I could do not to bust out laughing — or stick two fingers up and let him get a shot at that. And now . . . here you are. Another mug. Have a look. Go on, have a look what's inside the safe, and see if he would've been pleased with what he'd have found.'

I hesitated, not certain I could trust him. It was possible he believed he could rely on Spooner's doubtless high-level contacts, and thought he could shoot down a burglar with impunity, especially one with a hand in his safe. It was now agony even to consider presenting my back to him.

'Go on,' he encouraged, one corner of his mouth hinting at a smile. 'You can turn your back. I've never yet shot a man in the back.'

Still I hesitated. 'Face to face, though?'

'Oh yes.' He cocked his head. 'Uganda. Several.'

'Ah . . . I see.' I turned my back. Nothing happened. I reached my hand into the safe. There were several items in there, lying flat. I drew them out and turned. I glanced at him. Lips pursed, he nodded. His eyes glinted.

There was a certificate of insurance, possibly on his life. The probability was that, living the life he did, the premiums would be sky high. There was his pilot's licence in the name of Colin Nigel Hughes.

'You're Colin Hughes?' I asked.

'The very same.'

And there was a photograph. It was glazed and framed, what is known as a glamour shot, that's to say it was a head and shoulders study of a smiling woman, but glamorized by the application of careful make-up and a special hair-do and soft studio lighting. For a moment I didn't recognize her, but the written statement across the bottom corner quickly dispelled all doubt.

'Love you, Colin. Jennie.'

It was Jennie Tate. Startled, I looked up from it. The pistol was now an irrelevance. It hung limply in his hand. And he was enjoying himself. That would explain why he had been so forthcoming. Perhaps he had even planned this, or at least had been prepared for it.

Having heard that I had taken over from George Tate, he had wished to clear himself from any scenario I might be putting together.

'You wanted him to find *this*?' I asked.

For a moment he didn't respond. In fact, he appeared to be uncertain. He shook his head, perhaps to shake up his mind. 'Hell!' he said. 'I really don't know. Towards the end, maybe. Yes . . . towards the end.'

'The end being George's death?'

'No. Oh no.' He bent sideways and placed the pistol on a small glass-topped table. I noticed that the safety catch was on 'safe'. 'No,' he went on, straightening. 'It was after that. A different end.'

There was a gentle creak in the moment of silence between us, me standing there with my mind struggling to understand. A door that normally opens silently will more often creak when eased gently. I turned my head. Amelia was standing there in the doorway. Enter wife, bearing weapon. She was carrying the torch from the car, but not, as normal, with her hand high up towards the switch. No — with her hand firmly gripping the bottom end. As a weapon.

'I saw the light go on,' she explained.

'Come in, love,' I said, sighing. 'My wife,' I went on. 'Amelia.' He nodded, smiling. 'This is Colin Hughes,' I introduced him. 'He's Mr Spooner's chauffeur and helicopter pilot. We were just having a friendly chat.'

Her eyes were on the pistol. 'Friendly?'

Hughes laughed. 'There's nothing in the clip.'

Silently, as she came forward with the torch, handled more casually now, I handed her the photograph.

'But it's Jennie!' she cried at once, not even needing the message written across it. Then she saw it. 'Oh dear . . . '

'Mr Hughes was about to explain that,' I told her.

'Frankly . . . ' he began. 'Won't you take a seat?' he asked her, and she sat, somewhat primly, in a wing-backed chair. 'Frankly, I did think, at one time, of having that picture blown up a bit larger, and reframed. Then I could've substituted it for the Renoir in front of the safe. Now *that* would've given Tate a jolt. But no . . . I have to control my sense of humour. And it could have hurt her.'

'That mattered, did it?' I asked casually. 'Harming her?' I was looking round for ashtrays, wondering whether to light my pipe — and not seeing any. Yet I knew he smoked. Perhaps this room was used only for access to the safe. 'You didn't want her hurt?'

'At the beginning, it wouldn't have

mattered. She was just another female. But it was an assignment. The boss's instructions. Find out what the idiot's up to, he told me. Find out what Tate's doing.'

'It must have worried him,' I suggested.

He shrugged. With such massive shoulders he could express more than words. But nevertheless, he amplified.

'I wouldn't know about that. I just do what I'm told to do, and get paid for it. And he pays me well. Find out, he said, what Tate thinks he's doing, and what he expects from it.'

'Because George Tate might've located the money,' I suggested. 'Your boss would want to know about that. He'd want his money back.'

'You can bet he would. But Tate might've kept a chunk back for himself. He could always say: that's all there's left. So that's why he wanted Tate watched. That's what I reckoned, anyway.'

'You sound doubtful.' That was Amelia, involved now. 'It could more likely have been his concern about Adrian.'

'Sure it could.' Hughes glimmered a faint smile in her direction. 'Perhaps he feels things every now and then, like ordinary people.' Yet there was no sarcasm in his voice. He was genuinely considering the proposition.

'Smoke if you want to,' he said to me. 'The curtains are due for the laundry, anyway.' It was a strangely feminine remark for such a masculine man.

I hadn't realized the pipe was in my hand. I nodded. 'Thanks.' And began to fill it. 'So you took on this assignment?'

'Sure. I told you . . . his orders. But he left me to make up my own mind on how to manage it. Not keep an eye on Tate, I decided. He'd spot that. But get at him by way of his wife. It was easy — too damned easy. Tate brought it on himself, but what could he expect! He left her on her own for most of the time, the fool, and she'd surely have gone crazy, shut up on her own at home. Of course, she went out. Alone. In the evenings. A lady on her own — on the town! Oh dear me, that wouldn't do. And she was lonely . . . just waiting for a friendly smile.'

He turned to Amelia for her support and understanding, and smiled.

'I see what you mean,' she said, and I winked at her.

'She was taking risks,' said Hughes. 'She could've found herself in trouble. Could've done worse.'

I tilted my head. 'Oh, I wouldn't say that.' I turned, to see Amelia return my wink.

It was going along fine, and I'd extricated

myself from an awkward situation. Everything was friendly. 'So you picked her up and played her along, and asked to see her again . . . and again . . . and she told you what you already knew, that George was out late most nights, so that you two didn't really have to waste time in cafés and bars, staring into each other's eyes . . . '

It was deliberate. I'd guessed the truth; knew he wasn't going to admit it unless I prodded him. Yet I had miscalculated his mood. His shoulders firmed and he leaned forward, poised on the balls of his feet. His hands bunched into very dangerous-looking fists, and his face changed. It was now the face of a man prowling a jungle, of a man whose actions in the next few seconds could seal one fate or the other. He was on the edge of uncontrolled violence.

'Richard means,' put in Amelia smoothly, 'though he's very poor at words, that she and you fell madly in love with each other.' Her voice was gentle, the soft, awed tone of women discussing a true and glorious passion.

He relaxed. Shrugged. Said to me, 'By God, you came close to it there, my friend.' And his fists unwound like a spider awakening from a long sleep.

'I'm sorry,' I said. 'As my wife says, I'm bad

at expressing myself.'

He turned to her, his eyes glinting. 'I could make you a better offer, ma'am.'

She laughed. For a few seconds there might just as well have been only the two of them there. Then he shattered the mood by raising his palms and slapping them on his cheeks, as though reprimanding himself. But now — as I'd hoped to provoke — he was disposed to plunge into self-justification.

'I don't mind talking about it,' he admitted. 'Not now. It's all finished, anyway. It was over the moment Tate died. That underlined what we'd been doing. At the beginning . . . all right, so it was nothing more than a casual pick-up. It was what I'd been told to do. I was getting closer to Tate. But I wasn't doing it with too much enthusiasm. No great act. Make no mistake, I never pretended to be anything but what I am, never pretended to her. But she was easy to talk to, and she certainly didn't mind talking about her precious George. Precious? Yeah. She thought the world of him — or she was trying damned hard to go on thinking that. Look at it how you like. But fairly soon, we weren't talking about him. He never came into it again. We talked about us, and it wasn't a job for me any more, and anyway, I wasn't interested in George Tate's operations by that time. I didn't ever seem to get the time to think about anybody but his wife. And then there came the time when I realized I wanted her, and she was thinking on the same lines — and Tate was just an awkward nuisance between us.'

He took a breath, moved around the room a little, and glanced towards a corner, where there was a small cupboard.

'Would either of you care for a drink?' he asked, having talked himself dry.

'Thank you, but no,' we both said.

'Then I will, if you don't mind.'

'It's your home,' I reminded him.

He had the doors open and was pouring himself a fair-sized scotch, but he found time to glance back at me. 'Is it my home? Oh no . . . no. It's Marcus Spooner's, and he doesn't let me forget it.' He straightened. 'Your good health.' He downed it in one swallow, banged down the empty glass, and asked, 'Where was I?'

'You were working round to the day you killed George Tate,' I said.

'What! That's a damned lie.'

'Is it? You own a thirty-eight calibre pistol, and there was a thirty-eight hole in his van.'

'The police thought it was a twig. Twig! I ask you!'

'Jennie told you that?'

271

'The last time I saw her.'

'When was that?'

'Just after he died.' He became thoughtful, and paced a little out of the pile of his carpet. We waited silently.

'Never could understand women,' he admitted. 'I mean, you'd have thought, with him out of the way, everything'd be wine and roses. Y' get me? But oh no. It seems there's a lot happens when people are married. They get to know each other's little moods and excitements and fears and joys. Or so she told me. I wouldn't know. Part of your life, she said. And then, all of a sudden, with George dead, I didn't fit in. As a bit of fun on the side . . . safe fun 'cause she was married . . . then that's all right. It seems. I couldn't get the hang of that. But it ain't fun and it ain't on the side, when there's no husband around. It all gets serious, see. Don't ask me to explain. And for Jen, it was serious. She'd gotta have time to think about it. She said.' He shrugged. 'She's still thinkin'.'

There was a brief silence. His eyes flicked to a phone on a table by the door, as though magically, and because we were discussing her, it would ring, and it would be his Jen, and she'd say yes. Yes, Colin. Oh yes!

'What a pity', I ventured at last, 'that you killed him for nothing.'

'I told you — I didn't kill him.' His face was becoming flushed. I didn't dare to push him much further.

'All right,' I conceded. 'But there was the right-sized hole in his van. And you've got a gun, and you wanted him out of the way.'

He stared at me warily. 'I didn't kill him.'

'You took a shot at him.'

He shook his head. 'No. If I'd taken a shot *at* him, I'd have hit him.'

'Even when he was driving his van?'

'Sure. A rustle in the undergrowth, you turn round and fire — and you haven't got time to miss.'

I had given him the opportunity to slip that in. It boosted his ego, that memory, and he relaxed. He'd lived through it.

'But all the same, a shot was fired.'

'Yeah . . . well . . . ' He glanced at his drinks cupboard, then away from it. 'I'd been round there, see. George — oh, you didn't have to expect him before one in the morning, so we'd had quite an evening of it. She was ready an' warm enough at that time. Lord, but she was! But I hadda get out of there smart-like. For me . . . I reckoned I didn't care if he walked in on us and found us on her bed. That'd settle things for good-an'-all, that would. So I reckoned. But Jen, she was sort of scared of that, scared for him an' for me, though I couldn't understand that. So she shuffled me out, and it'd been great. Sure had. But out I went. Always takin' orders, I am, so I'm used to it.'

He broke off with a bark of bitter anger. Now he could no longer resist the call of his drinks cupboard. He poured himself an even larger whisky. 'Sure you won't . . . ' But expecting no reply. He turned back to us, holding the glass, walking round as he tossed down half of it, and then walking around again and using the glass to focus on, so as not to have to meet the gaze of either of us.

'I can tell y', it was really great, that last time. For both of us. Great. An' the bastard never even slept in the same bed with her! A waste. A wicked waste! So there I am, walkin' away from the house, all creepy like, keepin' in the shadows. Sneaky. It made it all into somethin' rotten, having to sneak. Me! Sneaking. Christ! But I'd left the Merc a coupla streets away, and before I got there, along comes that stupid van of his. That logo . . . d'you know . . . they call it The Prancing Prat.' He didn't glance at me, or he'd have seen my nod. 'That just about fitted him. A Prancin' Prat, that was George Tate. An' by that time, I was just in the right mood to see the end of Mr Bloody Tate. So I took a quick shot.'

So he took his gun on his amorous assignations! Perhaps he'd expected trouble. 'That was what I said,' I put in, to fill a sudden gap in his story. 'You killed him.'

'I hit the van.'

'But you fired at *him*.'

'No. No . . . oh no.' He was shaking his head, but halted it in order to throw back the last of his drink. He gulped. 'If I'd have fired at him, I'd have hit him. I fired at the van, jus' behind his head.'

'And just above?'

'An' just above. To scare him. To tell him: George Charles Tate, you're surplus to bloody requirements, mate.'

'All the same, you brought about his death. He went off the road.'

'Not my fault, that weren't.'

'You scared him, and he put his foot down.'

'He went off the road two corners further on. An' try provin' anything else. Just try. A twig, they said. A twig made that hole.' And he was nodding, nodding, as though never going to stop.

Now I understood completely what George had meant by, 'On both counts'. His investigations into one mystery had revealed another . . . well, not mystery, perhaps, because it had probably been very clear to him what was going on between his wife and

Colin Hughes. He might even have worked out *why* it was going on. Except that he could seriously have underestimated both the effect of his neglect on Jennie, and the effect of his Jennie on Colin Hughes.

'A twig?' I said, laughing lightly to dismiss that. 'A thirty-eight calibre twig?'

He laughed, joining me, the laugh uneasy because he couldn't see what I was getting at.

I put my hand in my jacket pocket. 'I'll see if one of these shell cases will fit the hole in the van, the next time I'm around there.' I showed him the three brass shell cases in my palm.

'Where d'you get those?'

'They're the same calibre as you use. Aren't they?'

'Lotsa people use thirty-eight.'

'So these ought to fit the hole in the van, seeing that they were fired from the same pistol.'

He cocked his head on one side. 'Y're guessin'.'

'I'm guessing it was your pistol that ejected these shell cases. Yes. Because you're the only one involved in all this who's got one, as far as I know. And because it neatly fits the fact that you pilot a helicopter, and it therefore fits the location I found them.'

His eyes searched for somewhere he could

sit. I had been guessing that he'd already drunk his limit before we'd arrived, and the last two had pushed him too far. Then he changed his mind. He didn't want to sit when I was still standing. Standing . . . and asking awkward questions.

'What location?' he asked. His eyes wandered. He was chasing his brain around to discover what I meant.

I took it very casually. Semi-drunk men can be unpredictable. 'The location I'm talking about is that place, house, site — call it what you like — where the boy Adrian was held. *That* site. It was there you fired three shots, at something or somebody.'

He was staring at me with his shoulders high and thrust forward, a fighting bull looking for an opening, staring at me from beneath his brows. He tried a tentative sneer, but he wasn't too good at it.

'Y're wrong. Wrong.'

'In what way am I wrong?'

'There was four. Four shots.'

'There should've been four bodies, then. You never miss, you said.'

'I aimed to miss. Just t' scare the bleeder off.'

'When was this?' I knew very well when it had been. I was only keeping the flow going.

'Y' know bloody well when it was,' he said,

as though he'd read my mind.

I examined the cartridge cases more closely, more intently. 'A long while ago,' I decided. 'They're corroded, rotting away in places. All right, so there were four. Finding three out of four's not bad — after sixteen years.' I beamed at him, to display how pleased I was with myself. 'Shall I try a guess?' I asked. 'Yes — I'll guess. The day the money was finally collected, the day they took it back to that old wreck of a farmhouse.'

I knew this to be incorrect. In that event, it would have to have been because he'd spotted them from the helicopter, returning in triumph. He would then have taken positive action. And *that* would have needed only three shots. One each. And he had used the singular. 'Scare the bleeder off,' he had said.

He shook his head, stubborn now, and difficult.

'The day after, then?' I offered, as a way out for him.

He nodded. 'Yeah. That'd be it.'

'That *would* be it? Make it more certain than that, Mr Hughes.'

He didn't seem to realize I'd slipped into my interrogation voice. I had demanded it. He looked away, and his voice held a careful tone, the weighing of each word being important. He had been prepared to talk to me, when it had been to clear himself from the sphere of my enquiries. But now it had become too close, too threatening, involving him from a new angle.

'All right — I *am* certain. The day after the money handover.' The hint of a slur had disappeared from his voice. 'Not *the* day of the hand-over. Whee . . . I'll never forget that. Spooner went really wild, and the missus — that was his wife, Reenee — she was near to hysterics. It'd gone on and on, see. Three weeks. Three goes at pickin' up the money, they had. Lordy, what a lousy lot they were! Fumblin' with the money, an' the missus near out of her mind. An' all the time — every day — there I was, out with the chopper, trying to spot the damned hide-out. But I hadda be careful, see. Careful. Because if they saw they were spotted . . . if I'd seen 'em headin' back to their hidey-hole, and they'd spotted me, they wouldn't have gone there. Not that stupid, they weren't. An' I had to keep high for that. And y' see, if they couldn't spot me, what chance'd I got of spottin' a car or the like, way down there? It ain't easy, y' know. A car — down there on the ground, it could be goin' fast. From up there, it's hardly movin'. So it'd been a dead loss all round, and I would get back and she'd pounce on me

— the missus would. Any news? Had I found where they'd got him . . . her Adrian? An' I had to say no. And she must've known, 'cause I'd been reporting back on the radio every damn second, to the boss. He'd have told her. You'd think he'd have told her.' He rubbed his hand over his face. 'I dunno, though.'

He had been going along fine, his story sharp and clear. Now he seemed to hesitate.

'And the day of the pick-up?' I asked quietly, leading him. 'You'd got a whole bus to watch, and you knew where it was starting from.'

'Yeah. Well . . . I suppose. The bus — that was easy. But they switched to the car, an' that wasn't so good. They drove into High Heath wood. Lotsa roads outa that, an' it goes on and on. I never saw 'em drive out.'

'We didn't get this information on our radio,' I said.

'Wasn't on your wavelength,' he dismissed it. 'On the boss's. Anyway, I lost 'em again, but it didn't seem to matter too much. Couldn't understand what I was supposed to be doin', anyway. If we'd found this hide-out of theirs, we wouldn't've dared to go near. It was Adrian, y' see. Get his throat cut, they threatened. An' now they'd got the money — so we expected to get the kid back. A phone call . . . you know. You'll find him

280

sittin' in a phone box somewhere. You know.'

It all sounded too dreadfully real to me, and it fitted exactly into what I could recall.

'You didn't go out again?' I asked. 'Later on that evening they collected the money?'

He gestured wildly. 'What was the point? We waited, waited. They fetched the doctor to the missus. But . . . no message. Not a bleedin' thing.'

There wouldn't have been. They had gone out on their booze-up. Not one tiny thought for the parents. 'So you didn't go out, even then, when there was nothing but silence?'

'It got dark.' He shrugged, managing to convey disgust.

'But . . . the next day?'

'We was still waiting there when the sun come up. The missus was up in her bed, drugged out of her mind by her doctor. Spooner shouts at me to get out on the job, *do* something, so out I goes. A dead loss, I think. A dead waste of time. An' me so knackered I can hardly see outa my eyes. But off I goes, tootling along in the chopper. Five hundred feet, maybe. Hopeless. Nearly clippin' the tops of the hills, an' my reactions not up to scratch. An' I gets one of them miracles you hear about. A car. Out in the wilds. One in a million chance, but I gain a bit of height. Could track him at a thou', then. Anyway, he gets to where he's goin', an' obviously it means somethin'. One feller gets out. On his tod. Me, I put the chopper down. I hold the gun on him, in case his mates was around. But it's all quiet. So I tell him to bugger off. Put a few shots over his head, an' he goes quick enough. Small fat slimy little bastard, he was.'

'Four shots, you said before. And his name was — is — Tim Craythorpe.'

'Can't see it matters now.'

'No. It doesn't matter now.' Oh, but it did! What I was concentrating on at that moment was that he'd slipped away from the exact truth, somewhere along the line. He had over-elaborated, as people do when they're unsure that their lies are being received satisfactorily. Now he'd been telling us about how he'd tracked a car, when he'd previously said how difficult that was. And surely he, with all his undoubted experience, would not have put his chopper down when there might have been two other roughs still inside the car — and he couldn't have known they weren't armed. I didn't push him on that point, but let him go ahead.

But he seemed to have ground to a halt. I had to say, 'Go on.'

'What else is there?'

'What you did next.'

'Oh yeah. After he'd gone, I went through the place. Oh . . . that was *it*, right enough. Empty rooms an' the roof fallen in, but signs in the cellar. Cookin' stuff an' food an' the like. Water. A stove. But nobody. An' I hadda go back and tell Spooner that Adrian had been there an' wasn't any more. No, he wasn't. An' all hell broke loose. He was on the phone to everybody — Chief Constable, Chief everythin'. And . . . nothing. The end. Finis, as they say.'

'No Adrian, no money, and no girl?'

He shook his head.

'But now that you know . . . *that* was why you were hanging around by Mrs Craythorpe's cottage!' I cried, realizing.

He was shaking his head doggedly. 'She must've been in that cupboard, *then*. The girl must. When I was in the house. An' I walked past. I musta walked right past that cupboard. I didn't know! I walked past it and never noticed it.'

'You wouldn't,' I murmured.

'No. How could I?'

'And you were wondering if it would be a good idea to pop in and tell it all to her mother?'

'Something like that.'

I shook my head. 'I don't think it would. Really I don't think she would want to know.'

He looked at me with uncertainty, reaching for a release from vague murmurings of any conscience he might have had. 'Really?'

'It wouldn't do any good.'

'It gives me the creeps, thinking about it.' He sounded morose.

'I know what it's like,' I assured him.

I wondered whether to slap him on the shoulder encouragingly, but decided against it. Like as not, he'd have had me on my back with a broken jaw, in pure reaction.

Quietly, we said good-night. He seemed not to hear. Out in the open air, so fresh and so welcome, Amelia paused.

'Richard,' she said, 'you're always doing that. You play things right on the edge. The very edge. One of these days you'll go too far, and fall on your face.'

'It's usually possible to talk your way out of anything.'

'Hmm!'

I lit my pipe at last, blowing smoke at the sky. Amelia said, 'Try explaining to Mary why we're late . . . again!'

'Oh heavens, yes!'

We headed towards the car and a hot meal.

13

As soon as we walked out of the gateway I knew that the hot meal was not going to be on the immediate agenda. A police car wouldn't be parked there unless they had business with us; unless a general look-out for that particular Granada had been put into effect. The passenger's door opened and a lean, young constable got out to confront us.

'You'll be Mr Patton, sir?'

'I am. Trouble, is there?'

'Inspector Brason has been trying to contact you. If you'll get inside you can use our radio phone.'

I slid inside. Usually I take up a lot of room, but I moved as far over as possible, so that Amelia could just wedge herself inside. It saved having to repeat everything that was said. The driver had already got through, and handed me the phone.

'Tony . . . it's Richard. You wanted me?'

'Where are you?'

'In car A64, outside Cumberland Hall. I've been to see Marcus Spooner, and we've had a chat with his minder. What's the trouble?'

'Can you get back — '

'What *is* it, Tony?'

I was using our usual technique, me holding the phone clear of my ear, Amelia with her head against mine. He said, 'It's Jennie Tate. She's taken an overdose of sleeping tablets, and she's in hospital. St Michael's. Tulip Ward.'

'Is she — '

'I don't know yet. If you could come . . . meet me there . . . I've got something to show you. Can you — '

'Of course,' said Amelia.

'That was Amelia, wasn't it, Richard? Right. The patrol car'll lead you. Tulip Ward. Remember . . . '

'All right. See you there.' I handed the phone back to the driver. Amelia nudged me. 'Mary,' she whispered.

'Do you mind?' I asked the officer. 'A private call,' I explained.

He shrugged. Amelia slid, out, for more room and for me to get free. I said quickly, 'I'll be a minute. Wait for me.' And Amelia took my place, and the phone.

Then I ran back to the dower house, rang the bell, banged on the door, and moved from foot to foot with impatience until a hall light went on and the door opened.

Colin Hughes had been at his whisky again. He seemed dazed and unsteady.

'What's up?' He narrowed his eyes, as though suspicious.

'I've just had word,' I told him. 'Jennie's in hospital. She seems to have tried to take her own life. An overdose. I thought you'd want to know.'

'Jesus!'

'She's at St Michael's. Tulip Ward. Got it? St Michael's and Tulip.'

'I've got it. But what the hell! Why'd she want to do that? I don't get it. Don't get it.'

I turned away. 'Think about it.' Then I ran back to the Granada, his shout following me. 'Is she . . . '

The patrol car had already done a three-point turn and was ready to head back towards Potterton. Amelia was just completing the same manoeuvre, behind the other car. Seeing me come running, she slid out quickly and went round to the other side.

'You to drive, Richard?'

'I think so, love.' I knew it could get a little disconcerting.

Off went the patrol car, blue light flashing but its siren silent. There was very little traffic out there, once we were through the village. But he piled on the speed, smoothly, gradually building it up, and I hung on grimly. His headlights, on full beam, gave me something of a lead, as I could see further ahead than if I'd been driving alone. But soon we came into the outskirts of the town, with the tail-end of the commuter traffic. Then — on went his siren. It wasn't an emergency for us; that was the other end. But the driver perhaps liked an excuse for using it.

In the leading car, I knew from experience, it can be very exhilarating, though your reactions, as the driver, have to be poised on a knife edge. You're travelling fast into what seems like a solid pack of vehicles, and somehow they recede, they part like a bow-wave a hundred yards ahead of the prow. Yet there's always the chance that one vehicle will fail to do so. A chance. It keeps you alert, behind that steering wheel.

It kept me even more alert. I dared not allow too much space between us, in case the fan of cars, in closing behind him, might do so into us. And, that close, I was unable to see far enough ahead to observe any hesitations or falterings in the clearing vehicles. So I had to maintain a constant distance behind, and hope the patrol car got a clear run.

It did. We slowed. He signalled a left turn, and we found ourselves in the car-park behind the hospital. We parked. We got out. Amelia said, 'Wasn't that exciting, Richard?' And I had to agree. The driver now had his window down and was leaning an elbow on it.

'That was a bit of good driving,' I said.

He grinned. 'There's an entrance over there, look — where that ambulance is.'

'Thank you.'

We began to walk towards it. A silver Mercedes Benz swung in as we did so, its headlights sweeping across us. How he'd done it I couldn't guess, and he had been half drunk. Though perhaps he would now be stone cold sober.

There was no need to ask for directions. It was a reasonably modern building, and much attention had been paid to signposting. Perhaps it had been overdone; you had to read so many indications in order to spot the one you wanted. But as we mounted the stairs to the next floor the destinations thinned down to a dozen or so, all flowers, and after we had walked a very long, straight and rather depressing corridor, there it was, right at the end. Tulip Ward. It was alongside Daffodil Ward. Later, I discovered that the staff called them, respectively, Female Intensive Care and Female Terminal. Tulip and Daffodil sounds much better. Spring. An awakening, not a dying.

In the waiting room, Tony was walking

around impatiently. At my shoulder, suddenly, was Colin Hughes.

Tony ignored him. 'Amelia.' A smile for her. 'Richard.' A nod for me. 'Glad you could get here.'

'Caught us just about to head for home,' I told him.

'Ah . . . yes. And this is?' He cocked an eyebrow towards Colin Hughes.

I introduced them. 'Inspector Brason, CID — this is Colin Hughes, handyman for Spooner, chauffeur, chopper pilot, minder and guard, and spy as required. He's got a personal interest in this, Tony.'

They eyed each other, not offering to shake hands. Hughes was busy with his, wiping his palms up and down his buttocks, on and on, his face a set block of chipped granite.

'I know you,' said Tony to Hughes surprisingly. 'I've read about you and your personal interest.' He turned to Amelia. 'We'd better find seats, I think. Not the bench. Over there, look. A table and four chairs.'

Thus, with subtlety, did Tony include our companion. I saw that this was noticed, and acknowledged with an inclination of the head.

We sat, Hughes restless, glancing towards the rubber swing doors at the other end of the waiting room. Tony observed this.

'It'll be some time yet,' he said softly, embracing all of us but with his eyes on Hughes.

'She's . . . how is she?' Hughes was nervous, tense.

'My latest information is that she's out of danger. Weak, though. Very weak.'

It was as though Colin Hughes had been punched in the belly. He made a slight sound and his face crumpled. We looked away. Relief, I supposed.

'Now,' said Tony, reaching forward for his briefcase and perching it on his lap. 'The next-door neighbour's dog got into Jennie's garden. The neighbour heard him barking, and went after him. The dog was at the french window, with Jennie slumped in a chair just inside it. That spaniel saved her life. The neighbour was very sensible and didn't hesitate. The doors were locked inside. She put a brick through a pane and reached inside. Jennie was sitting beside a table, with a glass of water on it and her bottle of sleeping tablets on its side, nearly empty. The neighbour phoned an ambulance and then us. So . . . here we are.'

There was a brief silence. Hughes got to his feet, moved around restlessly, then returned to his chair.

'I went along,' said Tony. 'Not strictly my

job, but I was informed. The little room George had been using as a bedroom had been turned over thoroughly. Jennie searching, I guessed. It's been a long while since he died, and at last she thought to search.'

'Or at last,' said Amelia quietly, 'she'd worked up her courage to search.'

'Yes.' Tony glanced at her, smiling. 'Anyway, what she found was scattered on the floor around her chair, and in her hand. She'd come across some of his photos, some of his more personal ones, I reckon, as they'd been hidden in the bedroom rather than his dark-room. For her to see, and not you, Richard. And there was a letter he'd written to her, in a plain envelope simply addressed: Jennie. No date. It could've been written any time, but my guess is shortly before his death.'

From his briefcase he drew out an envelope. I recognized it as one of those that George had usually used for his prints. There were about twenty photographs in it. Tony spread them out on the table (so that was why he'd led us to a table) like an optimist laying out a hand of patience. Nobody said anything. To Hughes they would have been upside-down. But he would have been able to see them for what they were, some of George's best shots from outside restaurant windows, when there had been no light behind him to ruin things with reflections. And he had moved around. The two occupants of the table were easily recognized: Jennie and Colin Hughes. They were smiling into each other's eyes. In some his hand was on hers on the table, in others she was leaning forward to whisper something to him. The following photo had Hughes throwing his head back, laughing.

'She found those,' said Tony, his voice colourless. 'Then she obviously read the letter.'

Hughes had reached across and turned one or two photos round to face him. He cleared his throat, then was alert at the word: letter.

Tony placed a single sheet of paper on the table in front of Amelia and me. Hughes remained silent and stiff, his eyebrows lowered, his eyes hungry. His hands were now on the table surface, fists clenching and unclenching.

Silently, we read it together, Amelia and I.

My dearest, darling Jennie,
   I am writing to you now because of late I have come to the conclusion that my life is in danger. Some small satisfaction can be drawn from this, in that it must be an indication that my efforts (which I know

293

you disapprove of and even believe to be slightly insane) are at last bearing fruit. I now have an idea, only a slight one, of what happened to the money and the boy, Adrian. But not to Sylvia.

Clearly, this must affect Spooner deeply, because he has seen fit to turn his minder on to me. I refer to Colin Hughes of course, my dear. I have not the slightest doubt that it is on Spooner's orders I am being closely observed and my activities monitored. Whether or not it was his own idea, I am now aware that Hughes is devoting much attention to you. Perhaps he feels you are in possession of my thinking on it, and my plans. You will understand that it was with such a possibility in mind that I have not confided in you of late. Believe me, my love, it has been agony for me to remain silent,

There the page ended. Tony solemnly handed over another sheet, much crumpled. 'She had this in a ball in her hand.'

It went on:

when I have longed to ask your advice and outline my actions, if only in self-justification. But how could I, when it was clear you had been led into some besotted notion that the man Hughes was cultivating your interest for no other reason but a personal one? Oh Jennie, my love, how could you have allowed yourself to be so misled! The man is a trained mercenary, a man who has killed for money, not out of anger or necessity or principle. Such men are womanizers. If he tells you he loves you, remember that he does so (that he claims so) only in order to extract information about me.

It is all false. It is a lie, my Jennie. The man is dangerous, and if I should die suddenly, you will know in which direction to look.

I do hope you never read this. If you do, please believe that I still, as always, love you, and have nothing but your interests at heart.

Your adoring,
George.

I looked up to catch Colin's eyes. He was staring at me like a rhino facing a hunting rifle, not yet knowing its calibre or its destructive power. I turned my attention to Tony, raising my eyebrows. He inclined his head. Silently, I handed both sheets into those capable and destructive hands. Colin forced himself not to snatch at them.

295

He sat there, face expressionless, but slowly his great fists clenched firmer and firmer into the paper, until it seemed that both sheets would be equally crumpled — even torn. Then he tossed them away from him, and the hands reached up to his face, fingers clawing as though in an attempt to drag the flesh from the skull, the horribly red lower eyelids pulled down. He seemed to make a groaning sound, then he sprang to his feet and began to walk around, unaware that the waiting room was filling, unaware of anything except his own pain, his arms swinging, fists flying around dangerously, as though he might find an enemy at whom he could fling them.

'There's your answer, Tony,' I said.

'I didn't ask a question.'

'But it's there, and I've got the answer for you. Spooner must've set him off to discover what George was after. In fact, I know that's so. George was full of ideas, so that when Spooner's man-of-all-duties took up with Jennie, it gave more information to George than it did to Colin Hughes. Your inheritance, Tony — the model helicopter. He knew that Hughes was Spooner's pilot, so he guessed that choppers came into it somewhere, So he left you a hint. But it was a hint to Jennie, too. There it was, sitting on the sideboard, shouting out to Jennie that George knew about her affair with Hughes. That was more than a wee bit cruel, don't you think? Anyway — '

'And did helicopters come into it?' Tony interrupted.

'One helicopter, yes. On the day after the hand-over, Hughes was out in it. He spotted a car. It went to the place — the ruined farm. He landed, and scared off the driver with a few shots over his head. That was Tim Craythorpe, from the description.'

'Shots? Over his head? That's illegal.'

I pointed. 'There he is, look. That's him prowling around. Go on, charge him with it. Arrest him — '

Tony gave me a twisted grin. 'Calm down, Richard. And then what?'

'Hughes searched the house — and there was nothing. It must have been in the same condition as when we found it, me and Phelps.'

'It doesn't help.'

'No,' I agreed. 'Not a bit.' But it might, just might, I thought, when I could get a confidential word with Tim Craythorpe.

Tony was packing away his photos and letter in his briefcase. It would be needed as evidence for the coroner, if Jennie failed to recover.

'I'll be in touch,' he said.

'Sure.'

He hesitated. 'You're still . . . involved in this, Richard?' he asked, his voice a little weary, I thought, but I hoped that I'd detected a hint that he was becoming reconciled to my activities.

'Still involved,' I told him. 'It's not finished.'

He lowered his voice. 'Then be careful, Richard, please. I could spare a man, perhaps — '

'No. It's all right. You're forgetting, I'm in league with Martie Machin's lot. Or Ron Phelps's — look at it how you like. But I'm safe from them. Frankly, it's Spooner I'm watching now.'

'Spooner . . . '

'Or his man. *That* man. Colin Hughes. Spooner didn't like George Tate investigating and sticking his nose in. Now he doesn't like me doing the same. I wonder why, Tony. You'd think he'd be grateful for any help he can get in clearing it all up. You might give that a thought when you've got the time.'

'Oh . . . time,' he said with exhausted disgust. 'What's that . . . time?'

Then he hoisted his briefcase under his arm, said, 'See you, Amelia,' nodded to me, and walked away rapidly before I could think of anything else to worry him with.

Hughes was still prowling, but now punctuated it with pauses, mostly in front of the round windows set in the swing doors, as though he might see her, as though she might raise her head and smile in his direction. It was only then that I realized that this waiting room, now fairly full, was strangely quiet. Usually there is chatter. Children run around, excited because momma's promised them a baby brother or sister. But here, silence. Intensive care. There's nothing to whisper about but hope and fear.

I asked Amelia, belatedly, 'Did you get through to Mary?'

'Oh yes.'

'And told her what?'

'That we'd be late. She said she was getting used to it.'

'I doubt she ever will.'

'What is it, Richard? Why are we sitting here? Can't we leave now?'

'Yes. I suppose we can. No point in hanging around.'

Yet I had an uneasy feeling that I ought to remain in this area, that there was movement in the background, something stirring, and I did not dare to turn my back on it.

'I'll just have a word . . . ' I nodded towards Hughes, who was still hovering near the swing doors, half approaching any nurses who came through but afraid to speak to them. He, who'd prowled the treacherous jungles, his life hanging on the thread of a split-second reaction, was afraid to speak to a clean, neat, inoffensive young nurse.

I approached him. 'Have you asked?'

He shook his head numbly, then gave me an apologetic, weak smile.

'I'll do it.'

I pushed through the swing doors. Nobody rushed at me in horror. I moved forward. There was an office on the left, the door open. Inside was a senior nurse; I don't know how to recognize their seniorities. I moved inside the door and cleared my throat. She had been examining charts.

'I wanted to enquire about Jennie Tate,' I told her.

'You're her husband?'

'No. She's a widow. I'm just a friend.'

She smiled. What a lovely smile she had! One could bear to look up from a bed of pain, just to see that smile. 'She's out of danger now. It was a close thing.'

'When . . .' I watched, and hesitated as she tilted her head. 'When will she be . . .'

'Awake? Able to speak and understand? Oh . . . tomorrow. I wouldn't expect anything before tomorrow morning. I'd be here about ten, if I were you.'

'Thank you.'

She nodded, glanced down at her upside-down watch, and returned to her charts.

I went back outside. He was on me in a flash. 'Well?'

'Nothing new. She'll recover. About ten in the morning, I'm told, that's when you can come back. Then . . . she might recognize you. She might even be able to talk to you. Might even want to.'

He shook his head. 'I'll wait.'

'It's up to you. She might not want to see you though, or talk to you.'

'But she could listen, couldn't she! She'd have to listen. I'll do the talking.'

I grimaced, nodding. That very pleasant smile I'd admired might well disappear if he said anything to upset Jennie. And he'd be out on his ear.

But I had the idea that what he had to say wouldn't upset her at all, and there'd be no reason for her to use too much energy in answering. A smile would do it.

14

We retraced our route through the long, long corridor and down the staircase. I asked, 'Did you manage to contact Mary, love?'

She glanced at me. 'Yes. I told you that.'

So she had; my mind was too deeply involved elsewhere. A meal would be waiting, but we were now two hours away from home. At Cumberland House we had been only an hour and a half. Time seemed now critical, my stomach being a large, rumbling void.

We reached the doors by which we had entered. This, apparently, was not the main entrance, as I'd seen one ambulance here when we'd arrived and now there was another one, unloading a fresh customer. Looking round, I realized that this was Admissions, and the section a little further along the corridor was Outpatients.

At the rear of the ambulance, they were struggling with a bulky object on a stretcher, trying to get it out of the ambulance and on to a trolley. To you and from me, but breathlessly. I hesitated, staring at the stretcher. There couldn't be too many people with a shape and weight like that in one town.

Amelia and I stood aside as they wheeled in the trolley. There was a bulging blanket over it, this shape, and what had to be a face sticking out at one end. The stomach was a heaving mountain. Groans accompanied every lurch.

'It's Martie Machin,' I said.

Amelia knew who Martie was, though she had never met him. Now that there was a face to look at, she didn't gain much of a true impression, as there was a great wad of cotton wool taped over his left cheek, and a similar, though smaller, padding over the right ear. This latter was double-taped with sticking plaster, as though the ear might otherwise drop off and be lost on the way.

'Martie?' I asked him, bending over.

'Mr Patton,' he wheezed.

They ran him into the wide passageway beyond. There they parked him against a wall, and said something to a passing nurse. She glanced at a clipboard in her hand, nodded, and went on her way. Martie was left there. They would no doubt collect him in due course.

'Been fighting, Martie?' I asked him.

'That little bleeder, Tim,' he whispered. It seemed painful for him to get one word out. As I bent my head closer I could hear his breath wheezing.

'You've been fighting with him?'

'Only talkin'. Honest. Leanin' on him a bit. Y' know.'

Martie leaning on you would be a serious matter. 'I can guess,' I assured him. 'What's he done?'

'Tellin' bloody lies.'

'Nothing new there. What about?'

'That night. *The* night.' He hesitated as a bout of pain seemed to assault him, his eyes narrowing. 'The night we got back.'

'The night of the booze-up?' I asked, just to get it right.

He nodded, then gasped with pain. 'Wouldn't admit nothin',' he sighed. 'He's got that money stowed away, Mr Patton. Reckon so. Wouldn't admit it. Leaned on 'im a bit, and the rotten sod pulled a knife.' He lay silent a moment. His chest heaved with the pain of speaking. 'Christ, it hurts,' he moaned. 'Always gorra knife somewhere, our Tim. All down me face, and me ear near off. The bleeder.'

'Where was this?'

'Pearlie's place.'

'Oh?'

'He was visitin'. Pearlie called an ambulance.'

I had a feeling of the pressure of time. They'd be coming for Martie any moment. I bent closer, reducing his effort and his pain. 'And Tim?'

'Pearlie hoofed 'im out.'

I could imagine. 'And where d'you reckon he'll be now, Martie?' I felt Amelia's fingers on my arm at that, her tiny protest at the implication.

'Got me in the guts, too,' Martie groaned.

'Where will Tim have gone?' I insisted.

'Back home. To his ma's.'

A small nurse, crisp and authoritative, thrust herself between us. 'Come along now, Mr Machin. We can't have you chatting here. They're waiting for you.' As though they were standing around, having a quick drag, waiting for the patient to amble in! I stood back. A white-clad porter grasped an end of the trolley, twirled it around with practised ease, and rumbled it away with its castors wobbling.

'He was one of that nasty gang, wasn't he?' asked Amelia.

'The one in the photos with Pearlie the Perv,' I told her.

'He doesn't look much lying down,' she commented.

'He wasn't at his best. Or worst.'

'Poor man.'

'Indeed,' I said, thinking furiously. Dissension in the ranks now, with doubts and suspicions coming between them? I wondered how I might use this to extract an item of truth from them. Certainly, the story of that pick-up day, and its following hours of darkness, just didn't hold together. The actions — or reactions — arising from what had happened didn't ring true. Not as I'd heard it from Ron Phelps, not as I'd heard it from Colin Hughes. Somebody was lying.

'Richard . . . ' So softly this was, from Amelia, as not to disjoint my thoughts. 'What're you thinking?'

'I'm wondering about Tim Craythorpe. How he is and where he is. He could've lied to them — his mates. They certainly suspect it now.' I stopped, shaking my head. It was I who had implanted that suspicion.

She was smiling gently. 'Have you got any change?' she asked.

'Loose cash? Yes. Why?'

'I've got an idea we're not heading straight home. There's a public phone just along the corridor. I'm afraid I'll have to ring Mary again.'

'She won't be pleased,' I told her gloomily.

'Nonsense. You know you've simply *got* to see this Tim creature, or you'll not be safe driving us home.'

For a couple more seconds I hesitated, then I plunged my hand into my trouser pocket and held out a handful of change.

She selected a few items, then she edged her way through quite a crowd of bustling visitors, along to the phone.

It isn't as though Mary's employed by us. Due to a peculiar quirk in Amelia's Uncle Walter's will, Mary had the right to her own portion of The Beeches, for life. It could have made that life very uncomfortable, but fortunately she'd become a close friend and she always felt she had to ensure our comfort and well-being, if only as a matter of pride. If we had been paying her, our tardiness wouldn't have mattered so much. As it was voluntary, her looking after us so possessively, she would be hurt to have her efforts wasted.

Amelia returned, smiling. 'One of her usual stews or goulashes or something. She says it will heat up again, tomorrow. If we're home by then.'

'Ah. Good. And what about us?'

'A sandwich in town, I thought.' She cocked her head. 'It's past shopping time and there'll be empty meters everywhere.'

I don't know how she manages to think of everything, nor how she can keep track of the passage of time.

'Unless', she added, 'you think you ought to see this Tim person first.'

'He can wait. It can wait.'

'And you're not forgetting his knife, Richard, I hope?'

'You heard that?'

'Oh yes.'

'Well, I'm not forgetting it. But this fight with Martie was at Pearlie's place. She would enjoy that. I don't reckon Tim'd dare to produce a knife at home, though, unless it's to cut his meat, of course.'

I drifted the car through the main streets, these now, at six thirty, almost empty of traffic, and with lines of empty meter slots each side. It broadened the streets, giving them a boosted impression of spaciousness and importance.

'There!' cried Amelia.

She hadn't been looking for cafés this time, but for restaurants. I glanced at where she was pointing. It looked cheerful and warm and half empty. We parked and walked back, and because we so rarely dined out in the evenings we made it a full meal, adding wine to it and gradually relaxing. The importance of Tim's welfare and his possible distortions of the truth now seemed distant and not very urgent.

'Now,' I said, as the waitress walked off with the bill and my credit card, 'how shall we tackle it?'

'Well ... I suppose we drive to Mrs

Craythorpe's, and if Tim's there you will ask him questions.'

'You'd want to be present?' I was thinking about the knife.

'Well, of course. And I'd like to see how she's progressing with her roses.'

'I may have to become stern with him.'

She laughed lightly, touching my hand. 'As long as you watch out for his knife.'

'You wouldn't rather sit outside in the car?'

'What! Down that dark, nasty lane! No, thank you.'

So that settled that. Lock Lane had no streetlights.

I had to try to remember how I'd managed to find Lock Lane before. You get to recognizing corners, buildings on corners, sets of traffic lights. But now it was darkness and everything looked different, and in that section of the town darkness really meant an absence of efficient street lighting. They ought to reverse the lighting arrangements, less perhaps in the spacious centre of the town and more in the depressing outskirts. Rapidly, we became pressed in by high and dead-faced storehouses, and too often we plunged down into black, cavernous under-passes, over which ran railway tracks or major light-twinkling roads, until the streetlights became older and smaller and more widely spaced. Very nearly, I expected to encounter a lamplighter, though he'd have been lonely in those echoing, mournful caverns between unending rows of terraced, sullen-faced tenements, and shops with boarded-up fronts.

Then I recalled my thoughts on it, about the difference between terraced streets running parallel to canals, and those running down to them. I decided we were now driving parallel, and as the next junction offered a downhill to our right, I took it. Fortunately, it was not the street down to the Blue Boar in Farend Lane; miraculously, as the houses thinned and became detached, then became cottages, I realized we were in Lock Lane.

'How clever of you, Richard,' she said.

'It's nothing,' I told her modestly.

I parked the car just beyond Mrs Craythorpe's, switched off the lights, and we got out. As I was locking the door I glanced up. Fleetingly, I thought I saw a shadow move, a shadow against shadows, but my eyes hadn't yet adapted. Quickly I moved round the car, to be at Amelia's side. The shadow moved again. Gently, I manoeuvred her until she was just behind my left shoulder.

Mrs Craythorpe's window was the only light for several hundred yards. It was not bright inside the cottage, but she favoured net curtains, and outside, against the unbroken blackness, it gave an impression of warmth as it flooded softly across the lane. With deliberation I moved forward until I was in the light, then stood still. Friend or foe? The shadow could now take the decisions.

It moved towards me and became a positive shape, then a shape I recognized. It was Ron Phelps.

'Still lookin' for your two per cent, Mr Patton?' His voice was jocular, but his implication sarcastic.

I didn't answer. He peered past me. 'It's Mrs Patton. Hello. This is no place for you, ma'am.' Gone was the aggression; gone was any attempt to dominate with fear.

'I've visited Mrs Craythorpe before,' she told him. 'I found her to be a gentle and interesting old lady.'

'Oh . . . sure.'

'He's in there, isn't he?' I asked. 'Tim. Come home.'

'Not to any big welcome, y' can be sure of that. He knows more than he's said. I know that . . . I know it.'

'Don't make wild guesses, Ron.'

'He told lies. It was the right place we got back to.'

'He said that. Said it was the right place. So he wasn't lying.'

His face was indistinct in the poor light, but he seemed to frown. 'Got the money, he has, whatever he was doin'.'

'Just wild guesses, Ron.'

'How long d'you think it'll be before his ma gets it outa him? The truth. Gets it outa him,' he repeated, as though it hadn't been clear.

'Is that what you're here for?' I asked. 'D'you want to force him into telling *your* truth? Don't you see — to get a bit of peace he would admit to anything, then deny it later. Go home, Ron, you're wasting your time.'

'Go home . . . ' It was said with such a tone of disgust that I wondered where he lived and how he lived. Had he got a bed-sitter — or did he live on the streets and sleep in his car at night?

'Martie's had a go at him,' I commented. 'Martie came off worse.'

'Yeah. A fool, Martie is. Thinks he's only gotta swing his bloody great fists, and that answers it.'

'Go home, Ron.'

'Get stuffed.'

'I'm not going to stand out here arguing with you . . . '

'Then bugger off.'

'I'm going inside to talk to Tim. If you're

intending to wait out here, I'll tell you what he's got to say for himself. Right?'

I saw by the changed shape of his shadow that he had shrugged. 'I'll wait.' It was as though he'd conceded something. 'But all you'll get is a load of lies. The same old thing. But you get this, Mr Bloody Patton.' A moving shape indicated that he had a finger poised, about to jab at my shoulder.

I raised my hand and swept aside his arm, then I walked past him with Amelia carefully on the other side. I banged on the door. 'It's Richard Patton, Mrs Craythorpe.'

'Come on in,' she shouted. 'It's open.'

I thumbed the latch, opened the door, and stood back in the tiny hall for Amelia to go ahead into the living-room.

She was there, as before, in her heavily cushioned chair and in front of her roaring fire, embroidery frame in her hand, needle flickering. She looked up and round, taking a second to focus. 'Hello, dear. How nice of you to call for another little chat.'

'We wanted to see you again,' Amelia told her. 'It's a pleasure, anyway.'

But I, as an ex-policeman, had different thoughts. 'You really ought to bolt your door after dark, you know.'

'It ain't bin bolted for nigh on sixteen years.' She nodded positively. So she still hadn't really accepted Sylvia's death.

Amelia went to her. 'Let me see how it's coming on. Oh . . . that's lovely. You've got that leaf just right! And is this going to be a yellow rose? How *do* you do it? Do you make it up as you go along?'

Clearly pleased, Mrs Craythorpe said, 'Not really. I can sort of see it there, on the canvas. Kind of see it. I just fill it in.'

'Yes.' Then Amelia shook her head, having nothing more to add.

It was the seeing of it that was the trick, visualizing the exact picture. In that lay her remarkable skill. And yet, though she was clearly more relaxed, it was only that she was gradually adapting to Sylvia's death, not that she'd visualized her picture. She had not yet been able to understand the facts of her death. When she did, she would have the picture, and would be able to fill in the details, her mental needle chasing the pattern.

But the atmosphere was certainly more relaxed. Even the fire, after the chill of speaking to Ron Phelps out there in the lurking, prowling hint of a mist, was managing to seem more cheerful. The only temporary shade was Tim, a shape barely tangible, leaning against a side wall and looking sullen. The impression was that he

314

would have preferred to melt into the wall, to seek shelter somewhere else, anywhere.

I said, 'I came for a word with Tim. We heard he was here.'

'Not with me doin' the asking,' said his mother, nodding firmly. 'But it's his home, if he wants one, but only 'cause his dad would want it. Y' hear that, Tim? Cat got your tongue, has it?'

'I ain't sayin' anythin',' he said moodily.

She turned her head sharply. 'An' you just be polite when y're spoken to by a gentleman.' She must have meant me, though I hadn't spoken to him. Then she focused her weary eyes on me, squinting because she was permanently focused on one short distance. 'What's he bin doin', then? The police after him, are they? Wouldn't be surprised. They can have him . . . ' She nodded solemnly, her thin lips pursed, her sniff disdainful. 'Between two slices o' dry bread,' she added.

'What d'you want?' Tim demanded, showing a little defiance.

'Well — to start off with — I want the knife you're carrying. Out in the open. And gently. If it comes out fast I'll break your arm.' I said this, I thought, in a reasonable voice, with no aggression in it.

'Knife!' cried his mother, half on her feet. 'Don't you come your knives here, my lad!

Not in this house. Let's have it.' She straightened herself, five feet three of next to nothing, and glared at him.

'Yar!' he grumbled, but he produced his knife, and, rather than hand it over meekly, he flung it in a corner. A flick-knife. I didn't think they were using them, these days.

Amelia had quietly drawn up a chair, and was seated where she'd sat before. She looked around at where the knife lay, its blade naked, and grimaced. Then she reached over and picked it up, tenderly, using one finger and her thumb.

'Give it to me,' said Mrs Craythorpe, and Amelia parted with it in relief. 'There!' cried the old lady, and it flew to the back of the fire.

And there went any evidence of the stabbing and slashing of Martie Machin, gone were any fingerprints, destroyed was any possibility of the forensic lab accomplishing any DNA matching with Martie's unwholesome blood.

I returned my attention to Tim. 'Martie's in hospital,' I told him.

'Serve 'im right.'

'I see no bruises on you.'

'He's careful. Squeezes, he does, the bastard.'

'It's known as squeezing it out of you,

Tim-lad. The truth. Martie didn't think you'd produced any.'

He stared down at his feet, moving the toe of one shoe in a circle, like a child. 'It were the truth.'

'May we hear a sample?' I asked patiently. 'This truth of yours — are we to hear a sample?'

'What I said before. Always said. Bad, is he?' Smiling at the thought of it. He tried for a giggle, to cheer himself up, but it didn't work. 'Serve 'im right.'

'Let's hear it. What did he ask?'

Now his mother had abandoned her embroidery ring, dropping it on to the seat of her chair. She didn't seem to notice she'd pulled the needle from a thread of yellow silk. It glinted in her fingers. She moved stiffly to stand beside me, frail, wasted, and bristling with anger.

'Tell the man.'

Tim ran his hand over his hair. 'Ain't anythin' he don't already know. We got back to the place — '

'This is the night of the booze-up?' I interrupted. 'Late? Midnight-ish?'

'Yeah. Lemme say it. Come back, we did — an' it'd all gone. No suitcase o' money in the hall, an' no sign of the other two. So we shouted, an' there was nothin', an' Ron says

317

to me to get down in the cellar and check, 'cause nothin' was goin' to get him down there. Scared, he was!' He jeered, his fleshy lips curling. 'So I did, an' they wasn't there, an' no money left. Nothin'.'

'That was what you told Marty, and then he squeezed you?'

'Told 'im a thousan' times, I had. Keeps askin' the same thing.'

'And you still insist it's the truth?'

'Yeah.'

'The general idea is that you could have been lying, that you'd laid it on for Sylvia and the lad to be quiet, and the money was hidden down there with them.'

'No. It weren't.'

'It could have been like that.'

'It wasna.'

'Or maybe it wasn't the right place, and you pretended it was. So that you could go back the next day — '

'No!' This was almost a frantic protest.

'Go back the next day to the right place and pick it up,' I said, because he hadn't let me finish.

'It's a bloody lie.'

'None of that language here,' his mother told him. 'Not in my house.' She held the needle up beneath his nose.

'Ma!'

'Let me,' I asked her quietly. 'You're saying, then, that you didn't go back to the real place, the next day, Tim — the proper place?'

'No. I didn't.'

'I can prove you did.'

'Didn't then.' Another touch of childhood had crept in there.

'You either found the correct place on the night before, and lied about what was there . . . or you found the wrong place and lied about *that*.'

'No! It was the right place. Nothin' there.'

'Tell the truth, you little heathen!' his mother cried, and she jabbed him in the arm with the needle. He gave a squawk. 'Ma!'

'Or the wrong place, and nothing there,' I persisted, having to repeat it to be dead sure.

'The right place!' His voice was rising.

His mother jabbed at his other arm. Embroidery needles aren't long. Sharp, but not long. Tim got the pointed first half-inch of it.

'Tell 'im the truth,' she shouted.

'It's the livin' truth, ma!'

'Which truth?' I asked.

'It was the right place, an' nothin' was there.'

She jabbed at his belly. He jerked, whimpering.

'If nothing was there,' I asked, 'why did you

319

go back the next day?'

'Didn't go back. Yow!' Another jab — his upper arm this time.

'I can prove you did. You were seen there.'

'Didn't!' A jab. A howl. 'Didn't go back,' he insisted desperately. 'Nothin' to go for.'

Jab, jab, jab. 'Tell 'im the truth. D'you hear me!' she screamed.

'It's the truth.' He held up both palms in supplication. Jab, jab. She put a hole in each. She'd had a lot of accurate practice with that needle. 'The truth!' he howled, tears in his eyes now.

I put a hand to her arm, restraining her, partly expecting half an inch of needle myself, she was so worked up.

'I'll put it to you again, Tim,' I said, weary of it now. 'You went back to the right place the next day to collect the money yourself — '

'No. Not the money.'

Jab.

'Then what?'

'I didn't!' he howled, and she hadn't jabbed him.

'Didn't what?'

'Didn't collect anythin'.'

It was a break. He was weakening now. 'But you did go back the next morning?'

'Yes,' he whispered.

'But found . . . nothing?'

'Didn't get the chance to look.'

'Why not?'

'Some bugger chased me off.'

'Language!' his mother said, still monitoring him.

'How?' I demanded.

'Come down in a chopper.'

'Like in the movies?' I asked sarcastically.

'If y' like. He did it, anyways up. Fired a gun at me.'

'How many shots?'

'Was I countin'? Three or four.'

'It was four,' I told him. 'I've got three of the shell cases here.' I showed them to him.

He seemed to sag. He'd had enough of his ma's needle. Perhaps he'd encountered it earlier in his life. I could even pity him in that.

'So you left smartly?'

'Y're too right, matey.'

'Leaving him to pick up the money, is that it? So what d'you suggest he did about Sylvia and the lad?'

There was a silence. His mother had turned away. She had seen evidence of the fact that he was at last telling the truth. Now she paused, not turning back, but with her head cocked. There'd been a mention of her central interest in this affair. Sylvia.

321

'Suggest nothin',' said Tim, more confidence in his voice now he'd settled on the truth. 'Didn't do anythin' with 'em, he didn't. 'Cause they wasn't there, see.'

'How do you know that?' I spaced the words a little. The answer meant so much to me that I didn't want the question misunderstood. 'How can you be sure of that?'

'Because we'd searched the place before, ya stoopid git. Everywhere, house and out in the open, wi' torches. An' I'd been down in the cellar twice more. Slipped down. To be certain . . . to be certain. That's why. They wasn't there, an' the money wasn't there.'

'So . . . ' I sighed. 'In that case, why did you go back, the next day, if you already knew there was nothing?'

He hesitated. His mother had reached her chair. She paused, and half turned back. Tim held up his hand and answered quietly, in a dead voice, ashamed now.

'Because I couldn't believe it, that's why. An' because she was my sister, see. My sister. Ain't I supposed to care what happens to me own sister?'

And because of his shame, that he should have had to admit to a private and secret affection for her, I knew it was the truth. Especially when I looked at him again, and tears were running down his cheeks.

Amelia was slowly getting to her feet. I could see she was distressed, as she failed to replace the chair from where she'd got it.

'That's it, then,' I said. 'Thank you.'

Neither of them answered. I held open the sitting-room door for Amelia, and heard Mrs Craythorpe say, 'Come'n sit by the fire, then. Don't stand over there, you oaf.'

We left quietly. Amelia said not a word until we were in the car. Then: 'That was cruel, Richard.'

'I thought the truth could be important.'

'It's what he'd already said, wasn't it?'

'Almost exactly. But I had to *know* it was the truth. Not something I believed to be the truth — but *know*. Or . . . ' I let it ride, and started the engine.

'Well?' she asked, as I did a three-point turn.

'Otherwise I couldn't take it to Spooner. Not with any confidence.'

'Hmm!'

Our headlights cut the night ahead. Nothing seemed to be stirring. There was no sign of Ron Phelps.

'And now that you're confident — what next?'

'We'll go and see Spooner again.'

'Now?'

'It's on our way home,' I said, logically I

thought. 'Only a little out of our way.' I was driving slowly as we sorted this out.

She gave it a few seconds of consideration. 'He wouldn't be pleased to see you, not at this time. They'll probably be dining. You can't intrude.'

'Oh yes I can. They can just stop their dining. I want to get it finished with, my love. Finished.'

'No hurry . . . surely.' She wasn't going to concede anything now. She was tired, and she knew I was tired.

But she didn't know I'd passed the tired stage long before. I was exhausted. Partly, now, I had to get it cleared away while I could still call on a few reserves of adrenalin. Mostly, it had to be finished because the situation was explosive.

'Bear with me . . . please,' I said, and because I'd never said such a thing before she clutched at my left arm, quite dangerously, really, and said, 'Of course, my love, of course.'

And because she'd never called me 'my love' before, I couldn't reply, merely pointed the bonnet in the general direction of Cumberland House.

But a shape moved from the shadows to the left, and walked into my headlight beams. It was Ron Phelps. I rammed on the brakes, winding down the window at the same time.

'You damned fool!'

I might not have spoken. He merely thrust his face close to the gap and breathed at me. 'Well? What did the bastard say?'

'He said it was the right place you returned to, the night of the booze-up. He said there was nothing there. He admits he returned the next morning — to check. Still nothing. And I know he was telling the truth.'

'Crafty sod. He fooled yer.'

'No. No, Ron.'

'Then why'd he go back the next day?'

I decided that Tim would wish his secret to remain so. In his cherished circle of louts, filial emotion would degrade him. 'To check, just to check! He couldn't believe it, himself.'

He turned his head to spit out his disgust. 'You're soddin' useless, Patton. The swine's still lyin'. I'll get the truth outa him. I'll get it!'

And he stood back.

Grimacing, I wound up the window and drove on. Phelps's breath had reeked of beer.

15

I turned into the drive at nine fifteen by the dashboard clock. Colin Hughes had left the lights on at the dower house, upstairs, downstairs, and in the hall; even the front door was open. We could afford the time for me to get out and go to shut it.

'There's a possibility', I explained, as I slid behind the wheel again, 'that he won't be coming back here.'

I wasn't sure about that, not about anything. The fact was that I was making excuses, now, for any small action that would delay us. I was aching to get it over, but not anxious to approach it.

I rang the door bell. Once again I heard nothing. It seemed that it might not have rung, as we waited and waited. I pressed the button again, leaving my finger longer in place. Then at last there was a sound, the sliding of bolts, the clittering of a lock. The door opened a foot.

'What d'you want at this time?'

It was a woman's voice, slightly wavering as though there might be something to fear. I couldn't see much of her, though the impression was of plumpness. Her hair was a mass of tight, white curls.

'Mr and Mrs Patton to see Mr Spooner,' I told her.

'He can't see you now, he's dining.'

'Tell him I must see him.' I had no quarrel with this woman, who must have been a cook-housekeeper or the like. I tried to sound calm and patient.

'Would you mind coming again in the morning.'

'I'm sorry . . . it must be now.'

She hesitated.

'Believe me,' I told her, 'it's very important to your employer.'

'Oh dear. I don't know. If you'll wait, I'll go and ask. But he'll be very annoyed. Did you say Patton?'

The door began to close, but I got a foot half in. 'We'll wait inside, if you don't mind.' If the door closed, it might never open again.

'Well . . . really . . . '

But my gentle pressure on the door decided it. She wasn't going to be able to close it against me. She stepped back. I put a hand to Amelia's shoulder, and she preceded me. I closed and latched the door behind us.

She stood there for a moment, a red-faced and dumpy woman, considered us from head to toe, and seemed relieved that we appeared to be respectable, though I could barely have reached a minimum standard by that time.

'If you'll wait here.'

She went away. The lighting was low in that vast and echoing hall, the shadows deep. I didn't see which door she disappeared through, but then there was a silence as the last sound soaked into the brickwork. It was broken at last as a chair clattered over. Now I located the door. It was flung open fully as Spooner swept through, carried forward by his anger. They dined in dinner jackets and black bow ties there. It might well have assisted the enjoyment of the meal, but at this time he seemed deficient, in some way diminished to the stature of a normal human who had to eat and drink like the rest of us. He clung to the formality of dress as a boost to his status.

'What *is* this?' he demanded, advancing on us with rapid strides. 'Don't you know what time it is?'

'After office hours, I know,' I agreed, trying to remain cool and calm. 'But I haven't been working office hours, and I'd like to go off duty and head for home. Shall we go into your . . . office, do you call it . . . and I can make my final report?'

I was aware that Julian Rennie had quietly followed from the dining-room. He was wearing a dark grey lounge suit, perhaps in quiet defiance. He seemed to hover on the edge of my perception like a wraith, quietly and unobtrusively, as he had from the beginning, an inconsequential appendage to Spooner, who was only now aware of his presence.

With his hand on the door knob to his office, board-room, lounge — call it what you will — and without turning his head, he spoke to him sharply. 'We shan't be needing you.'

He swung open the door, hand still on the knob.

'Oh, I think we ought to have him with us,' I said mildly. 'We'll certainly need Adrian.'

Spooner was very still, back straight, shoulders stiff. 'What did you say?' This was almost a whisper.

'My mistake, I'm sure,' I apologized. 'The last day or two the name's been on my mind, haunting me. Adrian, Adrian. Over and over. The centre of it all.' I was right behind him now, Spooner seeming unable to move. 'And it's the surname that's been tripping me up,' I went on. 'Adrian's mother . . . she was a Rennie, too. Or Reenee.'

Then he forced himself into moving, hand reaching for the light switches, then walking stiffly into the room and at last stopping and turning round. Those few seconds had allowed him time to arrange his features, but now he seemed rather older than I'd thought him to be. Perhaps it was the dinner jacket. There were creases down his cheeks that I'd not previously noticed; his eyes were sunken, weary, wary. The black tie and jacket reflected a hint of death; it was in his face. Defeat, to a person of Spooner's overpowering necessity to win, would be a kind of dying.

Gently, softly, Julian moved around the room, close to the wall, until he could watch my face. But I turned from them and gestured Amelia to a chair, as Spooner appeared to have forgotten to suggest it. I intended to remain on my feet.

'I want to tell you what happened,' I said. 'You ought to be the first to know. That day, the day the suitcase of money was at last in the hands of those three men . . . that seems a good point to start on. I have it in detail from all three, confirmed by what I've seen myself, and found out by asking. Every detail, I can substantiate. Right? No comments?'

'Get on with it,' he snapped.

'Very well. They finally got back to the place they'd been using to hold Adrian. How old was he then? Five, going on for six? Something like that. He was too young for those three louts to handle — they're none of them fathers — so they'd taken along the younger sister of one of them, not much more than a child herself, sixteen to seventeen. She was there to look after Adrian, and I've no doubt she did the job as well as anybody could, under the circumstances.'

'Is this getting anywhere? You've ruined our meal — '

'I think it's very important, the relation-ships. Naturally, the lad would have been upset and confused and frightened, and he couldn't have been very comfortable. There's a bit of difference between living here with a nanny and existing in a cold cellar with primitive living arrangements.'

'I'm not interested in your social com-ments.' He bit off the words tersely.

'Sorry. Of course you're not. To the nub of it, then. They — those three men — brought the money back to that place I mentioned. It was still daylight. They took the suitcase of money into the hall and opened it up. Sylvia — that's the girl — and Adrian came up from the cellar, which was their home, in order to see. The men went crazy with success. They grabbed handfuls of those tenners, stuck them in their pockets . . . and then they went off to celebrate. No thought of phoning you, no thought of releasing Adrian somewhere public, for him to be brought home. Oh no.

They went off to celebrate . . . and there's irony for you. They were celebrating their new-found wealth, and by the time they returned there wasn't any wealth to celebrate. The money had gone, the girl had gone, and Adrian had gone.'

I paused. Julian was moving slowly around behind Spooner, to where he could watch my face more carefully. Spooner made an impatient gesture.

'Is there much more of this?'

'It's taken sixteen years for the truth to leak out,' I reminded him. 'What's a few minutes now? Let me go on. There'd be one or two explanations of that situation, and that's what has been interesting me. Perhaps they'd gone back to the wrong collapsing building — that's one. It was midnight, and they were drunk. But one of them — Craythorpe, the brother of the girl — said no, because he went down to the cellar to look and the camping equipment was still there. Or he was lying, having previously arranged for all those tenners to be got down there a bit at a time by his sister. Sylvia. Did I tell you her name was Sylvia?'

I was deliberately thrusting the name of Sylvia at him, probing for a reaction. But all it was doing was making him more impatient. 'You did,' he snapped.

'You'll no doubt have heard . . . that's the girl whose body was found locked in a cupboard — by me.'

I stared towards Spooner, but my eyes were focused beyond him. Julian's hand had lifted to his face, as though to hide his expression, or as though he didn't wish to observe the picture I was trying to paint.

Spooner made an impatient gesture. 'Get it said.'

'Very well. Those three men searched that place with torches, the house, the outside collapsed sheds and barns. Craythorpe even went down to the cellar twice more, to check. But still . . . nothing.'

'Is there an end — '

'There's an end,' I assured him. 'Craythorpe went back alone, the next morning, still believing he'd made a mistake. But he didn't get a chance to check, because your man was there — Colin Hughes — there with your helicopter. And Craythorpe was scared away. Hughes sent him packing with bullets buzzing past his head. Now . . . this is the point. I now know that Craythorpe wasn't lying. It was the correct place, and it was empty. That I can now prove, and I'll do so, shortly, for your benefit. But your man, Hughes, was left alone there, on that following morning, and *he* went through the house, and also found nothing. Nothing.'

Spooner had been half-turned, making a gesture to his secretary, who'd made a tiny sound of distress. Then the eyes were back on me, bleak and unresponsive. There was anger in the set of Spooner's jaw.

'He didn't report this to me.' Heavy the thunder was behind that voice. 'I'll demand an explanation — '

'I have the answer. It's quite clear. That place was empty of money and Adrian, by that time. But Sylvia was still there, in the cupboard. But Hughes didn't know that. Did he?'

This, I made a direct question. But it was aimed at myself. It was a possibility I hadn't considered. I paused, wanting time, but Spooner urged me on, speaking in a dangerously suppressed voice.

'Say it . . . for God's sake say it!'

'I hoped *you* would.'

'Say it, damn you. No!' he said violently, because his secretary had moved, in slow tiny paces, to his shoulder. 'Keep out of this.'

Julian didn't answer. His eyes were on me, his lower lip quivering like a reprimanded child's. But he showed no inclination to retreat.

'The fact is', I said wearily, 'that the place was empty that morning, and that's been confirmed by two witnesses. And if the money and Adrian were there when they left for the pub the previous evening, and there was nothing left when they got back at midnight, then the money and the boy were removed between those two times. Not Sylvia. She stayed there, locked in her cupboard. And that leaves only one person who could have removed the other two. Colin Hughes, of course, with the helicopter. You'd have had him out, Spooner, every hour of daylight. And . . . I'd suggest . . . he spotted something down there, landed, and made the rescue. Adrian and the money. Isn't that so?'

Spooner stared at me. Agony was on his face, agony at the fact that he, who ruled his financial empire with words, could find not a single one to offer me.

'It's as you say,' Julian said gently, into the silence.

'And you are Adrian?'

'Yes.'

'Do you remember it?'

'I wish I could forget.' This he said in a tiny, childlike voice, as though being forced to recall it flung him back to that time.

'He had nightmares . . . nightmares,' Spooner burst out. 'For weeks after. Months. We had to have him in our bedroom, to get to him quickly when he woke up screaming, and try to get him back to reality. It was necessary to persuade him he was home and in comfort, not in a nasty cold cellar, and frightened by three vicious criminals. It was a terrible time.'

He had over-amplified. I guessed that self-justification had something to do with that.

'Not that!' Adrian put in, almost defiantly. 'It wasn't the cellar. That wasn't nasty, it was f . . . f . . . fun. Really, that's how I remember it. Sylvie made it fun. Sylvie . . . ' And shockingly he buried his face in his hands and his shoulders shook with the violence of his weeping. 'Oh Sylvie . . . Sylvie . . . ' he managed to say past his sobs.

I had taken him, in his guise as Julian the secretary, as an older man, possibly in his thirties. But this had been because of the retreating hairline — which necessity had possibly dictated, and which could have been induced with hair remover. The necessity would have arisen from the deception, if he was ever to live in this house again. Spooner had not reported his rescue, nor had he declared the recovery of his half a million pounds. He would not have been able to explain the one without involving the other.

'You say you remember it?' I asked Adrian, gently now. His distress was genuine.

He lowered his hands, glistening eyes appearing first above his fingers. 'I'd give . . . ' he whispered, ' . . . I'd give my right arm to forget.'

'That's a convincing offer.' I managed to smile. 'I'd have thought that now . . . '

'Because it was I who killed Sylvie,' said Adrian in a soft, flat voice. *That's* what I can't forget. The moment when I turned that catch on the cupboard door, I killed her.'

I heard Amelia draw in her breath sharply.

'This is ridiculous!' Spooner cut in angrily, having been silent too long. 'I'll not have all this talked about in my house. We never mention that time.'

'Perhaps you should have done,' I told him. 'For example — have you heard about the cupboard door catch?'

'Yes. A fairy story. A fancy running through a child's mind.'

'Will you let me say *one* word!' his son screamed, abruptly and chillingly, because his voice had risen piercingly to a child's falsetto. Almost, I felt, he might stamp a foot. Then he had control. 'I intend to say it.' His voice was stronger. 'Never, never, would they let me talk about it. They wouldn't listen. Silly boy. It's a dream, silly boy. Always that. So I'm going to say it. Now. And if you don't want to hear it, father, then do what you always do

337

when somebody makes a point you don't agree with. There's the door to walk out of, if you don't want to hear.'

Spooner stared at him in what I took to be anger, but perhaps it was only surprise. He shook his head. 'Say it if you must.'

Adrian took a couple of paces forward. It made it more intimate. It was his secret he was confiding.

'We were playing hide-and-seek. Oh, I remember it so clearly. We could just about get up the stairs. Scramble, scramble. There were kinds of heaps of sand and bricks up there. Just right for hiding. Hide-and-seek. It was *that* afternoon, after they'd brought back the money. I didn't know much about what was going on, just that I wanted to go home, and then Sylvie would hug and kiss me if I cried — and we'd play another game. But it was me who was on it that time. Me who got to hide my face and count up to a hundred. I don't remember if I could do that — count to a hundred. Anyway, I know I could count to twenty all right, so I did that, all slow and shouted out. Sylvie's rule, that was. Always making little rules, she was. Little boys get the littlest of the peas, when she opened a can. I remember — we sorted them. She made a game of that. Oh yes . . . I remember . . . it's like yesterday.' He stopped, as though

338

awed by that thought.

And maybe it was always like yesterday, to the Adrian who had tried to hide behind the trick of forgetting all the yesterdays. But now they were tossed aside. Almost with welcome, he burst through a whole fortification of yesterdays, until he could face the one he'd been dreading. Yet now, that dread had become a hope. A glimmer of hope. Because Sylvie was now positively dead, and there was no more having to face it all as a nightmare.

'I remember . . . ' Dreamily now, but he shook himself fully awake. 'The men had gone. Nasty men, that's all they were to me. They'd gone away, and the money was there. I knew all about money. I'd been taught about money, and it was all there. And Sylvie held my hand and told me, 'Adie,' she said. She called me Adie. 'Adie, look what you're worth. Isn't that a lot!' And I hugged her and kissed her then, because . . . because, as I told her, she was worth twice more, ten times more, a trillion times. Then we played hide-and-seek, and the cupboard was a favourite hide. But somehow . . . I don't know . . . I seem to remember thinking that daddy had paid all that money for me, which must have meant he wanted me back. That was all confusing to me — part of the nightmare. I thought at first, you see, that

339

daddy had paid for me to be taken away, because he didn't want me.'

Spooner drew in a short, shuddering breath.

Now that he was launched, Adrian poured it out. But he was sweating freely, interspersing his words with small, childish smiles and with glances at his feet.

'What's all this nonsense!' demanded Spooner angrily. 'I've never heard . . . ' But his face was grey.

'No, you've never heard.' There was now a hard disgust in Adrian's voice as he cut in. 'Because you've never had the time to listen. Well . . . listen now.' He returned his attention to me, flashing a brief, apologetic grimace at Amelia.

'However it was, I know I got the idea that if I was worth that much money, then I ought to be going home, and if nobody was going to take me . . . ' He shrugged that aside. 'It was Sylvie's turn to hide, and I knew she'd got in the cupboard under the stairs. I heard it close. And I was supposed — it was part of the game — to go all over the house, pretending. But this time, because I thought I was supposed to, because daddy had sent the money, I ran outside and right away from the house. And so that Sylvie couldn't come after me and grab my jersey and say, 'Got you, you little tinker,' I turned the catch on the cupboard door. *Then* I ran out. And Uncle Colin — '

'Uncle?'

Spooner shook his head. He'd said nothing relevant for quite a while. A man who always wins knows when he's lost, and remains quiet, contained . . . and bereft.

'Daddy's chopper was there, and Uncle Colin, as I thought of him, brought me home. Here. And nobody would believe me. Sylvie was in the cupboard, and nobody would listen. And go and get her out,' he whispered.

Abruptly, he turned away. This was his nightmare. I'd had the same one — talking to people, appealing to them, and they looking right through me and not answering. But his nightmare was one from which he couldn't wake.

'And somehow,' he said, his back to us, 'I've managed to persuade myself it wasn't true, that she hadn't been in the cupboard at all.' He turned back, a sudden angry whirl. 'But she was. All these years. And it was me who shut her in there.'

Then he gave a short, hunted glare, first to his father and then to us, with his head lowered, and turned away, walking rapidly to the door.

'Adrian!' his father barked.

But Adrian took no notice, when Julian would have stiffened to a halt. He opened the door, walked through, and closed it very gently behind him. Then we heard his running heels on the mosaic-tiled floor, his feet pounding up the stairs.

Spooner stood very still, staring at the door.

'And you?' I asked.

He turned slowly, his face blank. 'Me?'

'You did nothing about the girl.'

'When we got him back, the lad was screaming. About Sylvie, which meant nothing to us. And about a cupboard, back at the place. We couldn't make sense of it. What cupboard? And he wept and wept, and my wife was distraught, and I gathered that this Sylvie person was locked in. Shut. Fastened. I didn't know.'

'But you did nothing,' I insisted.

'I sent Hughes back with the chopper — a floodlight on it, because it was dark by then. But he came back . . . two hours later. God, those two hours! Came back and said he couldn't locate the building. So I sent him out the next morning. Nobody had had a wink of sleep. Adrian, yes — for a few minutes, but that was from exhaustion. Then he'd wake up, screaming again.' He shrugged. His voice was flat, emotionless. 'So I sent

Hughes back as soon as it was light enough, and he managed to locate the place . . . ' His voice tailed off.

'And chased Craythorpe off with four shots over his head?'

'Yes. So I was told. Do we have to go into — '

'And he found nothing?' I persisted.

'He found the cupboard.'

'He did?' I glanced at Amelia. Her hand was covering her mouth. 'And did he open it?'

'Yes.'

'And . . . '

'She was dead,' he said, now in a monotonous monotone. 'He shut the door and latched it again, and . . . ' He shrugged. 'And came back.'

There seemed to be an extended silence in the room. The words ran round the walls, and died away. But they left behind them their message.

'And still you kept it all to yourself?' I said at last.

'We had a distraught child on our hands,' he snapped, on the offensive now. 'We couldn't do anything for him that time wouldn't heal. I thought he'd eventually forget. Children do. I was certain he wouldn't if we told him the girl was dead. The idea was

343

to try to persuade him she'd got free and run away. And d'you imagine I dared report we'd got Adrian here! Would you have liked a child of yours, close to hysteria, having to answer the questions they'd throw at him? That *you* would've thrown at him,' he challenged. He made a savage gesture. 'He had brought about a death. By latching that door. They'd have had their experts on it, your lot, the police, and courts . . . '

'A child! They'd not do that. You're talking nonsense, Spooner.'

'I didn't dare risk it. My wife was close to a breakdown, too. No . . . '

'You could have — '

'No!' Now his voice was like a whiplash. 'I wanted quiet for him, no pressure, not the slightest suggestion that he could've known what he was doing, and no suggestion that it'd been . . . deliberate.'

'No one would suggest — '

'I knew how it would've been.'

'I don't believe this! You couldn't have kept his return secret — when we'd thrown in the resources of half the police force — for such a reason. I was *there*, Spooner. I know how it would've been. We'd have gone gently, quietly, hushed it up and kept the details from the press. Sylvia's death would've gone down as misadventure.'

He dismissed this with a lift of his head, a thin smile of contempt. 'I didn't think it advisable to risk it. Do you imagine I can't make my own decisions!' He was angry that anybody should challenge that ability. 'When Adrian was more quiet and more tractable, I packed him off with his mother to stay with her sister in New Zealand.'

'Your wife . . . '

'I never saw her again. But I made her a very generous allowance. She wrote that she didn't want me to visit them there. So she died in New Zealand — and Adrian came home to me. He was eighteen, and he'd aged terribly. Not simply grown up — but aged. So I took him back as my secretary — with minimal duties,' he commented sourly. 'And if it hadn't been for that pest George Tate, there need never have been any more trouble.'

'Of course not.' I was unable to keep an acid bite from my voice. 'No one else involved, was there? But you — you had Adrian back. Trouble there, yes, but he was alive, and you knew he was alive. Yet it didn't occur to you that the girl, Sylvia, might have parents. Her father committed suicide. Her mother has lived the past sixteen years with no lock on her door, only a latch, and bolts she never uses. That's so that she can hear the

345

latch thumbed up, and it might be her daughter — at last. And the bolts not thrown across so that Sylvia could walk back in. And because she didn't know her Sylvia was really dead, there's always been that minimum chance. This never occurred to you, I suppose? That woman waiting . . . waiting . . . '

I was piling it on, trying to provoke one small hint of an emotional understanding. I was wasting my time, though.

He flicked a hand. 'I'll make sure she's provided for. And if I can see her . . . I'll get her to understand . . . I had to do what I could for my son. Where does she live? Some wretched hovel . . . I'll lift her out of that . . . her own bank account — '

I cut in angrily. 'Oh, that's just fine! Money'll cover it, money'll cure all ills. But it's not going to get you out of this, Spooner. There's more to it than this pathetic concern for your son — your wife and your son — that you've been trying to get across. More. And there's only one thing more important to you . . . your money. Adrian's welfare didn't come into it, did it? Try to convince me that your main concern at that time wasn't your half a million pounds. Money! You make me feel sick.'

'How dare you! This is absurd. I find you offensive . . . '

'Not absurd. It was the blasted money. Go on. Tell the truth and shame the devil. The money.'

'It was mine. Why should I tell anybody . . . '

I very nearly threw a fist at his face, to silence him. In order to control myself I went on wildly, reaching for something that might harry him. '*Your* money — no! You're the expert on the twisting and turning of money, so how does this sound? You'd traded half a million for Adrian, and you'd got him back. So the money belonged to those three louts who took him. Happy thought! Perhaps they could take a civil action against you — perhaps I could persuade them to. Farcical! Outrageous! Oh yes. But if it got to court, and they subpoenaed me as their witness — oh . . . what I'd have to say under oath! Where would your reputation be then, Spooner?'

Strangely, he smiled. 'You're working hard for it,' he said, his lip curling round the words. 'Your two per cent,' he amplified.

I moved a pace towards him. He raised a palm. 'Two per cent, you told me. That's ten thousand. I'll give you a cheque. Adrian's enough of a secretary to be able to draw a cheque. I'll just get him . . . ' He moved towards his desk, and actually had his internal phone in his hand before I slammed it back again, my fist clamped on his wrist.

'Listen,' I said, very softly, very close to his face. 'Don't ever offer me any of your rotten money. Never. If I keep quiet about this, it'll be because too many people have already been hurt. But, at the snap of a finger, by heaven, Spooner, I'll ruin you.'

His eyes were steady on mine. Then he smiled. Nastily. 'You?' He snatched his wrist free.

'It takes very little,' I told him. 'This financial empire of yours, how delicately is it poised? You had half a million pounds returned to you. What you call your money, and which had to be filtered back carefully into your various accounts. Secretly. Laundering your own money.'

He walked away. Then he turned and faced me again, well clear of my fists. His eyes were gleaming, as though he felt a moment of triumph. 'If I kept Adrian's return silent, I'd have had to keep the return of the money silent. Just pretend I'd lost it. See sense, man. Your mind's in a tangle.'

I inclined my head to Amelia. She rose to her feet, not quite with her usual grace, I thought, but with a hint of stiffness. Tension.

She moved towards the door, but I hadn't quite finished with Spooner. Something he'd said . . .

'But if you fed your money back into your accounts secretly, it would still have appeared on your books as a loss. Yes? So don't tell me you failed to claim the half-million as a tax loss.' I saw the flicker in his eyes. It had struck home, straight and true. 'A trading loss, the outgo of funds for a consideration that'd failed. But . . . if I were to drop a word to my friends in the police, and they to the Fraud Squad, and they to the Inland Revenue — how long would it be before they pounce on *all* your financial interests and off-shore accounts, and start taking it all apart? Don't tell me — I know. Your kind of life is based on trust and confidence. It wouldn't stand the full glare of careful probing. Your empire could be destroyed, Spooner. You with it. And all because you were greedy. It wasn't enough that you got your money back — you found time to think up a tax fiddle. Your money, always your money — first and last.'

'Damn you . . . get out of here. I'm not going to listen to you lecturing me on what I do with my own money.'

'But it wasn't your money, father.'

The words, so telling in quietness, cut sharply in contrast through our raised voices.

349

None of us had noticed that the door had opened, but it was Adrian's voice.

We turned to face him. He stood in the doorway with one hand still on the door knob, the other holding a small suitcase. He was wearing a light raincoat, but was bare-headed. He had found time to collect his thoughts and his emotions together, and was calm, quietly dignified.

'I came to say goodbye, father,' he said, 'but I couldn't help overhearing. Do you really imagine my mother didn't tell me everything she could remember? Oh yes . . . I know she was almost unconscious for most of the time, but that was towards the end. Your doctors had her under sedatives or tranquillizers — God alone knows what. But she remembered the beginning, the ransom demand, and how the money was got together.'

'I won't have you saying — '

'I say it now, or I publish it in the newspapers. Choose. Go on, say which you'd prefer. It's always been you making the decisions.'

Adrian was quietly emphatic. A breaking point had been reached and surmounted. He was his own man. His fresh but already mature confidence needed no emphasis to back it.

Spooner snapped, 'Say it.'

'It wasn't your money.' Adrian flicked us a smile. 'My mother's, that's what it was. You couldn't raise the money, father, that's the truth of it. No liquidity, as they say. What was the reason? My mother didn't know that. Was it an important takeover — or fighting to prevent a takeover? It doesn't matter. But she knew you wanted that newspaper group in the USA. Whatever it was, you'd already clawed in every penny from your secret off-shore investments, and didn't dare to borrow. Spooner borrowing at that time . . . it would mean he was in trouble, and the other vultures would circle you, waiting. And you'd plundered God knows how many company and trust funds. No . . . the truth is that you weren't able to buy my freedom. So my mother did. It was her inheritance from her father. She could just raise it, and it left her almost destitute. My mother's money . . . and when you got it back . . . ' He shrugged, a magnificent contempt in the lift of his narrow shoulder. 'When you got it back she was drugged, mostly unconscious, and all she knew about it was that I was back. All that mattered to her.'

'I don't know why she'd tell you such a load of — '

'Let me say it. She never did know you got it back. It wasn't until I returned here that I found out. But you'd got it back, and not one measly, paltry pound of it found its way to my mother. An allowance! How magnanimous of you! You fed it back into your own accounts. And you sent us away to New Zealand — well out of the way.'

He smiled at me. He smiled at Amelia. His face was set when he faced his father.

'I simply put my head in to say goodbye, father. I hope we never meet again, but I want to thank you for the spendid education in high finance you've given me. I intend to devote all I've learned to destroying all you've built up. I'll just mention that I hate you with all my heart and soul. Good-night.'

He nodded to Amelia and me, and quietly closed the door behind him.

Spooner stood, very still and pale, facing the door. I had released his wrist before Adrian interrupted, but he still held the phone. Slowly, he replaced it. There was now nobody to answer it.

'But *still,* when it wasn't your loss, you managed a tax fiddle,' I said to him softly. 'No, don't deny it. I saw it in your eyes. You did well out of it — very well.'

'And you?' His voice was no more than a whisper. 'There's your loss, too. Your two per cent . . . of nothing. For your silence about this, I will — '

'For that,' I assured him bitterly, 'you can only hope and pray. Shame the devil again.'

Amelia was now holding open the door. I saw her lips move, but heard nothing. But I knew it was an appeal. No violence, Richard, please. She was very pale. I walked over to her and put my arm round her shoulders as we paced across that empty, echoing hall. She was shaking.

I closed the front door behind us. The night air seemed cool and sweet. Clearly, we could hear rapid footsteps heading around the side of the house. To the garages, no doubt.

But he got no chance to overtake us along the drive. I was in too much of a hurry to get away from there.

16

I took the Granada fast out of the drive, turning at last for home. But I wasn't fast enough to hold off the Porsche, which blasted past me, away from home for him.

'Stop a minute, Richard, will you,' said Amelia quietly.

Surprised, I drew to a halt. 'What is it, love?'

'Aren't you driving the wrong way?'

'I thought not.'

She sighed. 'You'll think of it half-way home, then you'll have that much more driving to do.'

'Think of what?'

'Spooner didn't tell *all* the truth, did he? And I don't think Colin Hughes did, either. Not the truth, the whole truth, and nothing but the truth. Don't you think?'

She was only dimly visible there, sitting sideways beside me and staring worriedly at me. I said, 'I don't understand. I suppose I must be too tired.'

'But Richard — think. The exact truth could matter. To Mrs Craythorpe it could matter a lot.'

I tried to shake my weary brain into activity, shuffling the facts around and taking a second look at them. Then I got it. 'Yes,' I said. 'I see.'

I used the verge to turn, and headed once more for Potterton. It was not so fast as our previous run, and not made with my usual confidence in my reflexes. I was making small errors: the wrong line through corners, and braking a fraction late. But we found the hospital car-park safely, and very dark and dreary it seemed, almost empty of parked cars because it was long past the official visiting hours.

We now knew the way, and there was no hesitation. Once more along that corridor, past Carnation and Primrose and Anenome. Ridiculously, I noticed that they'd spelt it incorrectly.

The waiting room of Tulip was now nearly empty. There was only a distressed woman in a corner, and Hughes walking round in circles. He saw us, and stopped, staring. He hadn't been expecting to see us there again.

'Well?' I asked.

He came over and clutched at my arm. 'She's showing signs of coming round.'

'Well then . . . why not go home and get some rest, and come again in the morning. About ten, the lady said.'

'Home!' he said. Then he seemed to shake himself free of his personal concerns. 'I didn't expect you back.'

'No,' I agreed. 'We didn't intend to. Not tonight, anyway. But we've been to visit your Mr Spooner, and what we've heard has raised a few points.'

He stared into my face for a few moments, as though feeling he might see those points laid out there. 'A lot I care for his points,' he declared with contempt. He turned for a moment and glanced at the woman in the corner. 'Her mother's had a heart attack.'

'Yes . . . well . . . we've got other things to talk about, Colin. Don't try to distract me.'

Amelia said, 'Oh dear.' She was referring to the woman in the corner, I thought. Or her mother.

'Distract you from what?' Hughes demanded suspiciously.

'What I wanted to say to you. To start with, there's a gap in Spooner's story. According to him, you found the place — this is on the evening that the money was collected — found the place, as I said, and you picked up Adrian and the money. That's clear enough, but it's a bit thin. Don't you think? Can you pad it out for me? More detail, please.'

He ran a hand over his hair. 'Detail, detail. Won't it wait?'

'Not really.'

'What d'you want to know, then?' He glanced towards the swing doors to the ward.

'It's all right, you know. They're not going to be calling you for some considerable time. You can dare to concentrate on what I'm saying. Let's start with how you managed to spot Adrian down there, anyway. He'd be no more than a dot.'

'Chance.' His heavy shoulders lifted. 'Sheer chance. I'd seen a car, heading away . . . away from somewhere, so I traced the track back to the place it'd come from, and damned if I didn't see little Adrian running out into the open. Moving things attract the eye, you know. You learn that — '

'Never mind. You spotted him running away from the house. Then what?'

'Well . . . I put down of course, and naturally he knew me. Knew the chopper too. But he was acting kind of funny. Hesitating. Not coming running to me. For a sec or so it looked like he was gonna turn round and run back. It was almost as though he didn't want to go home. When I ran after him and caught up with him and grabbed his arm, he kept shouting something about Sylvie, Sylvie. I couldn't make head nor tail of it. Anyway, I got him in the chopper. Had to stick him under my arm, and him kicking all the way. Got him in the chopper, as I said, and I had to lock the door on him. I hadda get back to the house of course. Well . . . there was the money, see. So I ran back there, and it was all laid out for me. A gift. A suitcase full of money lying in the hall. I just shut the case and hefted it out, and humped it to the chopper.'

Amelia touched my arm and spoke softly. 'The girl, Sylvia, could well have been alive at that time. Almost certainly, she'd be. Didn't she shout, Colin? Didn't you hear anything from the cupboard?'

He shook his head at her. 'Not a thing. Not a sound.'

But they had been playing hide-and-seek, and she would most likely have kept silent, whatever she heard. At that time, she could not have known that Adrian had turned over the catch.

'And Adrian?' I asked, getting back to the original story.

'When I got back to the chopper I began to wonder how I'd get in. He was hammering on the door, and when I opened it he was a struggling bundle of screams. Yelling about Sylvie and cupboards, and fighting and kicking when I tried to climb into the cab.

But I managed to get in, with a handful of my hair in his fist.'

'And you didn't go back to the house?' I asked, a bit of my weariness coming out in the harshness of my voice.

'I had to get on the radio to Spooner, to report in.'

'Of course. Spooner came first. So you didn't go back?'

'No.' He glanced again at the double doors, but there was no activity.

'I thought you said . . . oh, never mind. Why didn't you go back? Adrian was screaming at you, telling you that Sylvie was in the cupboard. Surely it had to mean something. I'd have gone back to check. Pretty well anybody would have done. But you didn't, apparently.'

'I'd got the boss on the radio. He said fly straight back to the house, and there was something in his voice . . . ' Again the shoulders lifted, but minimally.

'Didn't you tell him what Adrian was saying?'

'Tried to. He wouldn't listen. As far as he was concerned, we were talking about one of the gang, and the orders were to get away from there smart-like.'

'And Adrian?'

'It was all I could do to get it off the

ground, Adrian climbing all over me and punching me in the face and screaming at me to go back, go back.'

'But still you didn't.'

He shook his head. 'Nobody crosses Spooner. Never.'

I glanced at Amelia. Sad, sad, she looked, fingers to her lips, her eyes wide and swimming.

'And anyway,' Colin continued, 'the way I reckoned — once I'd got the hang of the hide-and-seek business — if she'd hidden herself in the cupboard, she'd be able to get out again. Sounds reasonable.'

Was he asking me that? If so, it was weak. Adrian would've said about the catch. Sure to have done. But Spooner wielded the power.

'So all right,' I said, trying to keep my voice level. 'You presumably got back to Cumberland House safe enough, and you delivered Adrian to the fond parents, to his mother, if she was conscious, and the money to Spooner. So why didn't you fly back at once? You couldn't have been more than ten minutes away, by chopper.'

'Eight.'

'So why didn't you?'

In the waiting room, silence was expected. We had been talking quietly, but now his voice rose, an echo of a past anger.

'Because Spooner wouldn't let me, not once he'd heard that we'd been seen by nobody. He stuck his hand out and demanded the chopper's ignition key. I was the employee. It was his chopper. I hadda give it him. It'd all gotta be secret, that was it. Don't you bloody well know him, Patton?'

'I think so. A little. I can guess why he wanted it kept quiet.'

'Huh!' It was a grunt of disgust. 'Because of Adrian — *he* said. Not wanting him pestered. I mean . . . I wanted him to get on the phone and tell the police we'd got him back. I was feeling kind of great about it — that I'd rescued him. Why shouldn't I? But no, we had to keep it all secret, he said. Somethin' about Adrian being so distressed . . . Tcha! What'd distressed Adrian was that damned cupboard back at the place. And I could've gone back there an' then and sorted it all out. Pestered! A lot Spooner woulda worried about that. Nah . . . I reckon it was something more important to him. And what's the most important thing in Spooner's life? His money, that's what.'

'What exactly do you mean by that?' I asked, no tone in my voice.

He shook his head. 'I don't know.' Then he demonstrated that in fact he did. 'Me . . . I reckon that in the ten minutes it took to get back and inside, he'd worked out some fiddle or other he could work with that half a million — if nobody ever knew he'd got it back.'

He certainly knew his man. It was a pity he'd been afraid to cross him. 'Well, that's really great!' I said. 'So you went along with it?'

He shook his head, shaggily, violently. 'It was dark, anyway, by the time we'd finished shouting at each other. So there was no point. I'd never be able to find it in the dark.' He smiled thinly, reaching for approval. 'But I went back the next morning. You know that.'

'Spooner told me he sent you back, that night, with a floodlight on the chopper,' I said to him, weary of arguing.

He sighed. 'A lie. We didn't have a floodlight, not then. I *did* go back the next morning.'

'I also know you were lying about *that*. The details don't mesh in.'

'Well . . . yeah. He'd had time to work out a story. I had to keep in line with that. How d'you know?'

'I've heard it all from him.'

He made a disgusted sound. 'Oh, that's dandy. He'll be insane when I get back . . . when I go . . . ' He shook that, too, from his mind.

'I didn't mean that, as it happens. I was talking about the man you shot at. He wasn't driving there, as you told it. Was he? He was already there when you spotted him.'

'How d'you know that?'

'I know he went there on his own. You would have no way of knowing he was alone, from the chopper. He got out, you said. In that case, you still wouldn't have known he'd got no mates in the car. Or that they weren't armed, No, Colin. You lied. You've got the experience. You'd have waited. You'd have been very cautious. You lied. Let's hear the truth — I'm so damned tired of lies.'

He looked across at the woman and grimaced, then to me he said, as though that second had given him time to make a decision, 'He was standing by the car when I spotted him. It looked like he was just going to get in. I put down. He didn't move. I wasn't caring if anybody was armed or not — there were only three of 'em, anyway. I could've taken them out before they knew it. No. I put down. He was on his own, standing there. I told him to go. Different words, though. Put four shots over his head, and off he went.'

'So you didn't really know whether he'd been in the house and come out again, or just arrived?'

'Well . . . no . . . I suppose not.' He spoke with caution.

'What *do* you know?' I demanded, my patience running thin.

'It's nothing.'

I poked him in the chest with my finger. I tried to shout in a whisper. 'Tell me! Tell me, blast you!' It came out all hoarse.

He looked at me with a hint of trepidation, at the aching suppression of my fury, no doubt.

'If it's any help . . . ' He shuffled his feet, looking down at them. 'If it helps you at all . . . I went inside the building. I had to check what Adrian had said. You've gotta see that. For me — for me! I had to find that cupboard. I mean, it could've been a kid's story.'

'And you found it?' Amelia whispered. It was not really a question; Spooner had said that.

'Didn't have to look far.' He grimaced. 'Sorry . . . but the door was wide open.'

Sorry? For whom was he sorry?

'And?' I demanded.

'She was in there. Dead. Don't look at me like that, Patton, I've seen enough dead people to know. She was dead and cold. Oh Christ — she was stone cold.'

'And then?'

'I shut and latched it again.'

I couldn't say anything; couldn't trust myself to speak. My fist was thumping, thumping against my thigh. Then at last I got it out, a weak voice because I'd used up too much in fighting against it. 'Do you realize what you've done? Damn you, Hughes, can't you imagine . . . sixteen years! Sixteen bloody years her mother's waited! For pity's sake, you could have told *somebody*.'

Then strangely it was he who was angry, his face red with strain and his eyes wild.

'Do *you* know, Patton, you with all your fancy words — d'you really know what Spooner's like? You don't! Let me tell you: if I'd said a word about his damned secret, he'd have had me hunted down. Yes . . . me . . . and d'you think I could've defended myself against *them*, the people he'd pay to kill me? Not a chance. Watch my back? Not every second, I couldn't. Anywhere in the world, he'd get me. Oh, leave me alone . . . leave me *alone*, will you!'

So that was why he'd been watching Mrs Craythorpe's cottage, wondering whether it was now safe to go to her and confess it all.

I touched Amelia on the arm. 'Shall we go?'

She hesitated, facing Hughes. 'I'm sure she'll be all right. Both of you. All right.' She reached across and touched his arm.

Then we left. The corridor seemed twice as long as it had been. Lily Ward. I hadn't noticed that one. Lilies are used in wreaths. Not a good name for a ward, I thought. I wondered whether to ask Amelia if she agreed, then I realized that my mind was skating around the problem, searching for something more pleasant than what I had to contemplate.

'The stars are out,' she said, as we stood beside the car, and I knew that she, too, realized. Therefore, I didn't need to consult her.

We got inside and drove to Lock Lane. I couldn't remember driving there, only that we drew up a little beyond Mrs Craythorpe's cottage, just past the soft sprawl of light from her window.

'Richard,' she whispered. 'What Colin told you . . . you can't tell her *that*.'

'No. I can't.'

I banged on the door. 'It's me and the missus again, Mrs Craythorpe,' I called out, in a hideous attempt to sound jovial.

'Come in. It's open.'

I thumbed the latch. Yes, it was still unbolted. We walked in. Tim wasn't there. She had finished the roses, and put them aside. What was emerging now was a white, trumpet shape. It could well become a lily.

She said, 'Sit yourself down, my pet.' To Amelia, that was. 'How nice to see you again'. She glanced round at me. 'The funeral's on Monday.'

Nothing was real to her. For sixteen years, reality had ceased to exist.

'We've come to tell you how it happened,' I said, warming my behind in front of the fire. I didn't need to explain what 'it' I meant.

'I'd like to know.'

'Sylvia got shut in a cupboard.'

'Oh — I know that. Somebody's said that.'

'Perhaps it was me.'

'More'n likely. But it doesn't matter now.'

'We just thought you ought to know it was an accident. A child's game that went wrong. Not intentional. The lad threw the catch over . . . '

'How terrible.'

'It wouldn't have been so . . . ' began Amelia, then she bit her lower lip to silence.

'For the child, dear,' Mrs Craythorpe explained.

'Yes,' my wife agreed softly. 'Yes.'

'But it's over now.'

'It is.' Amelia looked dazed.

'All over. No use crying over spilt milk.'

Then there was a long drawn-out silence, until she suddenly added, 'No need for you to rush away.'

She was gently hinting that she'd sensed our uneasiness.

'But we'd better go,' said Amelia. 'It's getting late. Tim'll be home . . . '

'Oh, I don't expect so,' she said, and she heaved herself to her feet. 'It's been nice meeting you.'

We smiled. I made a silly sort of salute; I thought she deserved one. We went out, and the latch clicked behind us.

'A wonderful woman,' said Amelia, breathing it.

'Indeed.'

We stood out on the roadway. Ahead of us the light was enough to guide our feet back to the car. And other feet, it seemed. Two of them were planted solidly, well apart. The light managed to seep upwards to the knees, no further. I advanced, reaching out to restrain Amelia. You never know. Now it was a complete shape, but with nothing positive about the features.

'He isn't home,' I said.

'Who isn't?' It was Ron Phelps's voice, but harsh and distorted.

'Tim, Ronnie. Not at home. I don't think he's expected. Did you want him?'

Now, I was moving slowly towards him, cautiously because there'd been a tone in his voice that had echoed anger and frustration, all in those two words.

'Bloody lyin' toad,' Phelps jerked out. 'All the way. Lyin'.'

'He didn't lie.

'The wrong place. He took us back t' the wrong place.'

'No he didn't. Ron . . . you've got to listen to me.' I touched his left arm. There was fury in the manner he jerked it away.

'I ain't listenin' to you, Patton. He lied, the little creep. All the way through. Went back, he did, the next day, to collect the money. An' Sylvia was there — and he killed her.'

'No, Ron. Why don't you try to understand? I'm trying to lay it out for you. He went back to — '

'Told yer. He went back. He said it. Said it to me.'

But when had he said that? 'Will you listen!' Now I had to hold on to his arm. He seemed to sag. I thought he groaned. 'Yes, Ron, he went back, but it was just to take another look round for Sylvia. That's all.'

'It's you now. You lyin'!' he cried.

I held his arm tighter, as he'd tried to pull away. The whimper could have been a suppressed oath. But I had to get him to understand.

'And he found her, Ron,' I went on. 'I've got proof of that. I can prove everything now.

He found her *then*, Ron. That next morning. She was already dead, in that cupboard. Stone cold dead. That I can prove, too.'

'And has he told anybody that!' he shouted, his face distorted. 'Has he said one bleedin' word . . . ' He seemed to stab a finger towards the cottage.

'He could well have thought it was better . . . ' He tried to pull away from me. 'Better not to say a word about it, with you three — '

'D'you know what? You make me sick, Patton. Sick to the guts. Let go of my arm, damn you.'

I didn't; I wanted him there, to hear this. 'Would he dare admit he'd been back there?' I demanded, quietly but intensely. 'You two wonderful mates of his would've assumed he'd gone back for the money — and you'd have taken him apart, a bit at a time, to get him to admit it. And killed him if he didn't. Or if he did. Admit it.'

'The truth. We only wanted the truth.' But it was a weak appeal.

'And he's never set eyes on the money — '

'Sod the money.'

I shook his arm in exasperation. 'I can prove all this. Prove it.'

'Leggo my arm,' he whispered. There was murder in his voice now.

I released him. He turned away, seemed to stagger, then he began a slow walk away up the slope. An uncertain walk, rambling.

I watched him sway out of the small spread of light, and realized my hand was sticky. Amelia stood back quickly as I dived for the car, wrenched open the door, and reached in for the torch.

It was blood on my hand.

I threw the beam after him. He hadn't gone far, was weaving along slowly as though drunk. Blood was dripping from the fingers of his left hand.

'Ron!' I called, but he moved slowly away. I knew then that Tim had been carrying a second knife.

I lowered the beam and scanned the road surface. The blood drops led back down the lane. I called to Amelia, 'Stay here. In the car.' And I began to run, down towards the locks, down towards the dim lights in the old gatehouse. Down as far as the nearest lock.

Panting, I leaned against the gatearm, for support. Then I stiffened my legs and forced myself to the edge of the lock and aimed the torch. The water was low. At the bottom, face down in what was more slime than water, lay Tim Craythorpe. Now all the urgency departed. His head was at a strange, impossible angle, yet he couldn't have broken his neck in a fall of no more than ten feet. There was no hurry. No necessity to raise alarms. An anonymous phone call would cover it. As Sylvia had been dead — no hurry to release her from the cupboard.

I turned away. The lane seemed steeper than it had been. Amelia ran down to meet me and took the torch from my hand. I hadn't been aiming it, anyway. She took my arm.

'If you can get us out of the town, I'll drive the rest,' she offered gently.

'Yes.' I would have agreed to anything.

We reached the car. Swaying, I watched Amelia climb in. I opened the driver's door, and paused.

Mrs Craythorpe was throwing over her bolts. They were rusty with sixteen years of disuse. But she managed it. Clack, clack! Nobody would be coming home.

I got behind the wheel and we drove away.

We do hope that you have enjoyed reading this large print book.

Did you know that all of our titles are available for purchase?

We publish a wide range of high quality large print books including:
Romances, Mysteries, Classics
General Fiction
Non Fiction and Westerns

Special interest titles available in large print are:
The Little Oxford Dictionary
Music Book
Song Book
Hymn Book
Service Book

Also available from us courtesy of Oxford University Press:
Young Readers' Dictionary
(large print edition)
Young Readers' Thesaurus
(large print edition)

For further information or a free brochure, please contact us at:
Ulverscroft Large Print Books Ltd.,
The Green, Bradgate Road, Anstey,
Leicester, LE7 7FU, England.
Tel: (00 44) 0116 236 4325
Fax: (00 44) 0116 234 0205

DUMMY HAND

Susan Moody

When Cassie Swann is knocked off her
bike on a quiet country road, the driver
leaves her unconscious and bleeding at the
roadside. A man later walks into a police
station and confesses, and they gratefully
close the case. But something about this
guilt-induced confession doesn't smell
right, and Cassie's relentless suitor Charlie
Quartermain cannot resist doing a little
detective work. When a young student at
Oxford is found brutally murdered,
Charlie begins to suspect that the two
incidents are somehow connected. Can he
save Cassie from another 'accident' — this
time a fatal one?

SHOT IN THE DARK

Annie Ross

When an elderly nun is raped and
murdered at a drop-in centre for drug
addicts, the police decide it's a burglary
gone wrong. Television director Bel
Carson sees pictures of the body, and is
convinced that this was a ritualistic
murder, carried out by a sadistic and
calculating killer. Then he strikes closer to
home, and Bel determines to track him
down. As she closes in on the monster,
she senses that someone is spying on her
home. And, in a final, terrifying twist, she
finds herself caught in the killer's trap
. . .

SAFFRON'S WAR

Frederick E. Smith

Corporal Alan Saffron, ex-aircrew, is desperate to get back into action, but instead he's posted to Cape Town as an instructor, along with Ken Bickers, a friend about as hazardous as an enemy sniper, who considers Saffron a jonah for trouble. Within half an hour of arrival, Saffron's jonah strikes, and he makes an enemy of Warrant Officer Kruger, who turns Saffron's cushy posting into total warfare. With recruits as wild as Hottentots, obsolete aircraft, and Cape Town's infamous watch dog, Nuisance, Saffron's sojourn in South Africa becomes a mixture of adventure, danger and pure hilarity . . .

THE SURGEON'S APPRENTICE

Arthur Young

1947: Young Neil Aitken has worked hard to secure a place at Glasgow University to study medicine. Bearing in mind the Dean's warning that it takes more than book-learning to become a doctor, he sets out to discover what that other elusive quality might be. He learns the hard way, from a host of memorable characters ranging from a tyrannical surgeon to the bully on the farm where Neil works in his spare time, and assorted patients who teach him about courage and vulnerability. Neil also meets Sister Annie, the woman who is to influence his life in every way.